# DEATH OF A
# BOOKSELLER

# DEATH OF A BOOKSELLER

### BERNARD J. FARMER

With an Introduction by
Martin Edwards

Poisoned Pen
PRESS

Published by Poisoned Pen Press, an imprint of Sourcebooks,
in association with the British Library
P.O. Box 4410, Naperville, Illinois 60567-4410
(630) 961-3900
sourcebooks.com

*Death of a Bookseller* was originally published in
1956 by William Heinemann, London.

Library of Congress Cataloging-in-Publication Data

Names: Farmer, B. J. (Bernard J.), author. | Edwards, Martin, other.
Title: Death of a bookseller / Bernard J. Farmer ; with an introduction by
    Martin Edwards.
Description: Naperville, Illinois : Poisoned Pen Press, [2023] | Series:
    British Library crime classics | Death of a Bookseller was originally
    published in 1956 by William Heinemann, London.
Identifiers: LCCN 2022029627 (print) | LCCN 2022029628
(ebook) | (trade paperback) | (epub)
Subjects: LCSH: Book collectors--Fiction. | Murder--Investigation--Fiction.
    | LCGFT: Detective and mystery fiction. | Novels.
Classification: LCC PR6056.A676 D43 2023  (print) | LCC PR6056.A676
    (ebook) | DDC 823/.914--dc23/eng/20220725
LC record available at https://lccn.loc.gov/2022029627
LC ebook record available at https://lccn.loc.gov/2022029628

Printed and bound in the United States of America.
VP 10 9 8 7 6 5 4 3 2 1

# CONTENTS

# INTRODUCTION

*Death of a Bookseller* was originally published in 1956. Long out of print, the novel has for decades been sought after by collectors of classic detective fiction. On the rare occasions when a jacketed copy in excellent condition turns up on the market, it is usually very expensive. This British Library edition will give thousands of readers a chance to find out for themselves why the story has achieved a kind of cult status among book lovers.

The appeal of the murder mystery is, of course, a key consideration, and the storyline benefits from the fact that the author, Bernard James Farmer, had himself worked as a policeman prior to becoming a novelist. He was also a keen bibliophile and his intimate knowledge of the book world gives his observations about book dealing and book dealers an air of authority.

Sergeant Jack Wigan is on his beat when he meets a book-man called Michael Fisk who has had too much to drink because he's celebrating the acquisition of a rarity, John

Keats's own, personally inscribed copy of *Endymion*. The two men strike up a friendship and Wigan develops a keen interest in books. His enthusiasm and technical know-how proves invaluable when Fisk is found dead in his study with a knife in his chest.

Wigan is asked by the C.I.D. to assist in their investigation, and a number of potential culprits emerge, including the glamorous but menacing Ruth Brent, who represents a determined collector with deep pockets. There is plenty of incriminating evidence against the prime suspect, Fred Hampton. Hampton is an aggressive and quarrelsome individual, and Wigan's colleagues feel a strong temptation to "screw him down" with the crime. But the sergeant, a deeply humane man, is not convinced that they have the right man. Justice and compassion matter to him even more than books.

Wigan's efforts to uncover the truth turn into a desperate race against time—in some ways, this is as much a "clock race" thriller as anything written by that American master of noir fiction, Cornell Woolrich. In terms of literary style, however, this gently humorous, well-crafted post-war British mystery is closer to the work of another author whose books have featured in the Crime Classics series, George Bellairs.

During the course of Wigan's inquiries, an amateur criminologist called Askew tells him: "The public...think book-collecting a nice harmless pastime indulged in by old dodderers. So it can be, but not always. It can be ruthless." This is no exaggeration. A high-profile real-life murder case in 2016 had eerie parallels to Farmer's fiction of sixty years earlier. A book dealer, Adrian Greenwood, was stabbed to death in his Oxford home as part of a plan to steal a rare first edition of

*The Wind in the Willows*, valued at £50,000. The killer, Michael Danaher, was told by the judge sentencing him that he must serve at least thirty-four years in jail. His crime prompted a television documentary and newspaper articles claiming to lift the lid on "the sinister world of antiquarian book dealing."

This novel, crammed with book lore, is an excellent example of a branch of the crime genre examined in *Bibliomysteries* by the American editor, publisher, and owner of the Mysterious Bookshop, Otto Penzler; it covers novels and short stories where a book, library, bookshop, book collector, manuscript, or book collection feature as a significant element.

Bernard James Farmer was born in Maidstone, Kent, in 1902, and although details of his life are not easily obtainable, in piecing together various fragments of his fragmentary biography, I've benefited from helpful information supplied by his estate, Jamie Sturgeon, Jeremy Carson, and John Herrington.

Farmer attended Sutton Valence School, where he first developed an interest in sculling and rowing, which became a lifelong passion and the subject of a book he published in 1951. On leaving school he attended the City and Guilds Engineering College in South Kensington and became a fully qualified engineer. At the age of twenty-one, he set out to work on an engineering project in Winnipeg. A major accident to his leg on site, however, landed him in Kenora hospital for some weeks; during that time he submitted to the *Saturday Evening Post* a short story, which won an award. This success eventually altered the course of his career.

On recovery he travelled widely throughout Canada, often living from hand to mouth, taking such work as he could find in order to finance his writing. His experiences are reflected in his first major novel, *Go West, Young Man*, published in 1936. Farmer was nothing if not versatile, and his CV included designing electrical machinery, working in a gold mine, firing a locomotive, selling insurance, and working on a section gang (which he felt was one of the world's worst jobs). He also published a number of short stories in the long-established Canadian magazine *Maclean's*.

The first story he contributed to *Adventure*, "Black Booty," concerned the Mounties, and in an accompanying note he explained that in writing about north Canada, he'd drawn on experience of a prospecting trip in Northern Manitoba. One of his greatest friends was a Mounted Policeman, and Farmer reckoned that "although a great deal of false sentimentality has been, and still is, written on the Force, it is easy to see they do a real man's work in keeping order in regions where man's duty towards his neighbour too often depends on how much he can get away with."

After returning to England in 1934, he met and married Myfanwy Armon-Jones, a talented singer and pianist, with whom he had two daughters. In 1936 he published *Go West, Young Man*, a novel based on his experiences of life in Canada. His second novel, *Frozen Music* (1940), stems from the years when he and his wife were living in Essex. During the Second World War he volunteered as a fire warden at North Weald Aerodrome, which was close to his home. After the war he joined the "J" branch of the Metropolitan Police Force. Later, he worked as a journalist, novelist, and short-story writer, occasionally writing under the name Owen Fox. In Britain, his short fiction appeared in the *Evening Standard* and other newspapers and magazines.

By the time he published *The Gentle Art of Book Collecting* in 1950, he'd been collecting first editions for years. He also published *Henty's Hundred: a biographical study*; the work of G. A. Henty is mentioned in *Death of a Bookseller*. It may have been Henty's influence that prompted Farmer to try his hand at writing fiction for children and young adults; among other things, he was a contributor to the *Eagle* comic. He is also credited with producing the first bibliography, privately printed, of the writings of Winston Churchill.

In 1952, he gave a broadcast talk on the BBC's Home Service (now Radio 4) wryly entitled "Authors Must Eat," in which he discussed the wide range of work he'd undertaken in order to supplement relatively meagre literary earnings. His other radio talks included an account of his seven years as a policeman.

In 1953, he published his first detective novel, *Death at the Cascades*, which introduced Wigan, at the time a police constable. This book followed three years later, while *Murder Next Year* and *Once, and Then the Funeral* appeared in 1958 and 1959, again with Wigan in the lead role. Farmer also wrote a series of young adult books featuring Tom Ward, a policeman's son who joins the force himself, and nonfiction. His last published work appeared in 1960, and after a period of declining health and a series of strokes, he died in London in 1964. Although he never established himself as a major literary figure, it's a pleasure to introduce *Death of a Bookseller* to twenty-first-century mystery fans and book lovers.

—Martin Edwards
www.martinedwardsbooks.com

# A NOTE FROM THE PUBLISHER

The original novels and short stories reprinted in the British Library Crime Classics series were written and published in a period ranging, for the most part, from the 1890s to the 1960s. There are many elements of these stories which continue to entertain modern readers; however, in some cases there are also uses of language, instances of stereotyping, and some attitudes expressed by narrators or characters which may not be endorsed by the publishing standards of today. We acknowledge therefore that some elements in the works selected for reprinting may make uncomfortable reading for some of our audience. With this series, British Library Publishing and Poisoned Pen Press aim to offer a new readership a chance to read some of the rare books of the British Library's collections in an affordable paperback format, to enjoy their merits, and to look back into the world of the twentieth century as portrayed by its writers. It is not possible to separate these stories from the history of their writing and as such the following novel is presented as it was originally published with minor edits only, made for consistency of style and sense. We welcome feedback from our readers.

*The scene of this novel is laid in London's world of second-hand books; but shops and characters are fictitious.*

# CHAPTER ONE

## A NEW HOBBY

There are many hobbies in the police. It has been said that if you want anything done from mending a tap or painting a house to growing orchids, some policeman will know all about it. The job itself being unproductive of anything except law and order (without which no other job could function), many policemen like to use their hands in their spare time.

Sergeant Wigan, like many others, began with gardening. Then, finding he was not particularly gifted with green fingers, he went on to home decoration and making useful articles in wood. Then when he was promoted to sergeant and moved to Sun Police District he continued these hobbies, but finding he still had some time to spare, he tried some mat-making. Then one August night events threw in his way the most interesting hobby of all.

He was returning from Late Turn duty about 10.15 p.m. and saw a man swaying about in the middle of the road. He appeared to be drunk.

Sergeant Wigan got off his bicycle. "Anything wrong?" he

said cautiously, for sometimes a person who seems drunk is in reality ill.

The man was about sixty and had a shock of untidy white hair. He turned blood-shot eyes on Wigan.

"Just been having celebration."

"You seem to have been over-celebrating," said Wigan.

"A little bit, Officer, but I'm not too bad. I can walk, and I won't give trouble. I promise you that, if you let me alone."

Wigan considered. Generally speaking, a "drunk" is not wanted in the "nick" unless he or she is violent or incapable; and this man seemed neither.

"Walk on the pavement," he said.

"I will, Officer. I live in Chelmer Square. It isn't far."

"I'll walk with you as far as there." It is no part of police duty to see persons "under the influence" home; but sometimes it may be a wise move; and the sooner this man were off the streets the better. So Wigan delayed his own supper, and in the darkness wheeled his bicycle beside the man, who was sobering up fast and could walk and talk in a reasonable way.

"You seem a decent chap," he said. "My name's Fisk—Michael Fisk. I make my living buying and selling rare books; and today I made the find of my life: Keats's own copy of his poem *Endymion*, with an inscription: 'From the author to the author, John Keats, 1818.' You can't blame me for celebrating."

"No," said Wigan, "but you want to be careful if you have a lot of money on you."

"Oh, I haven't sold it yet. It will go for auction at Sotheby's. But I thought I would have a few drinks. Usually I drink little but tea. Will you come in my place and have a cup of tea? I'm a bachelor. I'd like to show you my books."

Wigan accepted. Chelmer Square was a cul-de-sac off the main road with old-fashioned houses substantially built. "This place suits me," remarked Mr. Fisk as he opened the front door of No. 10. "We all keep ourselves to ourselves." He showed Wigan into his study while he went into the kitchen to make the tea.

The house generally might have struck a woman as being dirty and ill-cared for, but in the study the shelves and shelves of books were in excellent order. "Books are my life," said Mr. Fisk, as he returned with the tea. "I'm what is called a runner. I go here, there, everywhere, picking up what I can find in the first-edition line, and selling to other dealers or sometimes direct to a collector."

"It must be a nice peaceful occupation."

"Is it? I've been in the game for forty years; and I could tell you some stories. Some dealers and collectors have no conscience whatever. They would rob a graveyard to get a rare book they wanted. Do you know, Sergeant, there are men and even women who would cheerfully kill me to get what I have found today?"

Wigan thought this might be an exaggeration; but he was interested. He thought he would like to collect first editions himself. It was a scholarly hobby. It would brighten up his mind, dulled sometimes by the monotony of police duty. He said this to Mr. Fisk, who instantly responded.

"By all means. I think it's a very good idea. I know a prison warder who collects Kate Greenaway—she was a famous illustrator of children's books. He told me that his job would drive him crackers if it wasn't for some outside interest. Book-collecting, Sergeant, is the most interesting game in the world.

You never get old. You never know what luck will send. Each time you pause at a stall full of old books and look them over, you are beginning a new adventure. Book-collecting is—well, I expect you are off duty and want to get home. Call on me again, and I'll give you a few tips."

Michael Fisk, apart from his trade contacts, was a lonely man, and he liked to see Sergeant Jack Wigan, who formed the habit of dropping in for a cup of tea once or twice a week and imbibing, with the tea, knowledge of what is and what is not a first edition. But there were many lessons to be learned.

In the labyrinths of Sun, a town which dated back to the twelfth century, Sergeant Wigan on his leave days discovered several volumes which he thought might be valuable. He took a battered calf-bound book to Mr. Fisk for his opinion. They were now on companionable terms, and Wigan said: "Have a look at this, Mike. The date is 1746. I'm pretty sure it's a first."

Michael Fisk opened the volume carefully with his long, slender fingers. He inspected the title-page, then he said: "Jack, I'm going to tell you a story. A runner took a book to a famous dealer and said: 'I've got something rare here.' 'Yes,' replied the dealer, 'but customers who want it are rarer.'"

"Then my book is worth nothing?"

"Nothing whatever. It's a volume of old sermons, which in the trade are pretty well unsaleable. Your book is a first edition all right, and probably there never was a second, for obvious reasons. However, try again, Jack. That's what we all have to do."

"It strikes me," said Wigan, "that a runner needs plenty of guts."

"Of course he does. The public thinks of a bookman as a doddery chap with shaky legs and weak eyes; but in fact he must have good health, certainly good legs, and first-class eyesight, with or without glasses. And he must know what to look for. Take another look at my books. There's my Keats—you'll recognise that again: it's in what we call a contemporary binding, calf gilt. That is, Keats took his copy of the poem to a book-binder and instructed him to bind it in a special style. Many authors do this with their own works. But, generally speaking, collectors prefer original binding, whatever it may be."

"Like this?" said Wigan, taking from the orderly shelves a book bound in green cloth.

"That's right. That book is *Of Human Bondage*, by William Somerset Maugham. It's another book you want to recognise. The first edition, published in 1915, is very rare, and worth now about £40."

Completely absorbed, Wigan moved from book to book. At least he had a good memory, which Mike told him a book-collector needs.

"By the way, Mike," he said at length, "my wife thinks you need a good meal properly cooked. So will you come to supper next Sunday, when I shall be off duty?"

Instantly Mike became rather shy. "Well, thank Mrs. Wigan very much, but I doubt if I'm fit for polite society."

"Nonsense," said Wigan stoutly, "of course you are. We're only homely people, though Mary is a thundering good cook."

"Well, would you mind if I come to tea? I'm usually at

home in the evenings, because dealers do a lot of their business then, and sometimes one will call on me and buy a book he needs for a customer."

"Right. Tea it is, but prepare for the biggest tea you have ever eaten."

The tea was a great success, and Wigan and Fisk became close friends. "Matter of fact, Jack," said Mike one evening, "I dabble in the occult—the mystical and supernatural; and I've a number of old and rare books on the subject. I have even tried to raise the devil."

"Dangerous stuff," said Wigan.

"It probably is, and I don't want to drag you into it. But demonology is intensely interesting."

"I've known trouble to be caused," replied Wigan, "by simple table-tapping. Books on demonology ought to be burnt."

"So they were years ago, by the common hangman. But he couldn't get hold of them all. However, as I say, I don't want to drag you into it. Let's have a look at some more modern firsts. At the moment Kipling's stock is rather low. So is H. G. Wells's. But Chesterton and Belloc are worth having, and you want to look out for firsts of G. A. Henty, because the Americans collect him, and if you come across an early first of Lord Dunsany's, like *The Gods of Pegana*, it will pay you to buy it."

There was never a more generous man than Mike Fisk. He probably had his darker side, and he may have had some unholy vigils trying to raise the devil with the aid of some old black letter volume; but with the instinct of a gentleman he would not show this side to a friend.

"I've got a lot to thank you for, Mike," said Wigan.

"Bosh!" said Mike; and this was the last word that Wigan ever heard his friend utter, for when, the following Tuesday evening, Wigan being on leave, he battled through blinding wind and rain to Mike's house to show him a first of Lord Dunsany's which he had picked up in a near-by market town, Mike was dead.

# CHAPTER TWO

## DEAD

"He's been dead about seventeen hours," said the police divisional surgeon, after doing his tests, which included a thermometer reading taken in the rectum of the body.

"About two o'clock this morning," said the D.I., Detective-Inspector J. Saggs, from Brabant divisional station.

"That's what I make it. And the cause of death is probably the knife-thrust in the chest. But I can't say for certain till I do the P.M. There may be some other injury. From the poor chap's point of view it wouldn't matter much."

"Mhmm. I wish the dead could speak. Just a lot of books round him. I suppose there's the motive. What do you say, Sergeant? You say you knew the fellow and you collect books. Anything missing?"

"I can't see a valuable book he had—a Keats first edition which was going to the book auctioneers, Messrs. Sotheby, when their sales start again in October. You see that gap there—that's where it was. There may be other books missing but I don't see any gaps."

"Mhmm," said the D.I. "Lucky you've got a cast-iron alibi, Sergeant, or we might suspect you."

The D.I. was probably joking, but… Wigan hastened to repeat his alibi. "I was on station duty last night, sir, at Sun Station. I was inside the whole of my tour of duty from 10 p.m. to 6 a.m., and P.C. Wheeler on communications duty will confirm this."

"Of course, Sergeant. Of course. We must look for a real suspect. I may be glad of your knowledge later. Myself, I know nothing about books except that my wife reads a few from the public library. Well, we must get photographs taken and then we'll have Mr. Michael Fisk removed to the mortuary. The coroner's officer will arrange with you, Doc., about the post-mortem—whenever convenient to you. And the super-intendent will have to know and the D.P.P.—there's a hundred and one things to do."

The D.I. had the reputation in his division of being a clever fellow but an absolute man-hunter. When he got his hands on a man it was the devil's own job to make him let go. In the days of the Bow Street runners, he would have been the most relentless of the runners. He loved to make an arrest and get "chummy" "screwed down"; but there was a check on his activities. In cases of murder the D.P.P.—Director of Public Prosecutions—is always informed; and he advises, under the directions of the Attorney-General, as to when an arrest shall be made; and he then institutes proceedings.

But police do the preliminary work. The D.I. had a hard, hawk-like face, and, as somebody once said, "Maybe his mother loves him." His eyes gleamed now with satisfaction.

"Let me get at my facts. That knife will have to be

fingerprinted, but it looks to me as if the murderer wore gloves. And it rained hard all yesterday and all last night, and it's damn-well raining hard now. Mhmm."

Wigan was doubly glad later that he had a cast-iron alibi, because he was informed by Michael Fisk's bank manager that he had in his keeping Fisk's will, which was written on a plain sheet of paper but properly witnessed by bank officials and perfectly legal.

"I leave my books and everything I possess to my friend Sergeant Jack Wigan, of Myrtle Cottage, Greenhouse Road, Sun, County of Middlesex, who treated me with kindness."

Just that. And now the dead man's books were his. Mike had been a bit of a crank and he was the sort who flicked cigarette-ash into the butter-dish, and probably his devil-raising hadn't done him much good; but he was a man of fine character, and it was unlikely that he had any personal enemies and likely that gain was the motive for the murder. Wigan remembered a story Mike had told him early on in their acquaintanceship. How he had once, when nearly starving, come across a book which the trade classed as erotica—an indecent book which would certainly fetch five pounds in the right quarter, for there are customers for that kind of thing. It was in the tuppenny box and Mike had twopence; but he had shoved it back under the pile. "Damn it," he had said to Wigan, "I thought to myself that if I can't make a living selling decent books, I won't sell the other kind. They do any amount of harm, shoving some young man or woman down the road to moral degeneration."

Wigan had admired him for that. Not so many, in Mike's position as he was then, would have resisted the temptation to sell something filthy for the sake of a good meal. Mike had a fine mind. He wouldn't do anyone a dirty trick. Books were the motive, and Wigan would have liked to use his knowledge to try and track down the murderer. Apart from friendship, he had a further interest, for he had discovered the crime. He had banged on the front door. No answer. The door was locked. So Wigan had gone round to the back door and found that unlocked, as it well might be with Mike's casual habits. Wigan had entered the kitchen. He had proceeded to the study, switched on the electric light, and then seen Mike sitting in his old leather arm-chair with a knife in his chest. There was a fearful amount of blood: on the table before Mike, and on a book, a large tome—not the Keats first edition, which was small and slim—which lay on the table. Touching nothing, and without loss of time, Wigan had informed the police station, who had telephoned the D.I. at divisional station, Brabant.

But for a uniformed sergeant to investigate a murder isn't possible. The case passes at once to the C.I.D. Also Wigan had his own work to do, supervising his men on the beats for which Sun section was responsible. He could have done a bit in his spare time, but, whatever some crime stories may say, unofficial help is not welcomed. Saggs was in charge.

A week after the murder, the superintendent of the division sent for Wigan to attend the super's office at Brabant.

"You are a good sergeant, Wigan," said the super, "and I'm

sorry to take you off the streets, but the D.I. is at sea over this book-collector murder. As you attended the inquest, you know most of the facts. The knife-wound caused death; and the knife should be a promising clue. It is a large, strong, single-bladed folding knife of dark-blue steel, a type made for H.M. Forces during the last war, and sold now in government surplus stores all over the country. You might think it would be easy to trace such a knife, but it isn't. The trouble with a murder always is that no one has any reason to suspect the murderer beforehand; consequently, no one takes any particular notice of what he or she does or says. The forensic laboratory can't help us much beyond the fact that there are no fingerprints, because the murderer wore gloves. Blood on the knife is the blood of the murdered man."

The super's careful, rather old-fashioned utterance ceased; and Wigan wondered what was next. Maybe he was to be switched to the knife-hunt. But the super had something better.

"The book-collecting angle has revealed nothing yet to the D.I. He doesn't understand old and rare books. I understand you do?"

"I understand something about them, sir. Michael Fisk was my friend, and what I know he taught me. Since I met him I have taken up book-collecting as a hobby."

"Ah. Interesting hobby, no doubt. I want you to give aid to the C.I.D. From today you will do duty in plain clothes, and you will of course draw plain clothes and detective allowance."

The super smiled in the way that, thought Wigan, made the old boy so popular with his men.

"Solve the murder for them, Wigan. I'm a uniformed man,

and I'm always glad to give the uniformed men a leg-up when I can. The D.I. has asked for you. So—do the best you can."

"I will, sir. I will indeed."

"Right. Now report to the D.I.'s office. It's the third door right at the end of the passage."

The D.I., J. Saggs, was a worker. Wigan was impressed with the immense amount of ground he had covered.

"Wigan," he said at once, "I've got in touch with all, or nearly all, the second-hand book dealers in and around London. Some admit to having had business relations with Michael Fisk. None will admit to seeing him on the day of the crime. Now of course we have got to trace the Keats volume you say is missing. I'm going to have a notice inserted in the dealers' trade paper, *The Clique*, which is issued to the trade only. I want you to draft it out as best you can and send it to the editor, who I'm sure will give you every help. Any other suggestions?"

"I suggest personal calls, sir, unofficial. Fisk was what is called a runner. He roamed round, buying books, which he subsequently sold, often by personal call, to other dealers. Someone may know something. There are places, such as antique shops and furniture shops, which sometimes sell a few books but are not recognised book dealers. Runners always call on them because they may pick up bargains. They learn the gossip of the trade."

"All right. You be a runner too. Do you think you can do the part?"

Wigan smiled. "There are all types in the runners' world. I

know an ex-postman with a sniff; and there's a prison warder who spends his spare time hunting for books."

"So you won't look out of place. Right. I'm going to throw this part of the case on you while I concentrate on the knife. It's quite new, and someone must have bought it recently. It will mean an enormous amount of work calling at every possible store; but there it is—this kind of case always does mean work. Now you had better draft out your notice for the trade paper: make it as exact as possible so that any dealer offered the book will communicate immediately with New Scotland Yard, telephone Whitehall 1212, or any police station. You know the style."

Wigan began to fancy himself as a detective, and the D.I. was in an amiable mood.

"Can't the laboratory people, sir, give any help about the knife?"

"Not much. The manufacturers tell me that it was made in 1945 for the Commandos, but never issued. It was kept in store till early this year, when it was released for sale as government surplus. It is made of good steel and the single blade is very sharp. It went through the dead man all right. The only help the lab can give is that the person who owned the knife also kept in the same pocket a piece of India-rubber."

"Then it may be a bookseller's runner, sir."

"Why?"

"Because a runner usually has with him a piece of rubber to erase prices in books. He may buy a book for threepence and sell it the same day in the West End for three pounds. Naturally he will want to erase the first price."

"Good. That's helpful." The D.I.'s hard face expressed

satisfaction. "Now see what else you can do for us. And remember, always carry your warrant-card. Some men in plain clothes forget, and it will be awkward, Wigan, if I have to come and arrest you as a suspicious character."

This was the nearest J. Saggs could get to making a joke, and Wigan felt that he had indeed started off on the right foot as Aid to the C.I.D.

# CHAPTER THREE

## ANIMAL GRAB

There are sometimes plums in the police job. A beat constable is let loose for the day hunting for the owner of cattle which have strayed (and he has a nice country ride while doing so); another man is sent on a job which involves an interesting visit to some works; and now here was Sergeant Jack Wigan, released on this fine August morning from the onerous business of supervising his men on the section, to go and hunt books—something which he loved to do.

Wigan took the train from Sun to Liverpool Street, then a bus to Tottenham Court Road, a centre of the second-hand book trade. Wigan thought he would begin with Niger's, a big shop in West Road which Mike had told him he frequented. Niger's was a huge place—one of the biggest book shops in London. Wigan roamed round the shelves. Many people were doing the same thing; and a good proportion Wigan judged to be professional runners.

At one end of a book-room was a great unsorted pile of books which was added to from time to time as books were brought up from the buying department in the basement. Three men were engaged in looking for bargains in the pile. Wigan made a fourth. Then a woman came up and made a fifth. Wigan noticed that little courtesy was shown. It was like the children's game of Animal Grab. A tall thin man with a beard was on his knees and burrowing in the pile with a complete disregard of what anyone else might be doing. The woman stuck her elbows into Wigan, the better to get near the pile. The other two men, both dressed so shabbily that it almost seemed that they had put on the worst clothes they had, used their eyes and made swift darts at anything they fancied. Then they lounged against the shelves and examined their finds. If anyone wanted to get near the shelves, well, that was just too bad.

Wigan, using his eyes too, spied a book by G. A. Henty which looked as if it might be a first edition. The title was *With Roberts to Pretoria*, and the binding, pictorial red cloth with bevelled boards, was typical of the Henty books published by Blackie.

Wigan stretched out a long arm to take the book from the pile. The man with the beard spied what he was doing and instantly seized hold of the book too.

"Give that to me. It's mine."

As a police officer Wigan never lost his temper, and he didn't lose it now. He replied calmly: "Pardon me, it's not yours. I saw it first."

"You didn't! I put it with those I have decided to buy. Give it to me!"

Really, Wigan didn't see why he should. Any sensible person, he thought, who had decided to buy a particular book would put it under his arm; and thus ownership would not be disputed. So they both held a portion of Henty's *With Roberts to Pretoria*, and it was all very absurd.

"Give it to me! Give it to me!" The man with the beard grew more and more excited. His eyes blazed with passion. His straggling brown beard, which made him look like a caricature of D. H. Lawrence, stuck out like a tuft. Wigan judged him to be about thirty-five. He certainly wasn't a charmer.

"I'm not afraid of you," he said, "for all your size. I'll hit you in the face."

Niger's was so big, with so many floors and book-rooms, that it was not surprising that none of the staff had yet heard the row.

"Perhaps," said Wigan, "we had better call the manager."

But this didn't suit the man with the beard. He well knew that sorting over the unsorted pile was not allowed, except by the staff. In fact a notice said: "Please do not touch." The man with the beard had himself pushed this aside.

"No," he growled. "I don't want to do that. Give me the book." He gave a violent tug, but Wigan, who was stronger, just held on.

All this time the other three persons, the two men and a woman, rooted for treasures without regard to the dispute. Now one of the men looked up and said: "Better toss for it."

And this is what Wigan did with a penny. He decided to sacrifice the Henty in the cause of duty, and when the man with the beard called "Heads," Wigan told him he had won and handed over the book.

Instantly the man with the beard became less truculent. The passion in his eyes died as if a light had been switched off. "Thanks," he said, "that's decent of you. Sorry I was a bit quick-tempered. As a matter of fact," he added frankly, "I always quarrel with everybody sooner or later."

"When you've finished here," said Wigan, "let's bury the hatchet and have a cup of coffee together."

"Thanks, I'd like to." The man with the beard got a member of the staff to price his book, then he paid for it and he and Wigan walked out together. Over a cup of coffee in Lyons the man with the beard said his name was Fred Hampton and that he was, as Wigan had surmised, a bookseller's runner.

"It's a tough game. One day you may slave for hours and not make a penny and wear out shoe-leather. The next day you may make a few shillings and the third day nothing. So it goes on."

"That's what my friend Mike Fisk said."

"The bloke who was murdered, eh?"

"Yes. Did you know him?"

"Slightly."

"And did you quarrel with him?"

"I may have done sometimes. As I told you, I quarrel with everyone sooner or later. But what's all this leading up to? I didn't murder him." Hampton's eyes grew wary, and he stared hard at Wigan as if he were seeing him for the first time.

"You're a cop, aren't you?" he said.

"I am, though I was in Niger's hunting for books the same as you."

"You seem to know a Henty first edition when you see one. I suppose you are helping to track down Mike's killer."

"How did you spot me as a policeman?"

"Oh, well—you look like one. I can't say more."

"Have another cup of coffee, Mr. Hampton?"

"Thanks. If you wish." Hampton seemed fascinated by Wigan. Wigan fetched two more coffees from the counter; also a plate of cakes. Hampton looked as if he needed a meal. He was feverishly smoking a cigarette when Wigan returned.

"Look, Officer, if you want to know all that goes on in the book world you ought to see a girl called Ruth Brent. She's a smashing beauty, but don't let that deceive you. She's as tough as tough. If Mike held out on her over a book she wanted, she would—wham!—stick a knife in Mike without the slightest compunction."

"These are pretty strong words."

"I know. I suppose I talk too much, but I've had dealings with Ruth. She's buying agent for an American collector. I once had a three-decker Henty—that's what we call a three-volume novel—which she wanted for her boss, who among other things collects Hentys. I asked her twenty quid for it. She said that was too much. She would pay ten. I refused. And do you know what she did?"

"What?"

"She said she would have to get tough with me. She wasn't going to have her American swindled. She opened her bag—we were sitting in a café—and I thought I saw something bright. It might have been a razor; and, well, dammit, I made a hasty bargain for twelve pounds ten. I'm not very brave, and I didn't want to be disfigured for life. So she took the book. I took the money. And that was that. But I bet she asked her collector for twenty-five quid. I fancy she's his mistress when he comes over here."

Wigan thought that Hampton had revealed quite a lot about his own character. It was a wonder that this violent, excitable man who wasn't very brave hadn't got hurt before now.

"Where does Ruth Brent live?"

"Oh, she has a flat out Muswell Hill way. I've never been there. No fear. When I want to contact her I just phone. Tudor 10006. We meet at a café near the Marble Arch."

Wigan noted the number.

"Look, Officer, for heaven's sake don't say I told you. I don't want to get slashed."

"I shan't give your name, Mr. Hampton. Will you sell me that Henty you bought at Niger's, if it is a desirable first edition?"

Hampton produced the book from the bag he carried. He examined the title-page. "It's a first all right. Blackie & Son, 1902. And it's in fine condition—condition is everything in our business."

"What is a fair price to ask Miss Brent?"

"Well, her collector probably has it. *With Roberts to Pretoria* isn't a scarce book. But Ruth will buy pretty well any Henty first, provided it is fine. I should ask her two pounds."

"I'll give you two pounds now, Mr. Hampton."

"Thanks. This is my lucky day." Hampton became milder and milder. "I'm sorry I lost my temper, Officer. It's this bloody job. It's so frustrating. You get to hate people, though I love books. If you contact our Ruth, do be careful. She won't be afraid of the police, you know."

"I'll be careful. May I have your address, Mr. Hampton, in case I need your advice or anything?"

"Here's my card. But, for God's sake, don't make trouble for me. I have enough as it is."

Wigan was a genuinely kind man. "Why don't *you* act as agent for an American collector?"

"Well, I have one or two on my books. But they are so damned particular. They want so much for their money. Mint condition, and all the rest of it. And you can't buy the stock now. So much has gone overseas. It isn't like ordering groceries from a wholesaler."

Fred Hampton abruptly dried up. "That's all I can tell you, Officer. Thanks for the coffee. I think I'll go further West now. Players in Piccadilly have been asking for W. W. Jacobs first editions. I have several that may suit them."

"I wish you luck," said Wigan politely. "And, Mr. Hampton, if you find any more Henty firsts, will you let me know? I'll pay you a fair price."

"I have Henty's *Out on the Pampas*, Griffith and Farran, 1871. That is rare. I've been keeping it for a rainy day. Sometimes a runner has to eat his books."

"I'll buy that." Suddenly Wigan thought it would suit him best to offer Miss Brent a really rare book. He settled on the price with Hampton, and went with him straight away to his house in Islington to get the book. Islington as a district can best be described as being like the curate's egg—good in parts. Hampton's house, one of a long row, was in a part not good. Here he maintained a wife and two children and strove to do his best for them.

"My wife knows nothing about books," he said to Wigan, "but she's a good sort. She makes the money go round. I'll do anything for her and the girls."

Wigan spent some time in Hampton's study (a back room) examining his stock, which contained some surprising rarities. "You never want to flog a good book in a hurry," said Hampton. "The b——s will screw you down to the last half-crown."

Mrs. Hampton knocked respectfully at the door. "I'm sorry to trouble you, Fred, and the gentleman, but can I borrow your knife? I've broken the washing-line."

"I've lost it somewhere, Minnie. Ask next door. They will lend you something."

It is one of the worst aspects of the police job that sometimes you have to turn pleasure into business.

"What knife have you lost, Mr. Hampton?"

"Oh, just a knife. Here's your book, Mr. Wigan, nicely packed up. Ask Ruth fifteen pounds. Her collector ought to pay that. Damn it, why shouldn't he? All the money in the world, I dare say, and my Winnie and Elsie want new shoes." Hampton's eyes flared again. "I'd like to make the f——s pay with the point of a gun!"

Wigan walked thoughtfully away. He would have to report to the D.I. But of course plenty of men do lose knives. It was now six o'clock. A detective's day is never ended. Wigan went to the nearest phone-box to telephone Ruth Brent for an appointment.

# CHAPTER FOUR

## OUR RUTH

Wigan didn't pretend to be a connoisseur of feminine beauty. Mrs. Wigan had a pleasant face rather than a pretty one. And as a mature man he thought perhaps more of beauty of character than facial beauty. But his first sight of Ruth Brent, whom he had arranged to meet at 4 p.m. outside a café near the Marble Arch, gave him an eyeful, as the Americans say. She was tall and slim, she had corn-coloured hair like a shining helmet, deep blue eyes, and she carried herself like a queen. She was the kind of girl one expects to see on the stage rather than ordinary life.

"Good afternoon," she said, looking at the book Wigan ostentatiously carried, by arrangement. "You are Mr. Wigan?"

"I am. And you are Miss Brent? Shall we have some tea?"

They sat down at a table for two; and at once, after Wigan had ordered tea and cakes, she came to business.

"May I see the Henty book you spoke of? *Out on the Pampas?*"

Wigan unwrapped the book and handed it across the table.

She compared it carefully with a typewritten list she took from her handbag. "My collector has the very best advice," she remarked. She verified the publisher and date of publication. She collated the text and illustrations. "This seems a good copy," she said at last. "My collector wants it. What is your price?"

"Eighteen pounds." Wigan purposely made the price high. He wanted to see the alleged toughness in action.

"Eighteen pounds is too much," she said. "I can offer you fifteen."

"Perhaps I can get more elsewhere."

"I doubt it. My offer is a fair one."

Wigan said nothing. Square and solid, he just waited. Ruth's fingers went to her bag. The café was not full. No waitress was in sight. The table at which they sat was secluded. If she were going to "slash," now was the time for it. But she only took out a delicately-scented handkerchief. It struck him that he was a different type from Fred Hampton and that she had no intention of being tough now in a physical sense.

"My limit is sixteen," she said. "You must take it or leave it. But I advise you to take it, because I can bring you other custom."

"I'll take it, Miss Brent."

She opened her bag again and produced a thick bundle of pound notes. She counted out sixteen. "Please check them," she said politely. He did so. "Quite correct, Miss Brent."

"Can I pour you out another cup of tea, Mr. Wigan?"

"Thanks."

"You are new to the book business, aren't you? I've never seen you before."

"I was a friend of Mike Fisk. Perhaps you have heard that he was knifed in the chest?"

"I have heard something about it. I've been out of town. To Liverpool. I was given a tip that some Hentys were for sale there. I bought half a dozen, for which I gave a pound each." A gentle hint, thought Wigan. She finished her tea and put on a pair of new gloves. "By the way," she said, "who introduced you to me?"

Wigan was prepared for this. "Mike Fisk," he said. "He introduced me to collecting. Henty seemed a possible line, and he mentioned you."

"Extraordinary," she said calmly. "I never met him. Still, as you say, he knew my name, he must have done."

"He knew everyone in the book world. I would like to trace his murderer. He was my friend. Can you help me in any way?"

Ruth's eyes widened. He was conscious of her beauty, yet there was a coldness about her, lack of sexual appeal, lack of womanly warmth and charm. However, Wigan was a modest man and it occurred to him that Ruth wouldn't bother to charm a man like himself.

She was purely business-like. "I don't think I can help you," she said. "Anyway, I must be going. But first I shall ask you to sign a receipt. I have to account to my collector for the money I spend."

"Certainly, madam."

"Your full name and address?"

Wigan gave his home address at Sun. He signed a receipt for sixteen pounds, punctiliously offered twopence for a stamp, then she rose to go. "My collector is interested in any valuable book. You can always phone me. Will you let me pay for the tea?"

"Certainly not. It's been a pleasure to meet you."

"I hope we shall do further business. Goodbye." She walked out of the café like a goddess.

Wigan hadn't what the Victorians called "further intentions," but if he had he wouldn't have picked on Miss Ruth Brent, beautiful as she was. He wondered what the person she called "my collector" thought of her.

It was about twenty minutes on the Tube from Marble Arch to Liverpool Street, and, when he caught the train, about half an hour from Liverpool Street to Sun. From Sun railway station to Sun police station was ten minutes. Using the police private line, Wigan reported to the D.I. He had reported already that Fred Hampton should be questioned further about the knife he possessed or had possessed. He had little to say now except as regards his expense account. "I've made two pounds profit, sir, over a book I bought and sold. Can I give that to the police orphanage fund?"

"If you like," said the D.I. "Keep looking for that Keats book. That's what we want to find."

"I will, sir."

Wigan rang off. He had a word or two with the station officer, then he took his bicycle from the shed and cycled home. As he approached his front gate he saw a small motor-car standing outside. As he entered the gate, Mrs. Wigan opened the front door.

"At last you've come," she said. "There's a lady waiting to see you. If I didn't know you, Jack…" She left the sentence ominously unfinished. In his front parlour Wigan found sitting Miss Ruth Brent. He was dumbfounded, flabbergasted—any strong word you can think of.

"Why, Miss Brent, I left you—"

"So you did. I suspected, and I thought I would make sure. You're Sergeant Wigan, aren't you?"

"Yes, madam."

"And you're investigating the murder of Michael Fisk?"

"That is so. I'm helping to."

"You've been a little roundabout with me, Sergeant. You must have laughed at me buying your book."

Policemen get tired like other men. Wigan was tired. He wanted his supper. He went directly to the point. "What can I do for you, madam?"

"It's what I can do for you. If you had been straight with me and presented your official card I would have helped you before. I think a bookseller's runner named Fred Hampton may know something."

"I have already seen him, but why should you think he may know something?"

"He's an excitable man, and violent when he thinks he can get away with it. Then there's Charlie North—he's another runner. He keeps a barrow in the Old Kent Road. You should be able to find him there."

"Thank you. That is helpful. Have you any other suggestion?"

"There's Algernon Askew, another runner with whom I do business. He's a cultured man and understands more about books than anyone else I know. He's not the type to commit murder, but you might find him helpful. I'll give you his address." She opened her diary and did so.

"Thank you, Miss Brent. Any other suggestions?"

"Now I want something from you. When the Keats first edition is discovered, I should like to have the first offer of it for my collector."

"Cool," thought Wigan. "She fits her name—ruthless." He did not feel inclined to say that all Mike's books had been left to him by will. He would have no peace if he did. He replied:

"I cannot at present make promises of that kind. But I will bear your offer in mind."

Ruth left him then. Her little car buzzed away, and at last Wigan could eat his supper. Afterwards he said to Mary, his wife: "How did she announce herself?"

"She came to the door and asked for Mr. Wigan. When I said you weren't at home she said: 'Is he by any chance Inspector Wigan?' I said you are a sergeant. She then asked to wait."

"That young lady," said Wigan, "has got 'my collector,' as she calls him, on the brain. I'll have to find out where her collector was at the time of the murder. I think the pair of them would rob the British Museum if they thought they could get away with it."

# CHAPTER FIVE

## BY TELEPHONE

Ruth Brent was writing her weekly letter to her employer. "Darling Di," she began, "I have such a lot to tell you—"

The sitting-room of her expensive flat was delightfully furnished and comfortable. Everything was paid for by Dithan Dand, industrial magnate of New York City, who would probably have married her except that he had a wife and children already. He was a vital, vigorous man who had one of the best private libraries in the world and enjoyed the visits of learned professors to see his books. "This will make Professor Nickerlo sit up," he said to Ruth when she had secured for him, from some runner, a valuable book not hitherto known to the collectors of Henty and Hentyana.

Di's latest craze was Henty; and Di's wishes had gone out, through Ruth, to the dealers and the runners, who were scouring the bookshops, stalls, and junk-shops for Henty. As the whim took him, Di would pay flying visits, by plane, to London. He would then stay officially at a large London hotel. From there he could conveniently visit Ruth.

Di was a crackerjack—his own description of himself. When he wanted a book he had to have it, and it was Ruth's business to get it for him. She did not herself, nor did Di, know a lot about books; but there were always experts who did. Just now American collectors generally were crazy about G. A. Henty, the writer for boys, who was born in 1832 and died in 1902. It might be thought that British collectors would have the best collections of a British author. They did not. American collectors did.

Ruth continued her letter: "A runner named Michael Fisk has recently been murdered, and the police are busy. A cop disguised as a runner contacted me, and—"

The phone rang. Ruth answered it, and a muffled voice said:

"I have a book to offer you. A first edition of John Keats's poem *Endymion*. It is his own copy, signed by him. A unique item. What will you give?"

"Unique" was a word that Di loved. It meant that he would own something that no one else in the world could own. Yet Ruth did not instantly treat with the seller. She did not like auction offers, bidding one collector against another. Di was generous, but he didn't like throwing his money away. "Only saps do that," he told her.

"I prefer priced reports," she said over the phone. "What kind of offer do you expect?"

"Around £200," said the muffled voice.

"I must think it over. I'll contact my collector. Where is the book to be seen?"

"You must decide now whether or not to buy. If you decide 'yes,' my agent will be at the Marble Arch café, The Spinning Heart, with the book at half-past four precisely on Friday afternoon. You will give the money in one-pound notes, and he will hand you the book."

"I must contact my collector. I'll phone you back at half-past ten."

"That will be satisfactory. Phone Primrose 36489. It's a phone-box. I shall wait in it. Goodbye."

Ruth never asked who the seller might be. What did it matter? But she wanted to know something more about the book, so she contacted one of her sources of information, a runner named Connington who was employed by day in a library and did some quiet dealing on his own account.

"I suppose you don't see the trade paper," said Connington, when she had got him on the phone and given him the facts; "naturally they wouldn't sell it to you, for it's trade only. Well, the Keats first edition you mention is splashed in an advertisement put in by the police. Information about it is urgently wanted. It was stolen from Michael Fisk who was murdered."

Ruth did not trouble about this angle. "Do you think the book is genuine?"

"Certainly it is. Mike knew a lot about books. But I wouldn't touch it if I were you, Ruth. It's as hot as hot."

Ruth thanked Connington for his information and rang off. She next telephoned Di on the transatlantic telephone. It was of course a great expense; but Di had warned her never to save on matters of this kind. "Never save a hundred dollars and lose a thousand," he had told her.

Di was at home. "Well, honey," he said, "it's nice to hear your voice."

"It's nice to hear you, Di. I love you and always shall." She told him about the book.

"Buy it," he said. "My, I'd like to see Prof. Nickerlo's face when I show him Keats's own copy of the *Endymion*."

"It's stolen, Di, from a murdered man. You ought to know that."

"What the heck does it matter? When it gets in my library, I'll keep it safe."

"What price shall I go to above £200?"

"I don't mind £250. But if the guy gets tough and bickers around with other collectors, then get tough with him. He's on mighty shaky ground, it seems to me. A word to the cops and he will be arrested for murder. But it's the book I want. Send it by plain book post, open ends. That's the safest way. The chances are the packet won't be opened. If it is, I shall have to lose it. I'll risk the money. Of course put no writing in, certainly not your name."

"I understand that."

"I shall be flying across soon. I'm hungering to see you, honey."

"Me too, Di. I live for the times you see me. Good night, Di, and—I love you."

"Ruth?"

"Yes?"

"You're a clever kid."

The phone clicked. Di had rung off. Ruth put her receiver down. Slowly her face turned scarlet.

At exactly the time promised, Ruth rang the number given by the offerer of the book. The phone was answered by the same guarded, muffled voice as if the speaker was talking through a handkerchief—a common enough trick to disguise the voice.

"I'll buy the book," said Ruth, "for £250."

"Sorry, the price has risen. It's now £300."

Ruth smiled at the phone, and her lips were thin. Di wanted the book and he was going to have it—at his price.

"I'm authorised to offer you £250," she said mildly. "That's a fair price."

"I'll accept £300."

"Very well—if you insist. I'll meet your agent on Friday afternoon at four-thirty inside The Spinning Heart. How shall I know him?"

"You know him now. He's Fred Hampton, the runner. Just hand over the money, in one-pound Bank of England treasury notes, and take the book. You can examine it first if you wish. Goodbye."

"Goodbye," said Ruth pleasantly. What a fool Fred Hampton was to try that game with her! He would get £250, and not a penny more. She was pretty sure it was him on the phone; but if it wasn't, it made no difference. It was from Fred she would get the book—at her price.

Ruth had started life as a chambermaid in a London hotel, and risen to be buying agent for Dithan Dand by brains as well as beauty. The steps to the rise had been many, and not always savoury. For a time she had worked in a film company. For a time she had worked as pillion-girl in a Wall of Death act, waving a white kid-gloved hand in the air as jauntily as you please while the machine roared round and round on the vertical wall. On one occasion, however, the motor cut out unexpectedly and the machine fell from the top to the bottom. Ruth had strong nerves, but she decided to try something safer. For a time she worked as hostess in a night-club—the kind of club that police are anxious to close. It was here that she saw the razor boys at work, and a lot more besides, but Ruth was always what is technically called a good girl. She was ice to men until at last she met the man she wanted: Dithan Dand, millionaire, one of the most powerful men in the world. Men—she knew them backwards. Men who wanted to kiss, to pat. Men with all sorts of suggestions. But Di was a man she could love. She loved him. Di needed a secretary in Britain, and that became her official job.

If Ruth's beauty had a fault, it was her rather thin lips. She never laughed much. She had the film-actress's studied smiles. She smiled softly now as she thought of Di. She thought of the book Di wanted, and her smile became hard. Fred Hampton might need persuasion. For him she selected a razor blade. She wrapped it in tissue-paper. Just that. But she knew she could terrify him. Di would have the book at his price. £250 she would pay—and no more.

# CHAPTER SIX

## CHARLIE BOY

Charlie North, known far and wide in the book trade as Charlie Boy, was a most entertaining character. Most days when not buying stock he wheeled a barrow of books and "comics" to a pitch in the Old Kent Road, and was thus the humblest of all dealers: a barrow-boy. But he also had at home a small stock of valuable volumes which might have astonished the pundits of the trade who affected to despise him. There was a tendency to raise the status of the trade which was "antiquarian" not "second-hand." If you cut your neighbour's throat, you did so now in a gentlemanly way in the auction-rooms. But Charlie, between fifty and sixty, remembered when characters in the book trade were characters, not young ladies and gentlemen fresh from college; and as Wigan stood him lunch in a slap-up restaurant in Tottenham Court Road, Charlie Boy poured out story after story to entertain the detective sergeant—for so Wigan had introduced himself at the barrow. It seemed hopeless to attempt the fiction that he was just a runner. Charlie wanted to pack up at noon to do some buying at Niger's, so here they were, eating of the best.

"I remember Lavatory Jack, Sergeant."

"Why on earth did you call him that?"

"Because he was so poor that he had a pennyworth every night. He used to go in about midnight and he was out and about early next morning." Charlie laughed. "He used to pad the seat with coats, and he told me he always slept well. The secret was to keep his feet above his head. He was a card all right. And then there was One-Volume Joe—he used to buy up odd volumes, and if you wanted to make up a set you would buy from One-Vol. Joe. He was another card. And then I remember the aristocratic Carrington-Carrington Briggs. To see that toff round a stall, sporting a monocle, you would think he didn't know a first edition from a fifth; but he had the finest collection of old colour-plate books I have ever seen. Ah me, the book trade isn't what it was. Now I have to deal with young ladies who think me a dreadful rough-neck. High and mighty bitches, most of them."

"Do you know Ruth Brent?"

"Yus, I know her. A cool cuss. Buys for a Yank. She has always treated me fair, when I've got a book to suit her, but she won't pay big prices and she points out a mark as big as a pin-head. Yanks are crazy about condition."

"And Fred Hampton—do you know him?"

"Yus. Hasn't the guts of a louse, yet he's always quarrelling. It's his nerves. I'm helping you, Sarge, because Mike Fisk once did me a good turn. I was dead broke and I tried to sell him a book. He didn't say: 'We are not interested.' (Charlie imitated the West End accent). He said: 'I can't buy your book, but keep the flag flying, old son.' And he slipped me half a crown. That's the sort Mike was."

"We want to trace his murderer. The trouble is to set about it. The book business seems like a labyrinth."

"It is, layer upon layer, till at the top you get Messrs. Bettle and Bettle of New Bond Street who won't buy from a common runner like me except by post. I see the book trade paper. Do you?"

"I have seen recent copies of it."

"Then you will have noticed the bit, framed in black, about the Keats volume missing."

"I wrote it."

"Then I think I can tell you something. There's a rumour about that the book is being auctioned on the quiet. It will go to the highest bidder, probably a Yank. Why not track those who buy for the Yanks?"

"I've been in touch with Ruth Brent. In fact I sold her a Henty first edition."

"Her boss collects them. I've sold her some. Now, guv'nor, I'll give you a tip. She always meets her dealers in The Spinning Heart, near the Marble Arch. None ever goes to her flat. So, if I was you, I'd keep a watch on The Spinning Heart; and whoever meets Miss Ruth Brent may be worth watching too. I usually meet her at half-past four when I have anything to sell."

"Thanks, Charlie, I'll take your advice. I'll tell the D.I., and he will make arrangements with the proprietor of the café. Will you have a liqueur with your coffee?"

"I'll try anything once, guv'nor. I'll have an—an old brandy."

The old brandy loosened Charlie's tongue still more and he ranged over the book trade personalities. "There's a bloke named Connington who is as sly as sly. He's one of the cleverest bookmen in London, and he's quite well-off. But you wouldn't think so. He'll come and see me and worry me to sell him a valuable book, then weep and moan and complain that he hasn't got any money. Him! To me! Once I fell for that and sold him cheap some silk pictures by Stevens woven into book-markers, which he collects. The pictures was woven in, not printed on. That's the distinction of a good book-mark. Well, my lord so loved silk pictures by Stevens that he parted with his last ha'penny. That's what you would think. But I happen to know that he sold them after for about a thousand per cent profit!"

"Have you his address?"

"Notting Hill Gate way. His sister keeps a bookshop. Not a place for bargains. I never go near it. But Ruth knows all about him. He's one of her pets. When she wants to know about issue points, and her Yank don't know, she goes to Connington."

Charlie had another old brandy. Wigan didn't mind so long as Charlie kept sober enough to be coherent, for it would be charged to expenses.

Charlie drank. "Thanks, guv., you're a sport. Where was I? Oh, about the trade. Well, I've seen Joel Ferrow of Ferrow Brothers steal a vol. in the sales-room, then auction it after among the ring. Of course I don't mean Sotheby's: they wouldn't stand for that lark. I mean out-of-the-way places where books are going and the trade flocks down to pick up bargains. Joel is another card. You ought to meet him. He once gave me ten shillings for a rare occult work I didn't know the worth of and he did. Damn it, he might have given me more than ten bob. Later I heard it fetched pounds. But the trade isn't all bad. There's plenty of good bookshops, but they wouldn't be in your line—looking for the murderer of Mike."

"Do you do well now, Charlie?"

"Pretty good, guv'nor, when the weather's fine and I can push the old barrow out. Crime and passion is what they want in the Old Kent Road. I give it to 'em, and comics, which I buy cheap and stick together to make completes. But I won't sell obscene works, guv. I draw the line at that. I won't do it."

"Mike wouldn't do it."

"No. No, he wouldn't. I'm a bookman, guv., poor but honest; not a purveyor of filth. Now and then, when trade is very bad, I have to sell a meal ticket."

"What's that?"

"A valuable first edition which I keep at home. I still have a fine copy, signed by author, of Arnold Bennett's *The Old Wives' Tale*. That's what we call in the trade his high-spot, meanin' his masterpiece. It will fetch me a good price when things are bad. A real valuable book will always sell, come wars, depressions, strikes, or anything else. There is always money for a real treasure."

Charlie lit the cigar Wigan offered him. He was only a little man with a wizened face, no hair, and no teeth to speak of; but no one could say that life so far had broken him down. He puffed at the cigar with the air of a crown prince.

"I'd like to see your private collection, Charlie."

"As a copper or a collector?"

"A collector. I'm really fond of old books. I learned that from Mike, and that's why I have been chosen for this job."

"All right, guv. Sometime. Now, if I was you, I'd fix up that watch on The Spinning Heart without delay, or the Keats first, signed by author, will flit across the Atlantic before you can say Jack Robinson; and when next it turns up to the public view it will be in the library of Silas K. Blooming Dough; and of course it can't possibly be the copy stolen from poor old Mike and sold by his murderer."

Charlie finished his second old brandy. "The effing bastard," he added deliberately. "I'm honest, guv'nor. I thanks you for the eats and drinks. But I don't much like the police, and I wouldn't help you except that Mike once gave me half a crown when I was down and out. God rest his soul. There's a little R.C. church, Mister, down my way. I don't often go inside; but I'm going to light a candle to Mike's memory. May his soul rest in peace."

"Amen to that," said Wigan.

# CHAPTER SEVEN

## OBBO ON THE SPINNING HEART

Obbo—police slang for keeping observation—is a tiring and exacting job because concentration must never slacken for an instant. A man keeping obbo cannot leave even to answer nature's call without a relief, for the wanted person may appear within those few minutes. So whenever possible the job is done in pairs. Wigan took his turn at obbo on The Spinning Heart, which, by arrangement with the management, was done from inside a staircase at the side of the main room, a small window in the wall being admirable for the purpose. A curtain over the window and a slit in the curtain, and Bob's your uncle, as someone said.

This particular job didn't last long. On the second afternoon, a Friday, at half-past four, Miss Brent came in and sat down at a table for two. The management had further helped by re-arranging the tables, placing tables for two near the staircase wall. Ruth was about eight feet away from where Wigan watched with Detective-Constable Calder. She removed her gloves and lit a cigarette.

A minute later Fred Hampton entered the café. He was carrying a small parcel. He approached Ruth's table and sat down. "Good afternoon," he said. His words could be heard clearly by Wigan and Calder, whose window was about four feet above. The frosted glass in it had been removed.

"Good afternoon," said Ruth. "You have the book?"

"Here it is. Have a look at it."

Ruth did so most carefully, with every concentration. The first issue of the first edition, she had ascertained from Connington, should have two leaves of advertisements at the end dated May 1818. This copy had.

"This seems all right," she said at length.

"The price is three hundred pounds."

"I will give two hundred and fifty."

"But you agreed on the price with my principal. I can't possibly accept less. Look the book up in Book Auction Records, Miss Brent. A presentation copy has sold for three thousand dollars."

"I shall pay two hundred and fifty. My collector won't give more. There are marks on the cover. They appear to be blood. Do you want me to fetch the police?"

"Now look here, Miss Brent—"

"Two hundred and fifty." The book was in Ruth's hands. She put it on her lap. She opened her bag, a square-shaped one like a tiny trunk. She produced a bundle of new notes neatly secured with a rubber band. "Here is the money," she said. "You can count it if you like."

Fred Hampton realised what a shocking tactical error he had made in allowing Ruth to take the book before he mentioned the price. He became violently excited. "Give me my book back. Give it to me!"

Wigan was for leaving his hiding-place at once, but Calder, the more experienced detective, held up his hand. If they waited they might see and hear more to the advantage of the case.

Ruth had not closed her bag. Her fingers touched the razor-blade wrapped in tissue paper. Her eyes were cold.

"I advise you to sit down," she said quietly.

Fred's white face, his waggling beard—he might be a figure of fun; but at the back of his mind were his two girls, Winnie and Elsie, who needed new clothes; and he could gladly have strangled Ruth, so lovely yet so stony, without heart or compassion.

Ruth acted with calculation. There were others in the café, but they were absorbed in their own affairs. A waitress stood near. Ruth beckoned to her and ordered tea. Then the waitress disappeared.

"I have refused your offer," said Fred. "Give me back my book."

Ruth took the razor-blade from her bag. With a swift movement she leaned across the table and drew the blade down the side of Fred's face. A moment later his chin and beard were running with blood. She left the money on the table. She rose from her chair and moved quickly towards the door. She was stopped by Calder, who had as swiftly left his hiding-place.

"I'm a police officer," he said, "and I'm going to detain you on a charge of causing grievous bodily harm."

Wigan went to Hampton's side. He was crying that he had been slashed. The café was in an uproar. Wigan bound up Hampton's face with a handkerchief, but the bleeding from a razor-slash is hard to stop, and, using the café phone, Wigan summoned an ambulance.

"Satisfied?" said Calder at length to Wigan, when the ambulance had departed for the hospital and Ruth had been taken in a police car to the nearest station.

"Well, we've got the book—"

"Unless I'm much mistaken, we have also got the murderer of Michael Fisk; and so Detective-Inspector Saggs will think."

The next morning Ruth Brent and Fred Hampton were brought up before the magistrate. For the razor-slashing Ruth was heavily fined, with prison as an alternative. She paid at once and was released. In Fred's case the D.I. said he might have another and more serious charge to prefer, and he asked for a remand in custody for a week. The magistrate granted this, the present charge, being in possession of stolen property, being enough to hold him. As Hampton said he was without means, he was granted legal aid. A solicitor was present when the D.I. interviewed Hampton in his cell.

"I am making inquiries into the murder of Michael Fisk. You need not answer any questions, or make any statement, but anything you do say will be taken down in writing, and may be given in evidence."

Hampton turned to the solicitor. "What shall I do?"

"You can answer questions likely to help the police clear up the crime, but you need say nothing to incriminate yourself. I will watch the questions."

The D.I. then proceeded to show the enormous amount of work he and others had put in to trace the knife with which Fisk had been killed.

"Have you recently been in Bristol, Hampton?"

"Yes, I was there about three months ago."

"Why were you there?"

"I had a tip about a Henty collection. There is an antique dealer there called John Hood, who is very good to me. He wrote and said he had had some Hentys offered to him, and would I buy them. I said I would have a look at them, and I went down on a cheap train from Paddington."

"While you were in Bristol, did you buy a knife?"

"I bought one from John Hood. He had a boxful. They were government surplus."

The D.I. produced a knife similar to that used to kill Michael Fisk. "Was your knife like this?"

"Yes."

"And where is it now?"

"I don't know. I lost it."

The D.I. pursued his points relentlessly. This was the kind of case he liked: the building up of points of evidence until the accused was finally surrounded like a fish in a fishing-net.

"Why did you buy a knife?" he said.

"It would be useful in my business. They were a bargain at one-and-sixpence. John told me so."

"You would use it to cut books?"

"To open the leaves? I suppose you mean that. Yes, I would

use it for that sometimes if the leaves were better opened, as in a technical work where first-edition value doesn't usually count."

"And where do you think you lost your knife?"

"I don't know. I have no idea."

The D.I. glanced at the solicitor. "To turn to another point: where did you get the Keats book you were offering to Miss Ruth Brent?"

Hampton licked his lips. "It sounds fantastic, but I found it on my front step as I came home late one night. It was wrapped in a parcel. I opened the parcel in my study. I found ten one-pound notes inside the front cover of the book, and a postcard. On the card was written: 'You will offer this book to Ruth Brent on Friday the 27th at half-past four in The Spinning Heart. You will let her examine the book. The price is £300. You will keep £50 for yourself. The remainder you will hand to me in Niger's bookshop at 10 a.m. on Saturday morning. You will know me when I come up to you and say: "Have you the money?" Burn this card.' It was signed 'The Red Hand of Vengeance.'"

The D.I.'s face betrayed no emotion at all when he heard this. He said: "Do you engage in free-lance writing activities, Mr. Hampton?"

Hampton's white face turned scarlet. He replied: "I do. I make a little money that way."

"By writing fiction?"

"I write stories for boys."

"I see. And you burnt the card, as suggested by the, eh, Red Hand of Vengeance?"

"Yes, I burnt it with a match."

"And so with this book, advertised in your trade paper as

stolen from a murdered man, you kept your appointment with Ruth Brent?"

"Yes. I knew it was wrong, but I needed money badly. My daughter Winnie is going in for music. She needs a viola, a good one, and the price of that will be about £50. Now—she will never have it." Hampton looked as if he were going to cry.

"Have you any idea," continued the D.I., "who the Red Hand of Vengeance might be?"

"None. It was obviously someone in the trade, since he or she said he would be known to me. The writing was tiny printed characters. I wish I hadn't burnt the card now."

The D.I. made no remark. He turned to see that the police shorthand-writer was keeping up-to-date, then he said: "I should like to turn to another point, Mr. Hampton. Please cast your mind back to the day of August 9th, a Monday. What were you doing on that day?"

"I started out after breakfast, about 9 a.m. to walk to Sun, where I intended to see Michael Fisk. It may seem a long walk to you, but bookseller's runners are accustomed to walking. It is part of the stock-in-trade. Well, on the way I made various calls at bookshops or antique shops where they sell a few books. I wasn't in a hurry because I knew Mike Fisk wouldn't want to see me before 6 p.m. He probably wouldn't be at home. He would be out hunting, himself."

"Please pause for a moment," said the D.I. politely. The shorthand-writer caught up, then looked up and nodded.

"I got to Sun about five," continued Hampton. "It was a terrible day, raining hard all the way. I was pretty soaked. I had a cup of tea somewhere. I can't exactly think where, because my mind was on my work. I had had a letter from an American collector, and I wanted to get a book on demonology out of Mike. It wouldn't be easy because I didn't like him much and I knew he didn't like me. But I could make a good profit. So I walked towards his house. I knew where he lived—in Chelmer Square."

Hampton paused for the shorthand-writer to catch up. The solicitor poured him out a glass of water and gave him a cigarette.

"Ah," said Hampton, "that's better. Well, I met Mike on the road and told him what I wanted: Jean Bodin's *De la Démonomaniedes Sorciers.*"

The shorthand-writer spoke. "Will you spell that out, please?"

Hampton patiently did so, letter by letter. Then he continued: "I knew Mike would have a copy. He specialised in the occult. My Yank would pay a thousand dollars for it when he came to London, as he told me he intended to do, in September. Well, I met Mike on the road and told him what I wanted and he flatly refused to sell the book to me. He said: 'It's no good coming to me looking for bargains.' Then I flared up and called him a bloody selfish bachelor. And I thought of my wife and the girls and the constant need for money, and the blood went to my head as it does when I get in a rage, and I called Mike an effing bastard and a few other things. And he made no reply and walked off; and now my wife and the girls will be ruined." Hampton put his head in his hands.

"What did you do next?" said the D.I.

"I walked home. It took me hours because I was tired, but

I had earned nothing so did not feel justified in spending money on fares."

"Did you meet anyone on the way?"

"I saw cars. It was pouring with rain and I would have liked a lift, but none would stop; they just splashed me with water and went on."

"What time did you arrive home?"

"I was very tired and slept for some time in a telephone-box. I sort of dozed in the box. I got to Upper Street, Islington, at six o'clock in the morning. I remember a church clock striking. I got home a few minutes later. I made myself a cup of tea and went to bed."

The D.I. considered. Then he said: "You are a man of good education?"

"I went to a small public school."

"And why are you living now in reduced circumstances as a bookseller's runner?"

The solicitor interposed. "I cannot see, Officer, that you have any right to ask the prisoner that."

"Very well, sir. When you were having this altercation with Michael Fisk, Mr. Hampton, did anyone else see you?"

"I seem to remember a labourer passing. But it was pouring with rain, and he didn't take much notice."

"Thank you. I think that's all I wish to ask you."

"I'm in a mess, aren't I?" said Hampton to his solicitor when the D.I. had left.

"I'm afraid you are. I can't say yet what is in the police mind, but it may be something more serious than being in possession of stolen property, the Keats book."

"Well, I look to you to help my wife and daughters. I don't

want them to know I'm in trouble. Even if I have to go to jail, I still don't want them to know. On no account must Winnie or Elsie visit me in prison. Winnie is studying music at the Royal Academy. She has a scholarship. She's a really clever girl. But she must have a viola, and her teacher says that a good instrument is necessary. I don't know much about music myself, but I have been into the matter. What they call a trade instrument can be bought for £15, but a good one will cost at least £50. I suppose you couldn't lend me the money?"

"I don't think you have any right to ask me that. Have you no friends?"

"None," said Hampton bitterly. "When you stopped him, that copper was trying to prove that I am a man of bad character. The fact is, I quarrel easily. It's my nerves. The war made me worse. I had a bloody war job. I suppose I've sunk a bit, but I do understand books."

The solicitor sighed. He knew only too well the kind of client Fred Hampton was going to be. No profit, no credit, and quite possibly (though of course ethically this didn't affect the matter) the halter at the end. But the solicitor was the kind to do his duty without much geniality. Here he did show a little human feeling.

"Have you anything you can sell to raise money?"

"I have only a set of fourteen volumes of Kate Greenaway's *Almanacs,* including the rare one of 1897. But they are fine and should fetch £50. There is a firm in New Oxford Street who have always treated me decently. Will you take them there and get what you can for them?"

"Very well. But you must give me a written order to your wife to secure the volumes. What shall I tell your wife?"

"Say I'm detained on business. She is used to that. And look, while you are about it, there are one or two other books which had better be sold. Minnie will need housekeeping money. I'll jot down the titles. You don't mind, do you?"

"My dear sir, I am not a charitable institution. However, you can rely on me to do my best."

"Thanks." It was on the tip of Hampton's tongue to say that solicitors these days are dam' well paid: they have a Law Society to fix their own fees. But he refrained. If this lifeline failed him and the police still opposed any bail, what on earth could he do? How would Minnie and the girls be able to manage? Oh God in Heaven, he was in a mess!

Three days later Hampton was taken from the cell where he was on remand to a West End police station, where he was formally charged with the murder of Michael Fisk at about two o'clock in the morning of Tuesday, August 10th, 1954. He was cautioned, and replied to the charge: "I am innocent, before God."

The case was first heard by a magistrate. For the prosecution, the evidence was largely circumstantial; but again it was obvious that the D.I. and his men had put in a tremendous amount of work. They had traced the labourer who had seen the altercation between Hampton and Fisk; and the labourer said he heard Hampton say: "I'd like to punch you on the nose." They had further traced a newspaper man delivering evening papers to Chelmer Square and district who said he saw Hampton, whom he noticed because of his beard, standing at the front door of No. 10 Chelmer Square. He was delivering a *Star* to No. 8. He heard Hampton bang at the knocker, but what happened next he could not say because it was raining hard and he hurried across the road to deliver a *Standard* to No. 15. The time was about seven o'clock.

For the defence Hampton said that his answers to the D.I.'s questions were not altogether complete. He remembered now that he had called at Fisk's house to try and make him change his mind; but Fisk refused to let him in. He stood at the door and barred entrance. He said: "I won't sell you any books." He then closed the door, and Hampton began to walk home. There was nothing else he could do.

The prosecution's case was that Hampton had either been admitted to Fisk's house, or had later forced entrance, and had attacked Fisk with a knife, causing his death. The magistrate committed Hampton for trial at the Central Criminal Court.

"The fellow's easy," remarked the D.I. to Wigan, as they walked away from the magistrate's court.

"I wonder whether he really did kill Fisk, sir."

"Not your job to wonder, Sergeant."

"But the evidence seems a bit slim—so many gaps in it."

"We've got a few bits up our sleeve. I had a search-warrant issued and searched his study. I found in a drawer a half-finished work, grossly obscene. That won't do him any good with a jury. Then there were one or two pornographic works. Highly indecent. It all adds up to a character morally degenerate."

"Or he may have intended to sell them for the sake of his family. I seem to remember once reading a story in which a man with a face like Christ's sold dirty postcards to help a friend."

"Wigan, are you counsel for the defence?"

"No, sir, I'm only interested in justice being done."

"It will be done. It's my duty to screw the chap down and I will screw him down. I admit there are gaps. That confounded storm, the noise of the wind and rain, is against us. Fisk must have given a cry as the knife was driven in his chest. But I can't find anyone who heard it. Then what did they do between seven o'clock and two o'clock? Did they look at books? Did they eat? You're to go round Chelmer Square again, Wigan. Every soul in the place must be questioned. Also I want to find a pair of gloves. I couldn't find any at Hampton's house, yet Mrs. Hampton told me that Hampton did own a pair of brown leather gloves. Where are they? Every inch of ground between Sun and Islington must be searched."

Wigan made a shot at random. "Why not in the telephone kiosk where he said he slept?"

"Sergeant, I believe you've got it. I believe he did walk home, but he didn't take all the time he said. Ten miles from Sun to Islington. He could do it in four hours and still have a rest. Some stranger may have found the gloves, and perhaps we shall never recover them. But a G.P.O. cleaner may have found them. I'll contact the G.P.O."

The man-hunter was off on the scent again. With a strange sinking of the heart Wigan felt that he had put another nail in Hampton's coffin, and yet—the man was innocent. Wigan felt it. It was hard to justify this feeling, and the D.I. could hardly be blamed for pursuing the line he was pursuing. Wigan hoped that the gloves would be found. Evidence from them should be conclusive. Michael Fisk was killed by a violent blow delivered across the table. It was possible that the murderer's clothes would not be stained with blood; but almost certainly the hand that delivered the blow would be stained; and if the hand wore a glove... Wigan thought that perhaps he hadn't done Hampton such a bad turn after all.

The following day the gloves were found. Mrs. Hampton called at a North London police station and asked to see the officer in charge. She said she had brought with her her husband's gloves which the police were asking about. The D.I. at Brabant was contacted, and arrived within a short time. His face was grim-set as he entered the matron's room where Mrs. Hampton was sitting, but he strove to be pleasant. Judges' Rules laid down for police officers are strict about questioning, but if a prisoner's wife is idiot enough to offer evidence there can be no objection to receiving it.

"I understand, Mrs. Hampton, that you have brought here a pair of gloves belonging to your husband?"

"Yes, sir. I thought if I was fair and open with you, you would let Fred go."

"I cannot make promises, Mrs. Hampton, but I would like to see the gloves."

"Here, sir." She opened her bag. "Fred only has this pair, and he doesn't usually wear them in summer. He's such a one for losing things and leaving things about. I found them under the mattress of the single bed in his study. I expect they have been there since last winter. Naturally you wouldn't think of looking under the bed when you searched the house." She laid a pair of men's brown leather gloves on the matron's table.

"But I did look under the bed," snapped the D.I. "I saw no gloves then."

"They must have been there, sir, all the same. Anyway, I have brought them now. They were very dirty, so I have cleaned them up a bit."

"You *what*?" The D.I. almost gaped at the woman's incredible stupidity.

"Cleaned them up. With petrol followed by furniture polish. That's good for leather gloves. I do Winnie's and Elsie's, and very smart they look."

No real-life policeman ever loses his temper. At least, very rarely. The D.I. didn't lose his temper now. He was almost certain that those damned gloves weren't under the bed, but it was just conceivable that they had somehow stuck to the under-side of the mattress as he turned it over. Cleaned up, the leather yet had a crumpled look as if it had once been very wet; and the D.I. remembered the pouring wet night of the murder...

"Will you let Fred go now, sir?" pleaded Mrs. Hampton. "Any other gloves you found cannot belong to Fred. He only had this pair."

"I cannot let him go, Mrs. Hampton. It doesn't lie in my power."

"But he's really a good man, sir. I know you found nasty writing in his study; but he only did it for us to make money. It's so very hard free-lancing as he does. He ought to have a job with a regular wage, but that's hard to get at his age—he's forty-six—and he has no references after hitting the manager."

The D.I. tried to turn defeat into victory. "You needn't

answer unless you wish, Mrs. Hampton, but what manager did he hit?"

"The manager of the glass-works in Bolus Street. Fred couldn't get on with the job at all. He couldn't stand the heat, and he had a row with the manager; but the manager was a big, powerful man and Fred was sorry after that he hit him."

"I see. How long was your husband in the job at the glass-works?"

"About three months, sir. He got it from the Labour Exchange when we were very nearly broke. 'It will pull us out of the wood, Minnie,' he said to me. And it did. My husband is a hasty man, sir, but he doesn't mean any harm. He got the worst of it in the row with the manager."

"I see. When your husband returned home on the morning of Tuesday, August 10th, did he appear upset?"

"I didn't see him, sir. I was in bed. So were the children."

The D.I. began to wonder whether Mrs. Hampton was a cleverer woman than she appeared to be. Her large bovine face expressed nothing but anxiety at the trouble which had befallen them.

"I expect," said Saggs, "that you saw your husband's clothes after. Was there any blood on them?"

"No blood, sir. None at all."

"And on the gloves, before you cleaned them?"

"I didn't notice any blood, sir, but there may have been. My husband cut himself with his knife some time before."

"Curious," remarked the D.I., "if blood got on the gloves and they were under the mattress since last winter."

"I can't swear they were, sir. My husband was most absent-minded. He would put his things simply anywhere."

"I shall have the gloves examined," said the D.I. "The laboratory may be able to tell us something."

"Will they know if any blood on the gloves is my husband's?"

"I can't say. You say your husband cut himself. When, where, and how?"

"About a month before the Tuesday you speak of. He cut himself with his knife, very badly, on the forefinger of his right hand. He was trying to prune a little bush we have in the back garden."

"Anyone see him do it?"

"Not that I know of."

"Trying to prune a bush, you say. I suppose he was trying to cut with his right hand. Extraordinary he should cut the finger of his right hand?"

"Not extraordinary, sir. It just happened. The knife must have slipped. He came into the kitchen where I was working. His hand was streaming with blood. I bound up the cut. A bad one it was. Later when he had to handle his books he may have used his gloves then."

"Then put them back under the mattress. I see."

It was known in the neighbourhood where he lived (Brabant) that J. Saggs was not particularly beloved of his wife. Nor did his three sons seem to care much about him. Nor did his immediate neighbours. A grim-faced man, he kept himself to himself. He gardened a bit, played a little bowls with grave elderly men, with whom it was a point of honour not to discuss police matters with Detective-Inspector Saggs. Otherwise J. Saggs never seemed to cheer up at all. Yet now he was enjoying himself matching wits with a person who might be fully capable of taking care of herself.

"Mrs. Hampton: I suppose your husband isn't *left-handed*?"

"No, sir. Right-handed like me. He always has been."

"I see. Well, the crime it is my duty to investigate was committed by a right-handed person, so the doctor says."

Mrs. Hampton betrayed no emotion at all. "My husband is right-handed, as I say, but he hasn't committed no crime except to be in possession of a stolen book. But you know that."

"Yes. Your husband spoke of a parcel left on your front step. Did you see this?"

"No. But I wouldn't take any notice anyway. I never interfered with my husband's business affairs. I don't understand books. I never read, except a magazine or two that my daughters bring home."

The D.I. abandoned the topic. "When your husband left home on the Monday morning, August 9th, do you happen to have noticed if he wore his gloves then?"

"I didn't notice, sir. I have Winnie to get off—she's my eldest and goes to Baker Street. She is studying at the Royal Academy. Then Elsie, my second daughter, goes to work at a dressmaking house. She's very clever with her fingers, and sometimes she makes more than Dad does."

"She must be a help to you. I don't think there's anything else. Thank you for bringing the gloves, Mrs. Hampton. I must retain them. I expect you understand that."

"I do, sir. Good-day, sir." Mrs. Hampton knew better than to make another plea for mercy to the miserable old cab-horse, as she thought of Inspector Saggs. A good thing when one of *his* family were in trouble.

"I've done my best for Dad," said Mrs. Hampton to Winnie, when she had returned home.

"It's dreadful, Mum. They suspect Dad of murder. I know it. Everyone here knows it."

"They haven't found out at the Academy, have they, dear?"

"I don't think so. No one speaks of it. Hampton is a fairly common name."

"They mustn't find out. That would be Dad's wish. That's why he told us, through the solicitor, that on no account must we go to visit him. Whatever happens, he said."

"It seems so heartless, Mum." Winnie was a tall, serious-faced girl with beautiful long hands—the sensitive hands of her father. Suddenly she burst into tears. "I can hardly play on his viola. He—he bought it—"

"I know, dear. But you can make money too hard. I told Dad that when I found—well, never mind. Elsie won't talk. She says the girls don't know nothing yet. Thank God we haven't got a name like Beelzebub. The inspector never got no change out of me. I knew Dad's gloves must be found, and it was worth a walk to Sun to find them before the police did. You should have seen that copper's face when I brought them in! I petrolled them and I petrolled them, and I wish the scientist gentlemen luck trying to find stains. If they do, they're cleverer than I am."

"What do you think, Mum? Did Dad kill the book-seller at Sun?"

"I don't know, and that's a fact. But Dad was loyal to us and we must be loyal to him. If your heart is breaking, dear, put up a show before them snobs at the Academy. And like iron make up your mind. We mustn't go near Dad. Them's his instructions."

"I hope he knows how much we love him."

"He knows," said Mrs. Hampton.

# CHAPTER EIGHT

## SCREWING HIM DOWN

With care the police prepared their case for the trial. V. Belham, Q.C., was to lead for the prosecution and he must have every possible fact in his hands. Wigan, still attached to Brabant, as Aid to C.I.D., and working with the D.I. in his office, was interested in the attitude the D.I. took in the matter. Technically, police duty was to uncover the facts wherever they might lead, and at the beginning the D.I. had done this, keeping an open mind. But now sufficient evidence had been built up to justify Hampton's arrest and committal for trial, J. Saggs ceased to think that another might be guilty. With might and main he was bent on "screwing the man down."

Several times Wigan said: "Are you sure, sir?"

"What do you think the judge and jury are for?" was the reply.

With inexhaustible energy the history of the gloves was probed. Microscopic examination brought to light traces of blood on the right-hand glove which had impregnated the leather and was thus resistant to the act of cleaning; but it was not possible to prove if it was venous or arterial blood; i.e., if it came from a small wound or a large one. It is easy to get rid of blood by washing in cold water. Rain would do this. And beyond the fact that the traces of blood were human blood laboratory experts could not go.

The D.I. employed Wigan and others to re-examine minutely all the inhabitants of Chelmer Square. Somebody must have seen something. That was the theory that the D.I.'s experience led him to believe was correct, provided that one searched long enough. It was Wigan who called on a Mrs. Tray who lived in a house which overlooked the back of Fisk's house. She made the following astounding remark:

"I wondered when you would come to me. I have something important to say."

"But, madam, it was your duty to approach the police."

"It wasn't," snapped Mrs. Tray. "I haven't the time to run round after policemen. I heard detectives were calling at houses in Chelmer Square, and I thought to myself: If they haven't the sense to call here they can do without me."

Wigan consulted his notes. "It is almost certain," he said politely, "that a detective did call here. He interviewed the lady downstairs who is the owner of the house. She said she had heard and seen nothing unusual during the night of August 9th–10th."

"She's a jealous woman and would say nothing about me. The detective should have come upstairs. I'm a lodger, but I'm just as important as the woman who owns the house."

Wigan made no attempt to argue. Detectives can't be perfect, and probably the man who called here was a little at fault in not making a routine inquiry: "Are there any other occupants of the house?"

"Well, madam," he said mildly, "I have been fortunate. Your full name, please?"

"Ann Louisa Tray. Yes—T,R,A,Y. Tray. I'm a widow and I've lived here for about five years, but if I didn't happen to answer the door I don't suppose you would have heard about me. There are factory workers who can pay more than I do, and the woman downstairs wants to get rid of me. But I don't see why I should go. I'm comfortable here. I have my own little kitchen and use of bath. The woman downstairs goes out to work. She does very well, if you ask me."

"I expect she does," said Wigan in the same mild way.

"Yes. And I keep the hall clean for her. And I sweep the steps. But come inside. Come upstairs to my room. I expect with a policeman it will be quite proper."

"Certainly it will. I'm a married man with children. You can safely talk to me... Why, what a delightful room, madam, if you don't mind my saying so."

Mrs. Tray's rather acid expression became pleasant. For years Wigan had worked as a beat policeman; and no better training exists for getting on with people. He had been called to houses where husband and wife were fighting like the proverbial cats, and left them in sweet accord filling up a football pool. He was probably infinitely better with a difficult witness than the D.I. with his hardness which came through all he said and did.

"Of course my room is only small," said Mrs. Tray. "I get the Old Age—I'm sixty-seven—and my husband left me a little money. But I'm not what you might call wealthy."

"Your room is comfortable, ma'am. That's what counts. A man dearly likes a bit of comfort; and I expect you ladies do too."

Mrs. Tray beamed. "Would it be in order, Inspector, if I offered you a cup of tea?"

"I'm just a humble sergeant, ma'am. Sergeant Jack Wigan. It would not only be in order to offer me a cup of tea, it would be extremely nice. It's a hot day, ma'am. Summer at last after the appalling weather we have been having."

While Mrs. Tray was in her kitchen, Wigan stood respectfully looking out of the window. The house he was in was No. 9 of a row called Brompton Row and had probably been built about sixty years ago by the same builder who had built Chelmer Square. The builder's name was Collins, and he was known for the solid construction of his houses—perhaps one reason why nothing had been heard by immediate neighbours of Fisk's house, which was, from where Wigan stood, about a hundred and twenty feet away across two gardens: the back garden of No. 9 Brompton Row and the back garden of Fisk's house, No. 10 Chelmer Square. Wigan carried in his mind a plan of Fisk's house. Ground floor back: kitchen, pantry, and small living-room which Fisk did not use. First floor back: w.c. window, bathroom window, back bedroom, which Fisk used to sleep in. His study and store-room for his books was the front large bedroom which faced on to the square and was on the ground floor. A previous owner had had the house so, and Fisk had seen no reason to alter it. An old brass-knobbed bed which the previous owner had left behind Fisk had used as a sort of couch to lie upon among his books. The corresponding large room upstairs, facing the front, the previous owner had used as a drawing-room; and this Fisk had not bothered to furnish at all. A proper bachelor's house, as he had said to Wigan.

Wigan couldn't imagine what Mrs. Tray had seen. She was the wrong side to look into the study; and Fisk had been killed in his study, not in his bedroom.

Mrs. Tray returned with the tea daintily set out with an embroidered tea-cloth. Wigan sipped his tea in genteel fashion. He bit delicately at a crumby sort of biscuit with a cherry in the centre.

"Home-made," said Mrs. Tray.

"It's delightful, madam."

"And now I expect you're wondering what important news I have. Well, I saw the murderer washing his hands! I do not sleep well, and the noise of the storm kept me awake, the wind and the rain. I hope you approve of women smoking, Sergeant, because I smoke a lot. I like to sit at my window at night smoking and thinking of my husband and how different things were when he was alive and how he would stand up for me and not let me be put upon by the woman downstairs. But of course we had our own house when my husband was alive. We lived at Pinner."

Wigan stolidly bit at his biscuit. He knew better than to try and hurry a witness.

"Well," continued Mrs. Tray, "on the night you speak of, about two o'clock I couldn't lie in bed any longer. I know it's dangerous to smoke in bed and I never do it. I got up and sat by the window. I opened the window wider. The rain blew in a bit but I didn't mind that. I did not turn on the light. I lit a cigarette and looked across towards Mr. Fisk's house. I do think people should have certain windows covered with a curtain, but I know Mr. Fisk was a bachelor and I suppose bachelors don't bother. Anyway, I saw a light come on in the window which I knew to be the bathroom or—or the other place, but I think the bathroom. There was no curtain, only frosted glass in the lower sash, as is usual. I have excellent long sight and I could see clearly. There was a man in the room and he was washing his hands. I think his motions were consistent with a man doing that. The man was full-face to me, with slightly bent head. I think he had a beard. He raised his face once and I saw the beard. Mr. Fisk had no beard, so the man I saw must have been the murderer."

Wigan produced from his wallet two photographs, full-face and profile, taken by the police photographer when Fred Hampton had been committed for trial and hence was a prisoner.

"Is that the man?"

"Yes, I think it is… I can't swear to it because I wasn't near enough to see details of the face. But I think that's the man. I certainly recognise the beard. I will swear to the beard."

It was Wigan's duty to look after the legal side.

"There are other men with beards, madam."

"Then I will swear to *a* beard."

Then Wigan had to become somewhat less the homely copper. He had to ask Mrs. Tray to accompany him to Sun Police Station, where she was interviewed by Detective-Inspector Saggs with a shorthand-writer in attendance. Wigan was present. He noted that the D.I. was very careful indeed with a witness who might be torn to pieces by counsel for the defence. He was careful not to try and make her see more than she had in fact seen; but afterwards he was able to say to Wigan: "I think we are screwing him down."

The history of Hampton was traced from birth to the present day. He was born near Ashford in Kent. His father, now dead, had a small business which prospered; and he was able to send his son to a good school. Hampton's mother, also dead now, was a member of the Kentish aristocracy, one of the family of Selburns; and it was from his mother that Hampton appeared to inherit his fine-drawn nervous temperament. If he had carried on his father's business, all might have gone well with him; but he went out to Canada on some romantic notion. He lived there for ten years, but failed to prosper. While he was in Canada his father and mother died. The business was sold and the proceeds were sent to Montreal, where Hampton used them to start a bookshop with a partner named Bridge. This also failed to prosper. Hampton returned to England in 1930. He had neither job nor money. For a time he worked as a waiter, but his temperament made him quarrel with customers. He was tried in the cash-desk, and achieved distinction by flinging the till over a queue waiting to pay their bills. "I'm fed up with the bloody job," he told them. Naturally enough he was discharged immediately. It was after this that he began "flogging" books—a career open to anyone without training. He became very ill with strain and under-feeding. But the landlady of his lodgings in Islington stood by him. In 1934 he married her. During the war he worked first with a Heavy Rescue squad, but the job of hauling bodies and bits of bodies out of bombed buildings was too much for him, and he was moved to a warden's post. The chief warden did not give him a good character. "A more quarrelsome chap I have never met," he said.

All this Wigan was at liberty to read in the dossier "Frederick Hampton," which lay on the D.I.'s desk. Wigan was expected to add to it. "Find out what they say about him in the book trade," the D.I. told Wigan. Wigan did his best to find out the good as well as the bad. But there was little good. "Clever but cranky," said the manager of Niger's. "We don't mind runners, but once or twice he was a nuisance pushing customers about. I heard he had been a waiter and it was his way of working off bad temper. Still, I wouldn't like the fellow to hang, and if Niger's can be of any use for the defence, we shall be pleased to do what we can."

This was handsome, and about the best that Wigan encountered. At a fashionable establishment the manager said: "Mr. Hampton may have sold us a few books, but we do not care to be associated with him." Ditto, ditto, ditto, elsewhere. In fact Wigan found the big names rather "snooty." Yet in justice to them another character called Sniffing Sam seemed to get along well enough. "Poor Fred wasn't a charmer," said a bookseller in South-East London. And that seemed to sum it up.

Wigan was expected to tackle another angle. Why, if Fred was after a rare work on demonology, did he steal (assuming him to be guilty) a Keats first edition from Fisk? "Of course he may have made the demonology bit up," said the D.I., "but I'd like to have another look at Fisk's library. You come too, Wigan, and use your brains. There are so many loop-holes in the case."

From the time of Fisk's murder and its discovery, his house

had been sealed by police. At first a day and night guard was provided to keep away sightseers; but public interest always wanes in time; and the guard was later reduced to special attention by the P.C. on the beat, all reliefs. Near the entrance to Chelmer Square the D.I. and Sergeant Wigan contacted P.C. Thompson, Late Turn (2 p.m. to 10 p.m.), one of Wigan's own relief.

"Well, Thompson, how goes it?"

"All correct, Sarge."

"We are going to visit Fisk's house. Everything all right there?"

"Yes, Sarge. There isn't much doing now. Of course the neighbours keep away. They hate a murder in the square, and they will shoo away sightseers if they can. I think you will find our padlocks O.K. Shall I come with you?"

"Not necessary," said the D.I. So Thompson continued with his beat.

It was a mild September day, very pleasant in the tree-lined square. With his key the D.I. unlocked the padlock fastened to the front door. Then he unlocked the door itself. They went in. As every window was shut fast the house had a musty air. They entered the study. Everything was as it had been left after the body was removed. There was the table stained with blood. On it the blood-drenched book that Fisk had been reading when he died.

"Wonderful stuff, blood," remarked the D.I. "It's sticky, and there's nothing like it for retaining fingerprints. Pity the lab. people couldn't do more for us. My point is, if he was in the house from 7 p.m. to 2 a.m., what was he doing all that time? He wouldn't keep his gloves on. It isn't a social habit with men. And why did he take the Keats away?"

"Those points have occurred to me too, sir. I hope we are not trying to pin a murder on the man."

"Careful of your language, Sergeant. You will be a witness for the Crown. The court won't want to hear your speculations. Look at the books. Pick me out that *Demon de Sorcery*, or whatever it was that Hampton spoke about when he made his first statement."

Wigan carefully considered the shelves of books on the occult. "I can't see it, sir," he said at last. "Maybe Fisk didn't have a copy. It is very rare." Wigan felt bound to add: "That book on the desk, on raising the dead. The book with so much blood on it. Has it been examined for fingerprints?"

"Yep. No go. I don't suppose the murderer would touch it. What I want is a fingerprint before the murder was committed. I want to prove that Fred Hampton was actually in this room."

There was a gap from which the book on the dead had been taken. On one side of the gap was the bookcase wall. On the other was a book in ancient binding entitled: *Discoverie of Witchcraft*. Wigan took the volume out. He opened the volume at the title-page and studied it. Knowing him, Wigan, to be a religious man, Mike had said little to him about his works on the occult; but Wigan felt that this book, published in 1584, must be rare and valuable.

"I want definitely," said the D.I., "to establish Hampton's presence in the house. In the kitchen there are no signs of two men eating. Say Hampton sat in the small chair and Fisk in the round-backed one at the table. Hampton doesn't or didn't smoke. Right. No fag-ends. Then what did he do? That's clear, isn't it? *That's* what counsel for the defence will be asking."

"I understand that, sir. I think I can tell you what Fisk was doing."

"Oh, what?"

"Trying to raise the devil, sir, from that book on the table. Once I believe a bull came into the room."

"A what? Are you crazy, Sergeant?"

"No, sir. Strange things have happened in the occult world. I don't approve, so Fisk never said much to me. But he may have been trifling with the powers of evil while another man—perhaps Hampton—sat in that chair and turned over the leaves of this volume or another. Have you examined the floor for prints?"

"Yep. Of course. Hard-wood floor put down by the last owner. No prints."

Suddenly the D.I., with more imagination than Wigan gave him credit for, began to reconstruct. "Let's look at it like this. Hampton arrives at seven o'clock. He is admitted to the study here. Fisk says: 'Excuse me, old man, you'll have to wait a bit because I'm raising the devil by black magic.' Hampton waits. He waits till 2 a.m., then says: 'I'm tired of waiting.' So he ups with a knife and stabs Fisk in the chest. Then he seizes the Keats book and clears out. How's that? Absolute and utter nonsense. Now try this. Hampton calls at seven o'clock. He is not admitted. Fisk will not sell him books for his American customer. Hampton goes, but he doesn't go far. He lays in waiting, perhaps in some shelter which we have yet to find. He waits till past midnight, then he burgles the house and kills Fisk as he sits reading his book and raising the devil, or trying to. After which, perhaps appalled at the blood which is spurting from the wound, Hampton loses his nerve and takes the first valuable book which comes to hand. It happens to be the Keats book. How's that?"

"More probable," admitted Wigan.

"Of course it is. Now let's trek round and see if we can find a likely hiding-place. The man can't have been soaked to the skin, or there would have been water on the floor; which there wasn't."

About half a mile away on the road going north they found in a field an old shed. The roof, however, was still sound. The door was half-open. They entered and looked around. They saw an old plough and one or two other agricultural implements. "Never stand when you can sit," remarked the D.I. He went behind the plough and found an old box which would form a reasonable seat. By the box was a handkerchief rolled into a ball. After all this time it was still sodden. The D.I. picked it up and opened it out. It was marked in a corner: F. Hampton.

"Well, I'm hanged," said Wigan.

"He'll be hanged," said the D.I. grimly.


For the first time Wigan felt that Hampton really must be guilty, and he complimented the D.I. on his brilliant effort of deduction. But J. Saggs was not a genial character.

"Ha!" he said. "I've been thinking about your bull, Wigan."

"Not my bull, sir. I was only told the story. It materialised from what I believe spiritualists call ectoplasm. Fisk said it crashed about the room in a terrifying way till the power wore off and it disappeared."

The D.I. grinned sourly. "I suppose it couldn't have held a knife in its mouth?"

"No, sir," said Wigan shortly.

"Pity. I should like to see a jury's face when told about a ghost bull. It would make an ingenious defence for a murderer. 'I didn't kill poor Mr. Fisk, my lord. A ghost did it.'"

Wigan changed the subject. "I suppose he went up the side entrance and entered through the unlocked back door?"

"So I read it. In my experience it is more usual for amateurs to risk being seen entering a house from the front, or forcing an entry from the front. Only the experts use back gardens, and that after a lot of careful planning. Still, we'll have a look at the garden."

The back garden of No. 10 Chelmer Square was an oblong plot with grass in the middle and beds round each side. The grass was feet high and the beds were overgrown. Evidently, even allowing for the effects of time, Mr. Michael Fisk had not been a gardener.

"Now," said the D.I., "we can see Mrs. Tray's window. I expect she would see quite clearly a bearded face in the lighted frame of the window. Valuable piece of evidence that. Circumstantial, since she can't swear to the features, but it all adds up." The D.I. looked round at the overgrown waste. "We might find something more here. When a man of Hampton's nervous type commits a crime he is usually terribly upset afterwards. He may have been sick in the garden, or left other traces."

"Or in the lavatory upstairs."

"There are two, one upstairs, one down. The one down looks like a cupboard. I have had both examined. I have had the pipes taken to pieces. But these old houses have sound plumbing, and what with the rain water coming down, any material deposited would be soon washed away to the sewage farm, and from our point of view would be a hopeless proposition. If Hampton came out here, he wouldn't venture far in the storm. Why should he? Look about, Wigan."

They looked about. The D.I. was completely insensitive. He stooped and sniffed about, but he found nothing.

"Shouldn't this have been done before, sir?" said Wigan.

"It was. But I want it done twice. Maybe I have other reasons."

"You have had samples taken from the prisoner?"

"Of course I have." The D.I. gave a crafty smile. "Lie down on the ground, Wigan. I want you to call attention to yourself. Look like Sherlock Holmes with a magnifying glass."

Wigan did, a bit awkwardly. He was no actor. When he rose again to his feet, he looked up at the house facing the garden and remarked: "Mrs. Tray is at her window watching us."

"Ha! Is she now? Wigan, what have we got to make you wear a beard?"

"I noticed an old mop-head in the bathroom upstairs. I could tie that round my chin."

"Excellent. Go and do it. Then show yourself at the window. Make-believe you are washing your hands. Look across at Mrs. Tray."

Wigan did this. The mop-head was what might be termed a regular bachelor's mop-head—all fringe. It was made to fit on a triangular frame, and tied round his chin it gave a very fair representation of a beard. Wigan went through the motions of washing his hands, looking across at Mrs. Tray who was watching intently, cigarette in mouth. They then called on Mrs. Tray, and the D.I. said to her: "Madam, when you were seated at your window just now, did you see a man with a beard appear at the bathroom window in Mr. Fisk's house?"

"I did, and it was him." She pointed to Wigan. "Though he wore some sort of beard, I recognised him."

"Thank you, madam."

"We've got a live wire leading for the prosecution," said the D.I. later to Wigan. "We'll try and get him to make Mrs. Tray positively identify Hampton from the witness-box. That will fix him."

"Is that fair, sir?"

"Fair, fair! You'll make me talk about bulls again in a minute. Our job, Wigan, is to bring the murderer to justice, and don't you forget it."

# CHAPTER NINE

## SCREWED DOWN

Sergeant Wigan had not before attended a trial for murder, but in his service in uniform as constable and sergeant he had "been to court" (attended a court of summary jurisdiction) many hundreds of times; and he noted that procedures were in many respects similar, and were indeed based on common sense.

The Assizes for London were held at the Central Criminal Court, commonly called the Old Bailey; and the sitting was before a judge and jury: in this case twelve male persons, none of whom were challenged by defending counsel acting on Hampton's behalf. Counsel for the prosecution opened the case, after Hampton had formally pleaded "not guilty," then called witnesses, of whom Wigan was one, in support of it. But the wife of a defendant or prisoner is not a compellable witness; and Mrs. Hampton was not called. Wigan did not see her in court.

The case for the defence followed the case for the prosecution, and a point put to the jury was that a person is deemed innocent until he is proved guilty; and it is not for the prisoner to prove that he did not commit a certain crime. It is for the prosecution to prove that he did. After counsel's address witnesses for the defence could be called; and Wigan was interested to see if Hampton would be called to give evidence on his own behalf. He was not a compellable witness, and if he did not give evidence, the prosecution had no right to comment on the fact; but failure to give evidence would possibly have an unfortunate effect on the jury, since an obvious inference would be that the man was afraid to.

Counsel for the defence did call Frederick Hampton, probably thinking (so Wigan considered) that the whole burden of the defence rested on Hampton's personal statements; and therefore he had to be called in support of them, fantastic as they sounded, particularly in regard to his possession of the Keats first edition.

Hampton made a bad witness. He was shaking with nerves. If he wasn't guilty, he looked guilty; and though counsel for the defence led him quietly and sympathetically through his evidence-in-chief, his replies were aggressive as if he dared the jury to disbelieve them. And juries are only human. Probably the majority of the "good men and true" did disbelieve.

In his cross-examination by counsel for the prosecution Hampton had to admit that he had visited the shed on his way home. "I was soaking wet and I needed a smoke."

"Perhaps you were upset?"

"Of course I was upset. Fisk could have sold me books. Only he wouldn't."

When Hampton had finished his evidence, the manager of Niger's was called, and he tried to give a lever to the proceedings by stating that Hampton's "bark was worse than his bite"; and that, to his knowledge, two rows in the bookshop had ended in the mildest fashion. Counsel for the prosecution did not cross-examine, but evidence on Hampton's behalf regarding good character gave the right to call other evidence; and it was here that the evidence of the pornographic works was introduced. Also the written work Hampton was engaged on. "I have examined it," said a publisher's reader called by the prosecution, "and the work was not scientific nor could it be called work for the advancement of literature. It was some of the filthiest stuff I have ever seen."

"You are not trying the prisoner for writing indecent literature," the judge told the jury, "and the evidence can only be admitted as weighing against his general good character."

It was here that Belham, Q.C., pulled his dramatic trick. He recalled Mrs. Tray and asked her point-blank: "Can you identify the prisoner as the person with the beard you saw at the bathroom window?"

For a long minute Mrs. Tray surveyed Hampton's face. He was sweating badly and could not look her in the face. "No," she said at last, "I will not swear a man's life away. I cannot positively identify the prisoner as the man with a beard whom I saw. But I think it was he."

In his closing speech to the jury, Belham made the most of the knife ("He says he lost it. Where did he lose it? He must have some idea. But he hasn't"), the book ("proved to be in prisoner's possession"), and the handkerchief ("with the man's name on it, gentlemen"), and left Wigan at least with a bad impression. "The poor devil's a goner," he said to himself.

Counsel for the defence, who had called no evidence other

than that as to character (the manager of Niger's), had the right to the last word, and he made the utmost of the advantage. He spoke in quieter fashion than the aggressive Belham, but he was none the less effective. He accused the police, not perhaps of acting with deliberate unfairness and certainly not of manufacturing evidence, but of failing to follow any line except the chain of purely circumstantial evidence against Hampton. The knife he alleged he had lost: could not police inquiries have been made about that? The book he alleged had been left on his door-step: could not inquiries have been made about that? The defence was a complete denial of guilt. Somebody had committed the crime. It was not the defence's business to say who that somebody was. It was the business of the police to find out; and in this case, in the submission of the defence, the police had arrested the wrong person because circumstances seemed to implicate him.

Counsel took a sip of water. In his opinion (and no doubt the jury might think so too), Frederick Hampton was an unlucky man. He was a quarrelsome man, and he happened to have quarrelled with the murdered man just before the murder. He was an absent-minded man, and he had lost his knife—where, he didn't know; but it might have been picked up by the person who had killed Michael Fisk. He was a man engaged in a precarious livelihood, and to eke out his income he had in his possession indecent books and he was in process of writing an indecent work. But his motive was only to provide for his wife and family. No doubt it was wrong. But it was understandable. Again, for the same desperate reason he had undertaken to—"flog" was the word used in the trade—a book, the signed Keats first edition, which he knew to be stolen. There was no defence to *that*. But it didn't mean that the man had committed murder; and if there was doubt in the minds of the jury they should acquit him.

Wigan thought well of this speech, and Hampton himself seemed more at peace as he heard the quiet words of the counsel engaged to defend him.

The judge summed up. He took defending counsel's point about character and emphasised it to the jury. Then he dealt with the point about unsatisfactory evidence. Direct evidence was the best evidence. Hampton was found in possession of the Keats first edition, a unique copy known to be owned by the murdered man. That was direct evidence. Hampton's handkerchief, marked with his name, was found near the scene of the crime. That was direct evidence. It had been proved that the accused had bought a knife similar to the one used in the crime. That was direct evidence. Small pieces of India rubber had been found in the knife, and Hampton, as a bookseller's runner, carried a piece of rubber in his pocket. That was *circumstantial* evidence. In a court of law, circumstantial evidence may clearly establish guilt or innocence, and in any event it will usefully supplement direct evidence. Hampton was seen to quarrel with the dead man, he was seen to call later at the house of the dead man. Direct evidence. He was not seen to enter, the jury must note. Some hours after, at about the time the crime was committed, according to medical testimony, he or another man with a beard was seen to be in the bathroom of the murdered man's house. This last piece of evidence must be regarded as circumstantial.

Counsel for the defence, went on the judge, had accused the police of failing to follow up Hampton's statement, fantastic though it might seem. Where was the person who had given him the book to sell? Where was the person, if anyone, who had picked up the knife he said he had lost? Where was the bearded man who had appeared at the window, if not Hampton? The police did not know. They had not found out. But was it possible that they could find out? They could not collect every bearded man in England and put him up for identification by Mrs. Tray. They might honestly think they had got in the accused the right bearded man. Hampton's statement was not straightforward. He had altered it to explain further police discoveries. He was a free-lance writer; and even a writer of indecent works must possess imagination.

"The judge thinks Hampton did it," thought Wigan at this point.

The judge finally dealt with the difference in law between murder and manslaughter. Murder implied premeditation. If a man of violent temperament quarrelled with another man and hit him with his fist, and unfortunately he died as a result of the blow, the charge might be one of manslaughter: the intention was not to kill. But a man who carries a knife and produces the knife in a quarrel is presumed to know that a knife is a dangerous weapon. It can kill. So, if the jury believed Hampton guilty, there could be no question of reducing the charge. He was guilty, or not guilty, of murder.

The jury retired to consider their verdict. After about an hour they returned. Wigan had heard it said that if a jury find a man guilty on a capital charge they will not look at him when they deliver their verdict. If they find him not guilty they will. They did not look at Hampton now, and he was so white and shaken with nerves that he could scarcely stand up. Two policemen supported him in the dock, their hands under his elbows.

The judge asked the foreman of the jury: "Are you agreed on your verdict? Do you find the prisoner guilty or not guilty?"

"We are agreed. We find him guilty."

Before passing sentence, the judge asked Hampton if he had anything to say.

Hampton flared into violent speech. "I'm innocent. I never killed him. Someone has framed me. They have pinned this dreadful crime on me. I'm innocent, I tell you, I'm innocent."

The judge then called for the black cap and sentenced Frederick Hampton to be hanged by the neck until he was dead.

Hampton screamed with terror. He fought madly with the two policemen as they tried to persuade him, without violent measures, to leave the dock. "You're hanging an innocent man. Murderers! Murderers! You're hanging an innocent man!"

Wigan had to look away. The scene was so painful. But the hard-boiled D.I. never took his eyes from the frantic struggling figure who was at last carried, by the legs and under the arms, to the cells beneath the court.

"Murderers! Murderers! The bloody judge has no heart…"

Wigan wiped his sweating face. "Poor devil," he said.

The D.I.'s eyes contracted until they were two gleaming points of light, like dagger-points. "I said we'd screw him down," he murmured, "and we have."

# CHAPTER TEN

## CONSCIENCE

Sergeant Wigan was not an ultra-soft-hearted man as regards his work. On the beat, and on the section, he had done many acts of kindness. He had lent the public money on occasion. But if a person broke the law, then he or she must answer to the law. Particularly with regard to the Road Traffic Acts, Wigan had often had people ask him to let them off. "It's only little me, Officer. I just forgot I mustn't park here." And so on. But Wigan felt it was really wrong to "bend" the law, and he never did. It would be unfair to others.

But if Wigan wasn't foolishly soft-hearted, he was a strongly religious man. He had a conscience; and his conscience wouldn't allow him to forget Fred Hampton. Wigan was to return to the uniform branch at the end of the duty month (November), and the D.I., who was in an amiable mood, tried to make the last few weeks as interesting as possible. He put Wigan on a difficult larceny case; but despite the fact that the work needed all his wits, Wigan couldn't take his mind entirely away from the terrified struggling figure in the dock. Was Hampton innocent? Was he? It would be a dreadful thing to hang an innocent man, to plunge him into darkness from which no amount of fresh evidence could ever make him return.

Though he knew he would probably anger the D.I., Wigan brought the matter up again. "May I continue to work on the Hampton case, sir? In three weeks, if there is no appeal, it will be too late to do anything."

"No," said the D.I. briefly.

"But I'm not satisfied, sir. We're policemen and must do our duty by the man. It will be too late after. That's one of the chief arguments against capital punishment: if an innocent man is hanged there can be no restitution. I want to check all the facts and see if I can bring to light others. I'm asking this as a favour, sir."

"No," said the D.I. again.

Wigan hesitated. His next step was important. He could not of course be dismissed from the service because he asked awkward questions; but if he went right across the D.I. things could be made difficult for him—and goodbye to promotion to inspector. He didn't mind about promotion on his own account, but he had his wife and children to think of. An inspector now receives a very good income.

Wigan took a middle course. "Will you allow me to work on the case in my spare time, sir?"

"Wigan," said the D.I., "you are a good man and an excellent worker, otherwise I should be seriously annoyed. The trouble with you sentimentalists is that you never see another side. If I had my way, I could practically wipe out crime in Great Britain. I'd flog every person, man or woman, convicted a second time, and carry out every capital sentence without all this nonsense about psychiatrists and dual personalities. But of course the sentimental public wouldn't stand for it, so, neither will Parliament. Why don't you think of Michael Fisk? Wasn't he your friend?"

"Yes, sir, but I am not convinced that Hampton killed him. I've seen something of the second-hand book business, and I know some hanky-panky does go on. It's possible that he was framed and that the mysterious stranger does exist."

"So you know better than the jury, do you? They tried the man and found him guilty. That's all. Now regarding this larceny case: the servant says she didn't know her mistress had a diamond ring. I think she's lying, but, as we've made up our minds to charge her, we cannot by the Judges' Rules ask her any further questions without first giving her a caution—and that will stop the information we want. So find her boyfriend and get out of him what he knows."

Yes, the D.I. was tough all right, and clever, for the boy-friend promptly gave Ella the servant away. Perhaps he was tired of her. Perhaps he was shocked that she could steal. Anyway, he said that on a certain evening she had shown him the ring. And that was that. Ella had been screwed down.


Hampton's solicitor did lodge an appeal, which in any case would delay the date of execution. Wigan read this in his morning paper. He could not quiet his conscience. If the appeal succeeded or if it failed, the principle remained the same. If he believed the man innocent he should help him. Finally, one day about two weeks before his plain-clothes duty was up he asked the D.I. to authorise his immediate return to the uniform branch.

"Why this, Wigan? Don't you like us?"

"Yes, sir, but I wish to work on the Hampton case in my spare time, and if I return to the uniform branch I can do so without obligation to you."

"Wigan, you're riding for a fall. Remember, I've warned you. Our people don't like officers who try to do things out of the ordinary. Remember again—I've told you. But I'll help you to this extent. Stay with me till your month is up and you may do what you please with your time, provided of course that I don't urgently need your services."

"Thank you very much, sir. That's generous."

The D.I. sniffed. "It isn't really. Detective-Sergeant Tasker is back, and he and the constables can manage all the work there is now. I think you're an honest man, Wigan, but you've got a bee in your bonnet over Hampton. I suppose you've never seen a man sentenced to death before. Some carry on worse than he did. Some accept the sentence with dignity. But it's all the same in the long run, and so you'll find out. I don't for a moment think the Appeal Judges will let him off."

Wigan proceeded without delay to see Hampton's solicitor, who had small chambers in the City Road. He was a man who had started rather grudgingly, but improved as events went on. His client was his client. Wigan, who stated bluntly the reason for his visit, found himself, rather to his surprise, welcomed with a firm handshake.

"I'm glad you've come. I'm not satisfied with the verdict, as a man or a lawyer. But Hampton has been a most awkward chap to defend. He has been almost incredibly foolish."

"On what grounds, sir, have you based the appeal?"

"Generally unsatisfactory evidence, which the judge insufficiently pointed out to the jury. In my opinion, the prosecution gives Hampton in turn credit for too many brains and too few. He is clever enough to carry out a secret and ruthless crime, yet he makes up fairy stories."

"I think that too, sir."

"But the appeal may fail. It's hard to get over the direct evidence."

"I think he was framed, sir, and that's the answer to everything."

"Well, Sergeant, you're an extraordinary chap. I've never heard anything like this before: a police officer dissatisfied with evidence and working on the case on his own account. But good luck to you. *I* believe Hampton innocent because I've had a hand in his private affairs as well as this defence, and *I* don't think him capable of the crime."

"You mean he's not strong enough?"

"Oh no. That cat won't jump, and I didn't try it. He's thin and flat-chested, but sufficiently strong to drive that knife into Fisk. It's a murderous bit of steel. You're a big man and I'm a little one; but with that knife in hand I could kill you. I believe the wholesalers have recalled the blades and blunted them. Just as well. No, what I mean is that I am acquainted now with his personal character. He's got a lot on the debit side, but some on the credit; and he will do nothing seriously to imperil his wife and children. He's physically a coward and terrified of being hanged. He hasn't got a friend in the world except myself, yet he won't have his wife and children visit him. He's absolutely firm on the point."

"It shows courage, sir."

"Yes. It does."

"I'd like an order, sir, to visit him in prison. I'd like a talk with him."

"I suppose it will be all right… It's unprecedented really. But if we ask the Home Office officially there may be all sorts of difficulties. I think, Mr. Wigan, you have called on me just as a friend of Fred Hampton's; and as such I shall ask the Governor of the prison for an order to visit."

Most prisons are gloomy places, and, because the public turns its eyes away from what it doesn't want to see, they will probably continue to be. But Wigan thought he had never seen a gloomier place than the massive doorway and high black stone arch of Y Prison; and he thought too that all police officers and all judges should be compelled to visit prisons, just to see the kind of places their "customers" were sent to.

Wigan's order took him to the condemned cell. Wigan—of course in plain clothes—was plain Mr. Wigan on the order, and the warder who received him, one of the two on death-watch, treated him as he would any other member of the public. He was polite but careful, and he would not leave Hampton and Wigan alone together for a single instant.

"You can say what you like," he said. "Don't mind me. Just look on me as a piece of furniture."

Wigan knew this was intended for kindness, and he thanked the warder. Hampton sat on his bed. He looked small and shrunken, and his beard an untidy brush on his white face.

Wigan offered to shake hands, but the warder had to prevent this. "Sorry, sir, it's against regulations."

"That's all right. Well, Fred, I've come to help you if I can. You remember me, don't you? Wigan, the bookseller's runner?"

"You were a cop."

"That is true. But I've come to try and help you, and I'm risking my job to do it." Wigan looked at the warder, but he was taking no notice whatever. He might indeed have been a piece of the cell furniture.

"I believe you to be innocent, and I'm going to try and prove it."

A little life came into Hampton's lack-lustre eyes.

"You really mean that? On your honour?"

"On my honour. Now we've only got a little time. Who is likely to try and frame you?"

"I once had a row with Joel Ferrow, as I've had a row with so many people. It was in the auction-room. I would have got a lot for half a crown, but he stepped in and bid me up to ten pounds. Then afterwards, when I went to collect my lot, a bundle of books tied together, I found stolen the one book which made the lot worth-while. I accused Joel, calling him a thief and a swine. And he said: 'You wait, Fred. I'll get you. I'll stamp on you.'"

"Anyone else?"

"Oh, well, I've quarrelled with Charlie the barrow-boy, but I don't think he would put me here. Then I quarrelled with Ruth. I hate that type of girl. Sexless. All efficiency. And I quarrelled with Askew. As a matter of fact, we nearly came to blows in Piccadilly because we both arrived at a bookseller's at the same time. They were asking for Rider Haggard first editions, and I guessed he had a load as I had. And we jostled in the doorway."

Wigan smiled. "You are a lad, Fred."

Hampton smiled weakly. "I suppose I am. But all the time I'm thinking of my girls. They are two of the finest girls who ever stepped, and now what will happen to them when—"

"Don't think of that. I've got to speak plainly, and I want plain answers. Do you think Joel Ferrow bears you sufficient grudge to kill a man and put the blame on you?"

"It might happen. He's not the forgiving sort."

"Has he a beard?"

"Not normally. But he's got a long blue chin. He always looks as if he hasn't shaved. It wouldn't take him long to grow a beard if he wanted to."

"Now take the knife. You say you lost it. Where did you lose it? Don't you know at all?"

"I wish I did. But I'm careless about such things. One day I had my knife. The next day I hadn't. It might be anywhere. I might have dropped it in the street. I don't know. I can't think."

"Fred, you must think. I want you to do nothing else but think. Did you drop your knife in Ferrow's bookshop?"

"No, I don't think I did. I don't think I could have done. I didn't visit his shop. He wasn't the sort to sell me books. Once when I was outside looking at the stalls he came out of the shop and said: 'I don't want you round here looking for bargains.'"

"He may have picked it up. When do you remember having it last? Did you have it on the day you went to Sun to visit Mike Fisk?"

"I fancy I did. I fancy I put it in my pocket before I set out from home."

"Then when did you come to lose it?"

"I don't know. I know it was lost when Minnie asked for it when you came to my house."

Wigan patiently persevered. "When you were talking to Mike Fisk, you didn't take the knife from your pocket just to threaten him?"

"Oh no, I wouldn't be such a fool."

"You didn't take it out at all then, as far as you know?"

"No, I don't think so. It must have slipped out somewhere."

"And it was found by the real murderer, who used it to kill Mike with?"

"That's so. That's what I wanted the police to believe."

"What a hope!" said Wigan to himself; but outwardly he was as calm and patient as ever. His peaceful manner, which released Hampton from emotional tension, had its reward, for Hampton added almost casually: "I believe Mike Fisk and Joel Ferrow had a mix-up on their own account. I heard some rumour of it, but I don't know the details."

"I'll have to find out."

"You give me new heart."

"That was my object in coming here. But it would be cruel to make you think I'm Sherlock Holmes. I'm not that. I can only do my best. Now take the story of how you came into possession of the Keats first edition. I am to take that as true?"

"Oh, it was true all right. Of course I knew the book must be stolen. I've admitted that. But I was desperate for money. Winnie needed at least £50 for her viola, and there was my chance."

"And yet the person behind it took the chance of you walking off with the whole of the money, if Ruth paid?"

"I know. It does seem queer. As a matter of fact I would have dealt honestly."

"The manager of Niger's gave you a good character."

Hampton smiled bitterly. "About the only one who did. The other so-and-sos never raised a finger to help me."

"Skip that. I wonder who could have been behind it. Have you any idea at all?"

Hampton was becoming interested. He had thought himself abandoned to the blackness of the tomb; and now with a helping hand he tried to help himself. "I've thought and thought," he said. "Of course Harland, the solicitor, pressed me about it. He said that if I could prove anything we were saved. I know the 'Red Hand of Vengeance' sounds bloody silly. It does sound as if I made the whole thing up."

"If I remember rightly, the note stated that when you went to Niger's bookshop with the money on Saturday morning, and the writer of the note came up to you, you would know him—or her?"

"That's right. It did say so. I thought it might be Ruth herself. She's a monkey for tricks, you know. She would have made me sign a receipt for the money. And there was I: owner of stolen property which I had sold to her!"

All three were smoking, Hampton, Wigan, and the warder. For a time the dread purpose of the cell was forgotten. But the warder had to glance at his watch, and as he did so his mate, on guard outside the locked cell door, looked through the grill: "Time's nearly up, Charlie."

"I'm afraid I can't give you a minute over your time, sir,"

said the warder Charlie to Wigan. "The Governor is most particular. Of course he has to be. Quite likely he'll be along."

"I shall go the moment you tell me I must," said Wigan. As an official himself, he knew the advantage of being a model. But Fred took his remark the wrong way. "I expect you'll be glad to go," he said.

"Fred," said Wigan genially, "don't be a silly fool. From now I'm acting in your interests. I'll look into what you've told me, though I can't promise miracles. Would you like me to see your wife and daughters?"

"No. Harland's looking after them. I don't wish any contact with them at all."

"You're a plucky chap, Fred. Keep your heart up. Goodbye now for the present. I'll come and see you again."


The warder outside, after re-locking the death-cell, accompanied Wigan the length of the corridor. He seemed to recognise in Wigan another official, and was perhaps more open than he otherwise would have been.

"I hope he gets off," he said. "Between ourselves, he'll be a real terror when *he* arrives. Struggling, kicking, I know the type. It will be a dreadful business for us."

"I expect it will, if it comes to that. Poor chap, he's all nerves. Be as kind to him as you can."

"We always are that. I've been hit in the face and never hit back."

Wigan could think of nothing else to say. He shook hands with the warder, who handed him over to another, who escorted him to the prison gates. There he had to wait while his pass was carefully checked. Finally he left the house of gloom in a November afternoon, gloomy in itself.

"God, what a maze!" he said to himself. "I shall never forgive myself if I have raised the poor chap's hopes for nothing. I wonder where best to start. If I go to Ferrow and question him, likely enough he won't answer. If I threaten him I shall get arrested myself. I can't see myself getting much out of Ruth—even if she knows anything. Everyone is mum until poor Fred is hanged."

Wigan filled and lit his pipe. He found he needed tobacco, so he entered a shop near the prison to buy his usual: Wills's Cut Golden Bar. While he was inside the shop he saw an advertisement: "Niger's Shag is the best in the world."

"Is it indeed?" thought Wigan. Well, he might do a lot worse than try Niger's again. One inspiration might lead to another.

It was now about five o'clock. Niger's didn't shut till six. Wigan boarded a bus which would take him to West Road.

# CHAPTER ELEVEN

## AID TO SERGEANT WIGAN

Wigan arrived at Niger's at half-past five, and he went straight to the book-runner's paradise: the big pile of unsorted books on the ground floor. There he found Charlie Boy—Charlie North—alone, with a large bag beside him, rummaging for bargains.

"Hullo, Charlie! Any luck?"

"Not so far. When you can't sell you must buy. Book-runner's motto. And I've had a lousy day so far. I took a nice first of W. W. Jacobs to a shop I thought certain to buy it because they have a customer who collects Jacobs firsts. But would they buy? Not on your life. 'We are not interested,' said a——young squirt with an Oxford accent; and there goes seven and sixpence I had speculated."

"Bad luck, Charlie." Wigan had his second inspiration. "When you've done here, will you come and have tea with me?"

"Certainly, and thanks. You seem lucky for me, Mr. Wigan."

At tea in a café near-by Wigan proceeded to outline his proposition. It was that Charlie should help him in his fight to establish Hampton's innocence. "I may want a lot of your time and I'm prepared to pay for it. Will three quid a week plus expenses be all right?"

Charlie looked as if he were dreaming; but years of struggling for a living had made him sharp to take an opportunity before it floated off to somebody else. He accepted the first week's money which Wigan offered, folded the three one-pound notes carefully into his battered wallet, then he said: "What do you want me to do, guv'nor?"

"I'm convinced that Hampton is innocent. I've been to see him in prison. He seems to have quarrelled with nearly everyone in the book world, but especially with Joel Ferrow, Ruth Brent, and the runner Askew. I want you to find out more about it. It seems impossible for me to pose as a runner."

"You haven't got the life-and-death look, guv'nor. You can always tell a runner in a bookshop. He uses his eyes, not his hands or his feet. And he's quick. It takes years to get that quickness. I can go through a big shop in half an hour and know that I haven't missed anything worth-while, while the public—and that includes you, guv'nor, if I may say so without offence—flutters about from book to book and wastes time opening a book that I know ain't worth sixpence."

Wigan smiled. "I haven't got the commercial angle?"

"Of course you haven't. Does your living depend on it? It don't. Mine does."

"Well, Charlie, the chief suspect at present seems to be Joel Ferrow. Do you think you can find out anything about him and what he was doing at the time the murder was committed? What bothers me is how Fred's knife could have got into somebody else's possession. Yet it must have done if that somebody else killed Fisk."

"I don't know," said Charlie slowly. "I've followed the case in the papers, and it seems to me that it has been attacked from the wrong angle. That rare book of Fisk's that was stolen—the Keats first edition—where did it come from? Nobody has found that out. Suppose that Joel Ferrow and Fisk were both after the book, and Fisk won. Right. Then Joel goes to Fisk's place to get the book by any means he thinks fit. Joel's a tough nut. He attacked Fisk and killed him."

"With Fred's knife? How?"

"Because he finds that knife in Fisk's study. Maybe it is lying on the table. Say Fred dropped the knife and Fisk picked it up. Knowing our Fred and how violent he can get, Fisk would likely keep the knife until Fred calmed down. Or he may have picked up the knife and taken it home with no idea of who it belonged to."

"I suppose it's possible," said Wigan, "but it seems a most extraordinary chain of coincidence."

"Something of the sort must have happened unless Fred really did kill Fisk. Take the clothes a runner wears. All bits and pieces. At one time runners use to wear black, as a sign, so I've heard, that no mercy would be shown. You might own a first of *The Pilgrim's Progress*, say, 1678, worth a fortune; but if a runner could get it from you for sixpence he would. Now runners mostly wear rags and tatters, with the exception of a good pair of boots like I've got on now. Cost me £3, they did. Well. With clothes like that you can easily lose things."

"Why should a runner wear old clothes?"

"Oh, well, just a trick of the trade. You can pick up books

at beggar's prices. Not all runners dress so. Askew looks quite respectable—I suppose he thinks it's beneath him to dress like a tramp. But Connington, that I've spoke of, sometimes looks worse than a tramp. To see him hunting in West Road you'd think he was the Prince of the Beggars, and when he starts whining and moaning about having no money, you'd be sure of it. Yet in ordinary life Connington has quite a good job."

"I must look into this Connington. Hampton didn't mention him, but he may be another he's quarrelled with."

"Likely, I should say. But I've done something for you, guv'nor. Remembering our last conversation, I've got Connington's address. He does live with his sister at the Welcome Bookshop, Notting Hill Gate. The Ferrows live at Muswell Hill."

"Quite a few runners seem to live there."

"North London is good for books. West London is fair. South London is fair. East London is lousy."

"I see you know all about it. We will assume that Hampton lost his knife through a defect in his pocket; that Fisk or another picked it up; and that by a miracle of coincidence it was used to kill Fisk. And so the crime was brought home to Hampton. But Joel Ferrow has never, to my knowledge, been reported as being in Sun at the time of the murder."

"If you ask me, guv., the police have done nothing except pin the crime on Fred. Or they have done precious little. They took the obvious angle, and on the obvious the jury convicted Fred. As you have paid me, I am now your man; and I suggest that I pay a visit to the Ferrows' shop to try and find out something. Afterwards I should like to visit Mike's study. There may be something else missing beside the Keats first."

"I don't think so. I visited the study again with the D.I. I checked the shelves most carefully. There were no gaps I couldn't account for. One gap, a small one, was caused by the missing Keats first edition. The other gap, a bigger one, was accounted for by the volume on Mike's desk: the volume on demonology which he was reading at the time of his death."

"Ah yes, guv. Ah yes. Neat and sweet, hard to beat. Charlie's poetry. But I'll tell you something, but first I would like another dollop of tea, and do you think the exes will run to an egg on toast?"

"I expect they will," said Wigan, smiling. He went to the counter; and when he returned Charlie was primed up like a boiler with importance.

"Now, guv., I'll let you into a secret. A trick of the trade. You say no gaps. Right. You're a police officer trained to observe. So no gaps it is. But runners sometimes carry volumes in their pockets, volumes of no great value, but useful to fill a gap. I've done it myself. I see a first I want. I abstract the said first, at a convenient opportunity; and so that no gap shall show which will reveal the said abstraction, at least to the casual glance, say, of an assistant in the shop, I fill the gap with a volume of no worth from my own pocket."

"That certainly is a trick."

"Can you swear to all the volumes Mike had?"

"No. Mike told me he had about two thousand. I couldn't possibly remember all the titles."

"No. You haven't got the runner's memory. I have, but I haven't seen Mike's books. With all respect to you, guv., you really don't know much about books. There might be a weed among the flowers, a weed that no collector of Mike's standing would bother to keep, and you wouldn't spot it."

Wigan swallowed the insult to his book knowledge. "I think your idea is a good one. I think it will be best if you visit Mike's study before you see Ferrow. If a volume of false value has been inserted among Mike's books, and you spot it, there might be some clue as to the ownership."

"When you like, guv'nor."

"Now," said Wigan. "The keys of Mike's house are kept at Sun Police Station. The station officer will give them to me. I'll have to chance my arm about the rights and wrongs of it."

"What about light, guv'nor? I must have a good light."

"We'll take two police lamps. They are very powerful. The current may have been turned off by the electricity authority."

"I feel like a blooming burglar," said Charlie, as they stood in Mike's study. The current had indeed been cut off by the electricity authority. They flashed their torches about.

"I've spoken to the man on the beat," said Wigan, "so it will be all right. But we don't want to call attention to what we're doing. It's about nine o'clock and people will still be about. I'll draw the curtains."

He did so. Charlie shone his lamp on the book on the table.

"Is that what he was reading when he died?"

"Yes. It's soaked in blood. You can't read it."

"Blimey, I don't want to. But we ought to know the title. Can I raise the cover from the table? There won't be blood underneath."

"You can if you like. I will, and you can see if you can read the title."

Wigan lifted the book, crusted and soaked in blood, from the table and Charlie shone his lamp so that he could inspect the top cover. His face turned pale. "This is a queer set-up, guv'nor. Do you know what Fisk was trying to do?"

"I think he was trying to raise the devil."

"Yes. That's what that book means. Put it down, guv'nor. We don't want no more of it. Put it down quick, or I shall give you back your three quid and clear off."

"There's no need to be scared," said Wigan calmly.

"Isn't there? That's all you know. I go about a bit, and I've heard things. Things done in Soho. I've heard of a goat being raised, and it created hell before they could get rid of it."

"Fisk told me about a bull."

"Then he told you evil. Leave that book alone, and let's have a look at his other books… Crikey, what a collection of the occult. It makes your mouth water. There's books here I've never seen but only heard about."

Charlie stood still, using his eyes. He shone his lamp along shelf after shelf. Finally the ray of his lamp stopped. "Here's something to interest us. *The Pilgrim's Progress.* Umpteenth edition. Very nice volume, ain't it? Worth about half a dollar. If that."

"If a book was taken in place of it, how can you tell what book?"

"I can't, guv'nor. Of course I can't. But we may be able to find out something. I wonder why the Keats was taken and a gap left. No book to replace it."

"Perhaps whoever it was hadn't got another book with him."

"Perhaps not. Or he may have been deep. Very, very deep."

Charlie looked round uneasily. "I don't like this place, guv'nor. I wouldn't spend the night here for a thousand pounds."

"Do what you came to do and we'll go."

Charlie looked away from the blood-stained table and the blood-stained book upon it. "I wish you had cleared that lot away," he said.

"It will stay until the D.I. is satisfied that the case is finished."

"And that will be when Fred is hanged, unless we get him off. If I'm to scout round Ferrow's shop, guv'nor, I must know what to scout for. Most in the trade have a secret mark. Cost price, selling price. I expect Mike had. Maybe he didn't intend to sell his occult works; but some books he sold to make a living. Let's have a look over there... Carter and Mace. *The Tomb of Tut-ankh-Amen*. Three vols. Worth having. Mike never went in for trash. Now what's his price? Nothing on the front endpapers. Nothing on the half-title. He wouldn't mark the title-page... Let's have a look at the end. There you are—see! A tiny figure on the paste-down endpaper, bottom left-hand corner. You can hardly see it, but it's there. X. I bet you that means ten pounds—*x*, the roman figure for ten. That's about the right value for the book."

"You're a real expert, Charlie."

Charlie smiled, a cheery, attractive smile even with broken and blackened front teeth. "Thanks, guv., but I wish I wasn't here all the same. We've got what we came for—he marked with roman figures. I suppose we had better check with another book. He's got—I mean he had—some nice

Africana. Let's look at this one, *The Story of an African Farm*, by Ralph Iron—that's Olive Schreiner: Ralph Iron was her pseudonym. Two vols. 1883. That's the first edition. Now we'll look at the end of the first vol. Here you are: xv. £15!" Charlie's voice rose triumphantly.

Wigan was not shining his lamp. He had put it in his pocket. Suddenly, from no known cause, Charlie's lamp went out.

"Quick, guv.!" he shouted. "Shine your lamp. Christ, there's something terrible here!"

"Nonsense," said Wigan calmly. He had his religious beliefs, and they were proof against all superstition. He found his lamp and pressed the electric switch. The light came on. He saw Charlie panting and sweating. He was staring at the chair by the table, the chair in which Mike had sat.

"I thought *it* was coming," he whispered.

"It?" said Wigan. "The bull or the goat?"

"The corpse, guv., the corpse. I thought it was going to materialise."

"Charlie, you're an idiot," said Wigan.

"That may or may not be. You're a copper. You're not sensitive like me. Mr. Fisk—he wouldn't like his books being touched. He's been dead three months. My God, if he should come!"

"I'll answer for that. Mike was my friend. He would wish to see justice done. As for his books, they will come to me when probate is granted."

"Will they indeed? You're lucky, guv'nor, you're lucky."

Charlie was in a hopeless state of nerves. He was a little man: little hands, little feet. Wigan seemed enormous beside him. And Charlie seemed to think that Wigan, so big and solid, had no nerves and no feelings.

"You don't understand, guv'nor. What put me bleedin' lamp out?"

"Bulb gone, I expect. Give it to me and I'll fit the spare. All police lamps carry a spare bulb."

Wigan did fit the spare bulb, and Charlie's lamp lit again.

"Simple," remarked Wigan.

"He was raising the devil," whispered Charlie. He crossed himself. "He was sitting there reading the Black Mass. Blasphemies, guv'nor. Terrible blasphemies. Burn that book, guv'nor, and keep away while you're doing it. I think—"

"You think what?" said Wigan patiently.

"Nothing, guv'nor. I think we'll go now, if you don't mind. I can't *stand* any more of that bloody—I mean, I don't think we ought to disturb the poor fellow's books any further."

"That's all right, Charlie. I'm sorry you've had the ordeal."

Wigan carefully locked up. They went forth into the misty November night. At once Charlie recovered his jauntiness. "Tomorrow morning I'll go along to Ferrow Brothers and see what I can see. I've got a photographic memory for books. About nine months ago a very rare occult work by Lewes Lavater called *Of Ghostes and Spirites Walking by Night* was asked for in the trade paper by Ferrow Brothers. They had the want printed in blacks with a black border round it, very important. It was just the kind of rare work that Fisk might have, but I didn't see it among his books tonight."

"He might have supplied it to Ferrow Brothers in the ordinary way of trade."

"I don't think so. The want was printed week after week, until at last it ceased. Mike was shy of selling his occult works.

If he had the book and wished to supply it, he would have done so at once."

"That's true. But perhaps he hadn't got it."

"Lor' lumme, guv'nor, you are a blooming wet blanket. It's worth a trial. If Joel bumped Mike off, and Mike had the book, then Joel would certainly have taken it; and he wouldn't have flogged it as the Keats was flogged. I think the Keats was just a blind. Unique copy, simple to identify; and poor Fred was let in the cart."

"I should like to meet the famous Joel Ferrow."

"Big powerful chap. Ugly temper when roused. A real book-bandit, one of the old style. I remember him years ago. He was one of Lavatory Jack's pals, but you wouldn't think so now. The war gave the Ferrows their chance. After the war books boomed, and now the Ferrows have one of the biggest businesses in London."

"But he doesn't usually wear a beard?"

"He can grow one in two minutes, guv'nor. So can I. Visit one of the theatrical shops off West Road. Just chew on that."

As it was so late, Wigan offered Charlie a shake-down at his home. Charlie gracefully accepted, and charmed Mrs. Wigan by his easy manners.

"I'm an old campaigner, ma'am, and a bachelor. Your spare room will be like a palace to me."

"What a nice little man," said Mary Wigan when husband and wife were alone.

"He's more than that. I'm relying on him to get Fred Hampton off."

# CHAPTER TWELVE

## HUNTING AT FERROWS'

Generally speaking, the public are no use at identifying a person by mere description; and among other things Wigan charged Charlie to get if he could a photograph of Joel Ferrow which Wigan could show to porters and others. This seemed almost impossible, for Joel would hardly supply a photo of himself on request! But at one stroke Charlie solved the problem. "Ferrows issue catalogues, guv'nor, and in 1950 they had a slap-up cat. with a photo of both the brothers on the front cover, Joel Ferrow on one side of a big desk and Francis the other, with a pile of books between them. I think Lavatory Jack would have grinned. But there it is. I've kept the cat., and I'll give it to you if you meet me for dinner, on me if you please, after I've been to Ferrows's. We'll go to Lambeth together. That's where I live."

Immediately after breakfast Charlie thanked Mrs. Wigan, with much courtesy, for her hospitality, and set off for West Road. The establishment of Ferrow Brothers, antiquarian booksellers, was of considerable size: they had bought up two competitors. Though they did business on the grand scale now, they preserved tradition, the tradition of the tuppeny-box where all may delve for bargains, in that they maintained stalls in front. As Charlie arrived an assistant was busy setting out these stalls with rows of books. The assistant, Christopher Edwards, was called in the trade Corky because he had a false leg of cork and wood with a circular pad of leather nailed on the foot. Corky had a sly and subtle face and no good manners to speak of.

"'Morning, Corky," said Charlie.

"'Morning." Corky didn't give Charlie much welcome. Messrs. Ferrow bought mostly at auction now, and had no use for the humble runner bent on making half a crown. Corky flicked some dust from a book on to Charlie's boots.

"You're a charmer, Corky. Listen—I want something special for an American customer. Let me have a look at the inner stock, will you?"

Without a word Corky took Charlie down to the basement, where there were many book-rooms. To the uninitiated, there were volumes of great age and no doubt of immense value here; but Charlie knew there weren't. Really rare and valuable works would not be kept on a shelf where the public could get at them, open them carelessly, and destroy half their worth. Also rare and valuable works might be stolen.

Charlie didn't even bother to look round. "I'd like to see," he said, "Mr. Francis or Mr. Joel."

"They're busy."

"I still want to see them. It's important. My American will pay up to £300 for what he wants."

"And what does he want?"

"I'm not prepared to say yet. He's backing my judgment."

Corky's sly eyes gleamed. It was funny to see Charlie so important as if he had the wealth of the Incas in his pocket. Still, £300 was £300, and Ferrows had to make their profits.

"Wait here," said Corky. He stumped off on his wooden leg to a door marked "Private." He knocked, then entered. Presently he came out and returned to Charlie, who was ostentatiously studying a battered Henty first edition—small fry to the Ferrows, who could hardly bother with a modern like Henty. Yet their copy was priced £2–10s. "Cor luv-a-duck," murmured Charlie, "they make you pay for the air in here."

"Mr. Francis will see you."

"And what about Mr. Joel?"

"He's out—and what business is that of yours?" Corky couldn't stand any more of Charlie's airs, the blooming barrow-boy who had somehow picked up an American customer.

"Show me in," ordered Charlie importantly; and with a wooden leg which almost spoke Corky stumped his way to the private door. "Thank you, my man," said Charlie. So great is the power of the imagination, that Charlie almost believed that he had got an important American customer. His name? How about Horace K. Glassenberg?

The inner room, and the adjoining packing-room which had a frontage to the street, was where the main business of the firm was done. A big bookshop was like a cell within a cell within a cell. The outer cell was for casual buyers, necessary because many lots bought at auction contained perhaps two or three valuable books and a whole host of junk which had to be disposed of somehow. The next cell was for customers who wanted something more important and were prepared to pay a good price for it. The next cell was for customers who ordered from catalogue; and these customers might be distributed all over the world.

The inner room was lined with books worth thousands of pounds. At a table sat Mr. Francis. He was a large, fattish man with a pale face and a high forehead. He had a very short neck, which gave him some appearance of deformity. He was alone. From the packing-room came the sound of typewriters where girls were quoting books to customers and making out invoices to accompany the parcels of books packed by men. In the labyrinth that was the bookshop of Messrs. Ferrow Brothers, London, England, sat the brains of the two creators; and he turned a pair of dark, intelligent, Jewish eyes on Charlie. "What can I do for you?" he said.

"Important American customer, sir." Charlie hadn't meant to call Mr. Francis 'sir', but he had a kind of daunting presence.

"What's his name?"

"Well really, sir, you can't expect me to tell you that. You'd sell to him direct."

"Then what can I sell you?"

"My customer's wants are in your field: incunabula, occult works, old herbals—what the Americans term scholarly books. I'd like to look round."

"Very well." Mr. Francis knew that Charlie could be trusted in a bookshop. He wouldn't steal (Corky, the outer guard, could be trusted to look after that—he had eyes like a lynx), and he wouldn't mishandle books.

Charlie made the most of his opportunity. For the next

hour his eyes roved over the shelves. For appearance's sake he took out one or two books and more closely inspected them; but he couldn't find what he was looking for, a rare occult work that Mike might have owned. Mr. Francis continued his work: he was compiling the firm's next catalogue.

"Where do you price your books, Mr. Ferrow?"

"Our own mark. It needn't concern you. Ask the price of any book you select, and I'll tell you."

Charlie had an idea that Ferrows asked any price they thought they could get; and it was all locked up in the brain of Mr. Francis.

"I don't seem to be able to find anything, sir. I'd like to get a copy of Lewes Lavater's *Of Ghostes and Spirites.*"

"Then why didn't you say so straight out? You won't get that for £300. You're wasting my time."

"My customer's pocket is elastic. Like many wealthy Americans, he will pay almost anything for a book he wants. But I can't see anything rare enough to tempt him."

Then Mr. Francis made a significant remark. "I have a few more books at home."

Charlie perked up. By now he really believed in his American, a man with a fabulous purse able to buy on the scale of the late Dr. Rosenbach, who made a principle of never being outbid for any book he wanted.

"It may interest you to know," he said slowly, "that my customer will pay a thousand pounds for a book he wants, if I cable him first and he confirms by cable."

"Then why should he select *you* for an agent?"

Charlie puffed up his small chest. "Ah, sir, you jeer at me because I'm poor and I may sell comics from a barrow; but I do understand books—even the Latin titles. Books are my life. Have you a copy of the *Ghostes and Spirites*?"

"I may not have that, but I have other books as rare or even rarer. What would you say to King James I's own copy of his *Daemonologie*, published at Edinburgh in 1597?"

"Good God!"

"Precisely," said Mr. Francis. "But I don't allow any Tom, Dick, or Harry to see my own private collection; and before I allow you to do so, I must ask the name of your customer. You needn't worry—we shan't cut your commission."

Charlie was in a quandary, but only for a moment. He mentioned a past President of the United States.

"Well," said Mr. Francis, "this is most extraordinary. How did he contact you?"

"We all have our secrets, sir. I've paid dearly for mine, and I won't give them away."

"Extraordinary," said Mr. Francis again. "I must tell my brother Joel. When would you like to see our books? I live at Muswell Hill Grange."

"I should like to see them now, sir," said Charlie. He knew that unless he took instant action, his fraudulent statement would probably fall to the ground. The Ferrows might telephone the American Embassy and make a few discreet inquiries. Huge sums might be involved.

"Very well," said Mr. Francis. "I don't usually go home to lunch, but I will today and you can come with me."

Charlie thought of Wigan and the dinner appointment at the Lyons in West Road. "I'd like to go out, sir, and come back at one o'clock if that will be convenient."

"Quite convenient."

"Good lord," thought Charlie when he was outside, "what a pack of lies. I must have been crazy!"

The manageress of the Lyons Charlie usually frequented knew him well enough to accept a note for Sergeant Wigan: *"Am detained on business. Will meet you tomorrow same time same place."* Then Charlie returned to Ferrow's bookshop and afterwards set out for Muswell Hill with Mr. Francis in his car, an expensive limousine. Charlie knew there is money in books, and here was confirmation. The biggest dealers do not collect books first. They collect customers first, and books afterwards to suit them. This, thought Charlie, was probably the reason why Mr. Francis was taking so much trouble. He hoped sooner or later to find out the name of the important link between Charlie and his customer—for there must be one. Charlie wished him joy of the hope!

"Nice house you've got, sir," said Charlie, when they pulled up in the drive of Muswell Hill Grange, a tall old house standing high and overlooking the Cherry Tree Woods.

"It suits my brother and me," replied Mr. Francis. "We are bachelors. We have a housekeeper to look after us."

A light lunch was served by the housekeeper, who Charlie thought of as a close old dame, then Mr. Francis said: "Now to business. If you come into the study I will show you books I think likely to suit you."

Charlie said he would be delighted, but lining the study walls he saw only standard sets of Dickens, Thackeray, and Scott, which as a runner left him cold, for they were only of small money value.

"Sit down," said Mr. Francis, "and I will bring the books."

"I'll save you the trouble, sir. I'll come and see them."

Mr. Francis made no reply to this. In three loads he brought in a dozen books. Then he sat down and waited. One by one Charlie examined the volumes. He had excellent eyesight and the study was well lighted, but he looked in vain for Mike's secret mark. He wondered what to do next.

Mr. Francis observed: "Your customer should surely find something of interest among that lot. They are immensely valuable. Do you know the total value?"

"Something high, sir."

"£72,000."

Charlie was about to say "Cor blimey," then he remembered he was on his best behaviour. "It's a huge sum, sir. How on earth did you get them?"

"You have your secrets and I have mine. We have been lucky, my brother and I. Of course we have a flair for finding rare books."

Charlie wondered if the flair included murder. "I don't see Lewes Lavater's work, sir."

"I haven't that."

Of course, thought Charlie, Mr. Francis was far too "cagey" to give himself away. If he had stolen a book from Mike he might keep it for years. Booksellers often did keep a certain book for years to make in the end the most satisfactory profit. In fact Charlie had just wasted his time.

"I suppose," remarked Mr. Francis, "you are not romancing, are you?"

"Shouldn't waste my time, sir. I've got my living to earn."

"So I thought, or I shouldn't have asked you here."

"I'll report these titles, sir, to my customer and let you know."

"Very well."

Charlie grew reckless. "Sad affair about Fred Hampton."

"Yes."

"How's Mr. Joel, sir?"

"Very well, thank you."

Charlie rose to leave. He thanked Mr. Francis for his hospitality and said he would make his own way back to West Road, and thence to Lambeth.

Mr. Francis made a final remark. "Any business you introduce to us we will pay you ten per cent."

"That's generous, sir."

"I think so. Good afternoon."

# CHAPTER THIRTEEN

## THE B.M.

Because of Charlie's failure to keep his appointment, Wigan had time to spare; and with the thought of the desperate man in the death-cell ever in his mind, he was disinclined to waste. He decided to visit the British Museum, where, he understood, the runner Algernon Askew was often engaged in research. He would, so Charlie had said, look up obscure points of first editions for any collector who would pay him at the rate of about £3 a day. "He's a clever chap, Askew," Charlie had said.

Wigan entered the gates of the B.M., as it is familiarly called. At the office inside the building he applied for a Reader's Ticket, and was granted a temporary ticket, available for one day. Then he entered the great circular reading-room—one of the wonders of the world. Wigan was a modest man, and for a time he sat at one of the blue leather desks, getting his bearings, looking about him and thinking of all the famous men and women who had studied here. People, some of them strangely clad and perhaps coming from the far corners of the earth to this centre of learning, bustled about. Others sat absorbed with piles of books about them. Some appeared to be waiting for books to be brought to them. Wigan felt very much the humble copper. He gazed in awe round the vast dome and thought of Mike, who had often been in here and no doubt knew his way about the massive black leather-bound catalogues. A magnificently-dressed, dark-skinned girl who looked like an Eastern princess came in and stood uncertainly near him. Politely Wigan got up and offered her his seat. She said something to him in a foreign tongue. With the calm eye of the practised policeman he looked about and noted a desk marked ENQUIRIES. He directed her to this; and this made him think of his own errand.

He found the staff smilingly helpful. "What subject do you wish to study?"

Wigan lowered his voice—it seemed right to do so in such a place. "No subject at the moment. I wish to make contact with a gentleman named Mr. Askew, who I understand often comes here."

"Yes, he's one of our regulars. There he is—that very tall thin man in row D."

"Thank you." Wigan noted the request for silence and said: "I shall not transgress the laws of the institution by conversing loudly."

The member of the staff smiled. Good nature rather than pomposity is the key-note of the B.M. He instantly summed Wigan up as some sort of official; and he thought how amusing is human nature. However, his questioner looked a very decent man, so the member of the staff took Wigan across himself to D.8, where Mr. Askew sat, and effected an introduction. Mr.

Askew had just finished his work for the day, and he agreed to Wigan's favourite opening gambit—a cup of tea.

Wigan returned to his usual direct English. "I'm trying to clear Fred Hampton of the murder of Michael Fisk, and I ask your help, Mr. Askew."

Askew's long horse-face became animated. "That's *most* interesting. I believe him innocent too. I always have. I think he was the victim of an amazing set of circumstances. As a matter of fact, I'm an amateur criminologist—I specialise in books on criminology—and I've formed a theory of how the murder was committed."

"I should like to hear it. I'm a police officer. My name is Sergeant Wigan."

Askew almost dithered. "A police officer. Really! Well, my theory is that after Fred Hampton left the district of Sun, quite early and without entering Fisk's house, another person came on the scene, picked up Fred's knife, which he had dropped, and entered the house—quite possibly was admitted by Fisk. For a long time this person and Fisk conversed. At about 2 a.m. there was a quarrel and the person killed Fisk. Furthermore, I believe the person to be a woman!"

"Why so a woman, Mr. Askew?"

"Because—subject to your correction—the police never found any fingerprints."

"That's right, they didn't."

"Well, it is natural for a woman to keep her gloves on in a house, if she wishes. A man would never do so. It would be unnatural."

"That's true. Can you give a name to the woman?"

"I don't care to do that."

"I will. Ruth Brent?"

"She is a possible."

"But if so," said Wigan, "it seems extraordinary that she should meet Fred at The Spinning Heart to buy from him a book she must have stolen herself."

"Extraordinary, but not impossible. The public, Mr. Wigan, think book-collecting a nice harmless pastime indulged in by old dodderers. So it can be, but not always. It can be ruthless—no pun intended, I assure you. A book sold by Fred would establish a point in its history. What we call provenance. That means the history of a book. Collectors, especially Americans, like to know the provenance of a book. They talk about a Huth copy, a Widener copy, a James-Smith-Robinson-Brown copy, and so on. American dealers sometimes add a whole string of names; and a buyer then has a pretty sure guarantee that what he buys is genuine. But I didn't mention Miss Ruth. I don't want to bring undeserved trouble upon her. There are other women in the book trade, you know."

"Such as, Mr. Askew?"

"Oh well, Searle Connington lives with his sister, who runs a bookshop herself—the Welcome Bookshop in Notting Hill Gate. She is an expert in old coloured-plate books and recently sold Audubon's *Birds of America* for four thousand pounds."

"I am beginning to realise what vast sums are involved."

"Oh yes, prices are high. And they are rising."

"Any other women occur to you?"

Mr. Askew laughed. "I feel like an executioner. I really cannot name any others."

"Fred Hampton will hang if nothing is done."

"Well, there is—strictly between ourselves—someone who is womanish. Searle Connington. He is a man, of course, of the highest morality, but he does like to dress rather like a woman, though in a somewhat ragged way. I think 'womanish' is the right adjective to describe him."

"And he habitually wears gloves?"

"He does so—yes. Some collectors prefer to handle books with gloves on. One's fingers sweat, you know."

"Yes, though I've seen notices in bookshops asking customers to remove their gloves... I suppose it's the difference between the expert and the casual. I must meet Mr. Searle Connington."

"You can easily do that. He was in the B.M. when I left."

Mr. Askew performed the introduction, then tactfully withdrew. Wigan, who reckoned himself a good judge of character, thought that, apart from his theory, which might or might not hold water, he could eliminate Askew from the inquiry. He was a runner of the best type: cultured, clever, and devoted to books. He might be interested in criminology; he would never commit a crime.

Wigan repeated his tea gambit with Searle Connington, who outdid even Wigan in his love of tea-drinking. He ordered a large pot, and was most particular that the kettle should be brought to the pot and not the pot to the kettle. Also the cups must be warmed—the secret of a good cup of tea. Wigan thought "womanish" the wrong adjective to apply to Connington. He was rather an old maid. But he had force of character, and a pair of sharp, shrewd eyes. Though the day was not cold, he wore a pair of white cotton gloves. He kept them on in the café.

"Now let's hear what you want from me," he said, when he had added two lumps of sugar, one large, one small, to his cup.

"I am trying to clear Fred Hampton on a charge of murder."

"Bit late in the day, aren't you? He'll be hanged shortly."

"Where were you, Mr. Connington, on the day before Mike Fisk was killed? I mean the day, Monday, August 9th?"

"At a sale in Barnet. I dabble in antiques as well as books. There were some fine old glass paper-weights which I fancied."

"I understood you are in regular employment?"

"Yes, my good sir, I am. But my employment happens to be a library and bookshop. Bookshops are interested in sales. Q.E.D., if you understand what that means."

"I do understand. Barnet is not far from Sun."

"My good sir, my dear good sir, if you are accusing me of murder you are wasting your time. Quite a number of the trade were present. After the sale, which ended at four o'clock, we adjourned for what is known as, ah, the knockout, which means that we put up again lots among ourselves."

"Of course I'm not accusing you, sir. That would be most improper. All I'm trying to do is to find out general movements on the day. Can you name any other book dealers who were present?"

"Oh, representatives of several big West End firms. I remember Joel Ferrow looked in."

"And Miss Ruth Brent?"

"She was in Liverpool, I believe. But I had a watching brief on her behalf. She is interested in Henty first editions, but none came up."

This confirmed what Ruth herself had told Wigan about being in Liverpool. It began to look as if the trade generally had alibis except poor Fred Hampton. But Wigan ploughed heavily on.

"What time was all business finished, sir?"

"About six." Mr. Connington's eyes twinkled at Wigan. "We all went home then. Sales are exhausting, Mr. Wigan. Tempers are apt to get frayed. Personally, after buying a couple of paper-weights at an exorbitant price and missing others that I wanted, I was far too done-up to think of travelling to Sun to murder Mike Fisk. I dare say the same thing applies to others present."

"Sir, I'm not accusing you. I couldn't possibly do a thing like that, or even think it, without a formal caution. I'm only after information. Do you always wear gloves?"

"Always. I suffer unfortunately from acute perspiration in the hands. Most detrimental to books."

"Does Mr. Joel Ferrow wear gloves?"

"I've known him do so. Is *he* one of your suspects?"

"He might be. All connected with the trade are suspect until the matter is cleared up."

"Dear, dear, I thought Fred Hampton was convicted."

"I think him innocent."

"And on your suspicion we must all squirm again on the pin of uncertainty. You're taking a lot on yourself, Sergeant."

This was just what Wigan was doing, and if Mr. Connington complained to headquarters matters might be awkward for Wigan. But it isn't the sharp-tongued man who usually complains. Wigan tried doggedly for some *fact* which would give him a lead.

"As far as you know, did Mr. Joel Ferrow go home after the knockout?"

"As far as I know, yes; but his way home could take him through Sun, if he wished to make it."

That would apply to everyone present, including Connington himself; but Wigan was too wise to make the comment. "I suppose, sir, he didn't give you or offer you a lift?"

"No. I have my own car, Austin Seven, number XX 18273. Ferrow has a Jaguar, number GIG 31954."

Wigan made a note. "Thank you, sir. You're a good observer."

"Have to be. It's my trade. I reckon I can spot a bargain with any man in England. Good-day to you. Thanks for the tea."

Wigan got on the phone to Headquarters, Motor Vehicle Records Office. "Can you give me the owner of a Jaguar private car, No. GIG 31954?" He waited a short while, then with admirable precision came the answer: "Mr. Edward Maile, The Street, Little Franting, Surrey."

"Can you give me the owner before him?"

"Mr. Joel Ferrow, Muswell Hill Grange, London, N.10."

"When did the car change hands?"

"September 1st, 1954."

"Can you give me the date of manufacture and any other particulars?"

"The car was first registered on June 15th, 1952, in the name of Joel Ferrow, address as before. Engine capacity 3,442 c.c. All-black saloon body. No other distinguishing feature."

Wigan thanked the giver of this information, then he considered matters over a pipe—he thought he had had enough tea for one day. It was surely suspicious that Ferrow had sold a first-class motor-car so soon after the crime. Yet, of course, why not? Men do sell cars in a capricious manner. He might even have bought a newer-model Jaguar for the sake of flourishing his increasing wealth. Heavy traffic went through Sun, and it might be too much to hope that any constable had taken particular note of GIG 31954 on August 9th–10th. Yet someone might have seen Joel Ferrow. It remained to get his photograph from Charlie.

# CHAPTER FOURTEEN

## STRANGE THINGS HAPPEN AT NIGHT

"I'd like to burgle the house," said Charlie next day when he reported to Wigan.

"You can't do that. You'd only get arrested. And so should I if I attempted it."

"I thought you might be sort of privileged."

Wigan laughed. "A queer idea you've got of cops, Charlie. At the police training school a usual question asked is 'What is the chief requirement in a police officer?' Some say courage, some tact, some intelligence. The correct answer is honesty. A dishonest policeman is a contradiction in terms. I can't possibly agree to anything against the law, even to free Fred Hampton. The only thing we could do is to apply for a search warrant, and I know that would be hopeless. No magistrate would issue one on the slender evidence we've got."

"Well, guv'nor, it's up to you. We may as well give up. Somewhere the Ferrows have a secret store of books. If they stole one from Mike it will be with them; and unless they are absolutely insane—which they ain't—they will keep the book until Fred is dead and gone."

"Charlie, we will offer a million pounds for a rare occult work, so rare that no other collector in the world will have it. I think your fiction is too thin and bound to be discovered; but we can find a real American collector—the man for whom Ruth Brent is agent."

"He's Dithan Dand, the millionaire business man."

"Then he really can pay a million pounds. Good. Now I want you to get in touch with Ruth and tell her a tale, and make it convincing. You will know what kind of book to offer. But it's vital that the book should pass through our hands, so, when Ruth bites, you will go again to the Ferrows and inspect the cream of their stock, and this time it will be the cream. I'm relying on the lure of money."

"We may not be able to prove that any book they offer did belong to Mike. As a bookman, Mr. Francis would certainly collate any book in his possession—go through it leaf by leaf to check for any defects. If he saw Mike's mark he would certainly rub it out. A minute with a rubber would do it. Gone for ever."

"I know there are objections. It's taking a long chance, but we must take any chance. I've made arrangements for you to come to Sun Police Station and inspect the Keats first edition, a unique copy known to have belonged to Mike. Look for any mark in that."

In the little C.I.D. room at Sun Police Station Charlie sat at a table with the Keats volume, brought out of the safe, before him. With his long slender fingers he opened the volume, and almost instantly said:

"Look, guv'nor—£350, on the front paste-down endpaper. By heaven, I think we may have foxed them. That's what Mike *paid* for the book. That's not his handwriting. It's a former price. He left it in, and the murderer left it in. Now let's see if we can find his selling price..."

He took out a magnifying glass and went through the volume leaf by leaf. "It's a first issue," he remarked, "of the first edition with two leaves of advertisements at the end. Now let's see..."

Wigan waited, humbly aware of how little he himself knew about rare books.

Inch by inch Charlie scrutinised the leaves with his magnifying glass. "Got it!" he said at last. "Look, mister, VM. That means five thousand—five thousand quid. That's what Mike hoped to get for this book. And I should say it's worth it, every penny. Keats's own copy. £300 was a ridiculous price, and the only explanation is that the volume is 'hot'—stolen. I think the whole thing was planned to let Fred Hampton in the cart."

Wigan voiced an objection. "Why leave the original price in? Surely a fresh buyer would see it and think he was paying through the nose?"

"That's only what the ignorant public would think," said Charlie impatiently. "You offer them a penny pamphlet several hundred years old. It's marked 'One Penny' and you ask ten pounds. 'Coo,' they say, 'it's marked One Penny and you ask ten pounds. You are a blooming swindler.' Of course the original price has got nothing to do with it. At one time the Keats first did fetch £350. That's all that means. In years to come the five thousand will be out of date, and ten thousand will be more the mark. Rare books are rising all the time."

Wigan felt corrected. "Well," he said, "there's hope that an even more expensive item will still have Mike's mark in it."

"Your million pound touch is a good idea," said Charlie. "The big sum always fetches collectors. The great American collector and dealer Dr. Rosenbach knew that. He was never frightened of high prices. I remember when he paid a hundred and fifty-one thousand dollars for the Bay Psalm Book. The newspaper men were saying 'Cor blimey' and 'Cor luv-a-duck,' and things like that, and do you know what the doctor told them? The price, says he, was very reasonable! And I bet you that within hours some super-business-man collector was falling over himself to offer the doctor double. So Dithan Dand may do the necessary."

"Then off you go to Ruth," said Wigan. "The sooner we do it the better. If we can get in our hands a book with Mike's mark in it I shall go over the D.I.'s head, if necessary, to the Public Prosecutor. Get a written offer from Ruth. That ought to convince the Ferrows. Otherwise, they won't let any book out of their hands without the money; and neither you nor I, Charlie, have a million pounds."

"Cor blimey, guv'nor!" said Charlie. "I don't half feel queer dealing in millions. Six quid a week is my mark. When I've made that I usually pack up. By the way, here's your catalogue. That's Francis and that's Joel. Nice pair of mugs, aren't they?"

"I'll offer this round," said Wigan, "while you are busy with Ruth and the Ferrows."

It was about 11 p.m. when Charlie walked up Muswell Hill. It was a fine clear night, and the light on the summit of the television mast on Alexandra Palace shone out like a great star. Charlie walked slowly with the slouching gait peculiar to tramps, book-runners, and others who use their feet a lot. Neither tramps nor book-runners waste effort in raising their feet from the ground. His appointment, made by telephone, was for eleven-thirty. When he reached Muswell Hill Grange the time was eleven-thirty to the dot. Charlie rang the bell.

The great Joel himself opened the door, a blue-chinned, black-haired man in the prime of life with the build of a prize-fighter and the air of a buccaneer which clung to him from the days when he raided the auction-rooms and flogged his bargains in a sack. But as a concession to respectability he now wore the black coat and striped trousers of the conventional business man. He also sported a white waistcoat with pearl buttons.

"Come in, Charlie," he said. "We've got something good for you."

"Thank you, Mr. Joel." Charlie dropped the "sir" as befitted a man with millionaire customers.

"Would you like a cup of tea first?"

"I would indeed. It's cold tonight."

Charlie was shown into the same room as on his previous visit. The housekeeper brought in a nice equipage of tea and biscuits, and Charlie helped himself with appreciation. He expected something extraordinary in the way of books. Mike had a reputation in the trade of getting hold of rare books and manuscripts; and Charlie thought he might be shown an original manuscript—something of immense value. Mike had few friends and didn't talk much. Neither did he issue catalogues as some private dealers did. It was conceivable that the Ferrows might be reckless enough to show some-thing they had stolen from Mike. A million pounds is a lot of money, as Sergeant Wigan had said.

Mr. Joel came in. There was nothing in his hands. "So, Charlie," he said genially, "you're a blasted copper's nark, are you?"

"I don't know what you mean, Mr. Joel."

"Oh yes, you do. We know all about it. You and your stories. Me and my brother, we didn't bump Mike off; but we don't like snoopers round our books. We don't like it, Charlie. See?"

Charlie had plenty of courage. He was five feet nothing but he had done his bit in the 1914 War and could boast his row of medals with the best of them. He rose to his feet and watched closely Joel's huge figure. He might be able to dodge out of the room when the other made his murderous rush.

"You know what we would do with you in the old days, don't you? We would throw you out of the window. I've seen it done in the auction-rooms. And there weren't no fare back to town. I'd be more annoyed, Charlie, only I was an effing runner myself once, and I suppose you're getting paid for it."

"I don't want to see the wrong man hang."

"That's none of our business. Now clear out before I forget myself, and tell the copper you're working for that we'll tear him in half if he interferes with us. Now get."

Charlie walked out. "Thanks for the tea," he said.

"I've been a runner myself, and in want of a cuppa."

Charlie stood in front of the wrong side of the front door. "We shan't get no change out of them," he said to himself.

He was walking down the drive, which was over-shadowed with trees, when there was a rustle in the bushes below them. A dark-clad figure came out.

"Good God," said Charlie, "*you!*"

"Yes, me. I want the book you got from the Ferrows."

"I haven't got no book. They wouldn't give me nothing. They turned me out."

"I still want the book you got." The blade of a knife gleamed.

"Now look here, Ruth," said Charlie, "you're too damned handy with your weapons. I heard about you and Fred Hampton and your bleedin' razor-blade on his face. I tell you I've got nothing. If you don't believe me, walk in and ask them. They turned me out. They knew it was a sell to try and help Fred. Now put that knife away, there's a good girl."

Charlie wasn't afraid of Ruth or any woman. Women were easy to manage with a bit of soft soap. He looked at Ruth's hard, beautiful face and actually patted her hand. "You're a double-crosser, you are," he said.

"I was afraid you would double-cross me, and Di Dand does so want something unique."

"Those blooming American collectors, I hate 'em. They spoil the book trade. Half of them ain't got no feeling for fine books. They just speculate in them as they would stocks and shares."

"Di has one of the finest collections in the world."

"And how many books does he read? Tell me that."

"I love Di," was Ruth's answer.

"Ah well. And meanwhile poor old Fred will hang. Did you do Mike in? Did you, Ruth?"

"No, I didn't. How could I? I was in Liverpool buying Henty books for Di."

"Ah. And somehow I don't think Joel did it. He's not such a bad old cuss. He could have bashed my head off tonight, but he let me off."

"How will you get back to town, Charlie?"

"Walk, I suppose."

"I'll get my car out and run you back."

"Did you ever love anybody, Charlie?" asked Ruth as she was driving him back to Lambeth.

"Me? No. I'm too fly for that stuff. Where does love get you? No cash and a bunch of kids to bring up. I'm happy in my digs all by my lonesome. If you can't marry D and I should forget him if I was you."

"I can't forget him. I shall never forget him. I will do anything for him, anything."

"He seems a pretty hard customer by all accounts."

"There was a write-up of him in 'Talk of the Town' last week. All about his career. How he had worked as a navvy on the Canadian Pacific railroad. I was so proud."

Charlie was silent. He let Ruth talk on. She was in a rare emotional mood, about as rare as Lavater's *Ghostes and Spirites*. Charlie knew that the chance might never come again. He sat and smoked while she drove slowly through the streets, as silent and deserted as London ever is, and told him things she had never told anyone before. She spoke freely to the little man at her side. Charlie was a Roman Catholic, and he knew the meaning and the relief of the confessional.

"Here we are," he said at length, as she stopped before his lodgings. "Good night, Ruth, and thanks for the lift."

"Sole result of the night's work, guv'nor," said Charlie next morning as he met Wigan by arrangement. Charlie offered a copy of last week's "Talk of the Town." It was open at a full-page portrait of Dithan Dand. He certainly made a startling picture—the personification of human power.

"He may bear looking into, guv'nor. He flies back and forth with the greatest of ease, like the daring young man on the flying trapeze. He may have done Mike in and fixed with Ruth the business of the Keats. He and she together would stop at nothing. She was an actress once and a knife-thrower and lots of things."

He gave Wigan a full account of the previous night's adventures, then added: "I was Ruth's confessional. But there's nothing secret about me as there is a priest—not when an innocent man's life is at stake."

"He doesn't seem likely," said Wigan. "A man of his wealth can buy any book he wants."

"Not unless the owner will sell. Mike could be obstinate and independent. He would tell a millionaire to go to hell if he felt like it. You haven't read the article yet, guv. Dithan Dand lost his right hand in an accident. He wears an artificial hand with a glove on it. But he could pick up a knife with it and stab Mike."

"I'll try his portrait round," said Wigan. "I haven't had any luck with Joel Ferrow's. I showed it to Mrs. Tray, and all she could say was 'I don't think so.' She still thinks the man she saw was Fred. Matter of fact, she's very distressed. Her evidence went far to convict Fred. It's an appalling thought if the man is innocent. She will help if she can. It's the beard— one can't get over that."

"As I've said, any person can wear a beard for the price of a shilling or two. Even—even Ruth Brent. The girl was an actress."

"I can't prove anything. I'm all at sea, and I'm very much afraid I shall have to tell Fred so."

Wigan took the photo of Dithan Dand to Mrs. Tray. She studied it for a long time. Then she said: "I don't think so. Really, I don't think it was him at all." She made an obvious point. "He's got a big face."

It was true. Dithan Dand was a big man and his features were on the same scale: handsome, but rather gross and certainly large.

"The face I saw," continued Mrs. Tray, "was smaller, much more ordinary but with a beard."

And for the present Wigan couldn't get over that.

# CHAPTER FIFTEEN

## THE SANDS RUN OUT

On the day that Sergeant Wigan finished his service as Aid to the C.I.D. and rejoined the uniform branch, Fred Hampton's appeal to the Court of Criminal Appeal was heard and dismissed. The decision was final, with the exception that the Home Secretary could, if he thought proper, grant a reprieve from the capital sentence. Harland the solicitor, who was now firmly Hampton's friend, did all he could and at once wrote to the Home Secretary, stating that in his opinion there was, through extraordinary circumstances, a gross miscarriage of justice. But Harland didn't think it would help to organise a petition in any way; and he had to say this to Fred, who was nearly frantic with fear.

"You won't take the trouble," said Fred.

"I will take any trouble. But we need positive proof that you are innocent, and it's that we can't get."

Fred wept. "I can't think any more. That bloody copper has forsaken me."

Wigan, on his leave-day, got another order to visit Hampton. He found the death-watch exhausted with the effort of trying to interest the man in some small game, like draughts, and trying to calm his fears.

"We can give him a cup of something before the end," one of them said privately to Wigan, "but even then I dread the job."

"I've got to die! I've got to die!" shouted Hampton to Wigan.

Wigan swallowed. Speak he could not. At last he said: "I've come to ask you more questions. For God's sake answer them, man. I've worked and worked and made no headway. The Ferrows weren't seen at Sun on the day of the crime. Neither was anyone else connected with books, so far as I can find out. Can you think of any other person who may have killed Mike?"

"How the hell do I know? I'm not the——police. The devil may have killed Mike for all I know."

"The devil—what do you mean?"

"What I say. He was trying to raise the devil, you know; 'Resurge, Satanas, et omnes diaboli,' and all the rest of it. And if he did raise the devil, the devil may well have killed him. And left no fingerprints."

"It's fantastic," said Wigan.

"So's the whole bloody case. Little did I think, when I tried to chisel a book out of Mike, that I should come to this."

Wigan remembered that others had hinted at the same thing. "I'll look into it."

Fred turned his white face with its feeble little beard up to Wigan. "You might hurry yourself," he said.

Wigan changed the subject. "I hear your family are doing fine," he said. "They are living in the country now and Harland drives the girls to town every day. He's being a real friend to you, Fred."

At once Fred grew calmer. The thought of his wife and children, safe from this appalling mess, was the only thing that could calm him.

"He tells me Winnie's making progress," he said. "The viola's a good one."

"She may get on the B.B.C. There's no saying how high she may rise. Do you know anything about Dithan Dand?"

"Oh, that b——r. He's a pal of Ruth Brent's. Got all the money in the world. He's over in the U.S.A., so I can't see he comes into it."

"He could fly over in forty-eight hours."

"Yes, but for what purpose? Ruth buys him books. She was buying the Keats for him. Why kill when he could buy?"

"That's what I think. I can't see any reason, unless Mike held out on him. Mike could be independent."

"He bloody well could. But if he sent the book for auction, Ruth could have bought it there. I know she does bid against the trade."

"Then you really have no other thought but the devil killing Mike?"

"Yes, with my knife, curse him. Mike messed about with things he didn't understand and got his lot. That's how I read it."

"Then why the stolen books? For, with Charlie's help, I have discovered another book to be missing, probably an occult work."

"Someone entered the study after, found Mike dead, and pinched the books."

"But who?"

"I just don't know. I can't answer that. You're free. It's for you to find out, if you are the pal you say you are."

He said no word of thanks to Wigan for what he was doing, but Wigan didn't expect that or alter in the slightest degree his calm manner towards Fred.

"I wish I had the money to employ a real detective," added Fred peevishly.

"We shall do all we can, Harland and myself and Charlie North."

"How does he come into it?"

"I'm paying him to help."

"You must think a lot of him. But he's a sharp little cuss. Why can't he find the person who left me the Keats to offer?"

"He has his suspicions, but it's so hard to prove anything. Those foreign words you quoted: what do they mean?"

"'*Resurge, Satanas,*' etc.? They're Latin, and mean 'Arise Satan, and all devils.' They come from the Black Mass."

"And you really think Mike could raise the devil?"

"He could have a good try. I know animals have been raised before now, including one which kicked up hell. If you raise from hell you get hell. But I can't see the devil leaving me a book to flog."

"I wish Mike was here to tell us."

It was a silly remark, and Fred made Wigan feel it. "Wishing won't get me out of here," he said. "I expected more than that when you offered to help me. Offered—I didn't ask you."

"I'm going to help you, Fred. Fix your mind on that."

Fred began to weep again, from weakness and hopelessness. "Soon *he* will be here. My God, I shall never be able to face it."

Outside in the corridor the warder looked at Wigan. "Any luck?"

"None whatever."

"It's fixed for Thursday, December 16th, unless he gets a reprieve."

"Does he know?"

"The Governor has had to tell him, through the chaplain, that the appeal was dismissed. It would be cruel to do otherwise. He won't be told about the execution until the night before."

"The law is all against me," said Wigan. "If I could burgle a few houses I might get the evidence, but how can I do that?"

"Search me, chum," said the warder. He returned to his weary duty of guarding the condemned man, who must never be left alone for a single instant, by day or night, lest he die by suicide before the law claimed its penalty of death by judicial hanging.

Wigan went straight from the prison to the office of Mr. Harland and told him about the devil-raising theory which might at least account for the death of Mike Fisk.

The solicitor listened attentively, then he said: "I can't put that forward to the Home Office, I simply can't. It's the worst possible defence. Bill Smith kills Ted Jones. 'I never done it,' says Bill Smith. 'A ghost did it.'"

"It's not quite as bad as that. Mike was playing with

dangerous weapons in the form of books which deal with the Black Mass. He was trying to raise the devil, and perhaps he did it."

"Yes, yes, but all the evidence is against Hampton. He quarrelled with the man, he almost certainly owned the knife which killed Fisk, and he almost certainly was seen at the window about the time the crime was committed. We can't get over that, and, between ourselves, I can't see the Home Secretary getting over it. He has his duty to do. If he reprieves one murderer he must reprieve all, unless there are mitigating circumstances. The jury made no recommendation to mercy."

"Well," said Wigan, "will you consider seriously what I have told you? Isn't there an expert in the psychic world who can help us?"

"The greatest expert is probably Sir Manson Wood. I will telephone for an appointment. I will tell him what you have said. If my reasoned appeal fails, there may be just a slender chance." The solicitor removed his glasses and put them on again, as if the case would look better that way.

"That's all I wanted to hear. I suppose Mike's house and its contents belong to me now?" Harland was acting for him in the matter.

"As soon as the police remove their seals. I doubt whether they will until the case is finally closed."

"But I can raise money on the expectation of the books? I will pay any fee Sir Manson asks."

"He won't ask a fee. He is a director of a prosperous publishing house, and he conducts his psychical studies as a hobby. But mind you, Wigan, even raising the devil won't help us, unless the devil is accommodating enough to sign a written confession. Go out and get me something concrete: something I can use to knock to pieces the circumstantial chain of links against Hampton."

Wigan decided to apply for annual leave so that, freed from eight hours' daily tour of duty as a uniformed sergeant, he could devote his time entirely to Hampton's interests. The number of men who apply for the early part of December is not large. Mary Wigan was hoping this year for some Christmas leave so that she could visit relatives in Devon, and of course if Wigan applied for two weeks from the 6th to the 20th this would knock Christmas leave on the head; but she stood solidly behind her husband. "If you think you ought to do it, Jack, then you must."

Wigan began his application in the time-honoured way:

"To S.D. Inspector,—Sir, I respectfully request permission to take two weeks' annual leave from," etc. To his surprise his application did not return to him marked 'Granted'. Instead he received an order to attend the S.D. Inspector's office. The S.D. Inspector was a man of few words, and he started abruptly: "What's this I hear, Wigan, about you trying to get Hampton off?"

"I think the man has been wrongfully convicted, sir."

"The jury decided otherwise. I shan't grant your application. To do so would land you, and us, in a mess."

Wigan was standing rigidly to attention. He said respectfully: "Then I have the right, sir, to carry my application to the Superintendent."

"Certainly you have the right, but I hope you won't do it.

Look, Wigan, we all like you here. You're a good sergeant. You make your men toe the line, yet they respect you because you are fair. I know all about that. And now you've got a crazy bee in your bonnet. I followed the Hampton case myself and in my opinion the man was rightfully convicted. Motive, weapon, time, and stolen goods in his possession—all there."

"I feel the man is innocent, sir. I'm quite sure he is, and, given time, I hope to prove it."

"Do you, Wigan? I wish to heaven we had never lent you to the C.I.D. I suppose there are others who know a bit about books. I suppose the case has upset you."

"More than upset me, sir. I believe there has been a gross miscarriage of justice."

"You believe. Well, Wigan, I shan't grant your application; and if you appeal to the Superintendent I shall add a strong note giving my reasons for refusal. In the face of that I don't think the Superintendent will grant you leave."

Wigan didn't think so either. For a moment he thought of resigning from the police, but to do so would bring harm to his wife and children. After a moment he said with formal respect: "Thank you, sir. I will accept your refusal of my request."

The S.D. Inspector was much relieved. He said, man to man: "I know these murder cases are difficult. I expect the poor chap's in a dreadful state. But, damn it, he ought to have thought of that before he killed another man."

Wigan made no reply. He did not salute as he was not wearing his helmet. He turned smartly about and marched from the room.

The S.D. Inspector stopped him at the door. "Wigan, I'll

try and get you Christmas leave. Go away with your wife and children and forget all about it."

"Thank you, sir, you're very kind. I know you mean that kindly, but I shan't be applying for Christmas leave."

"Oh, well. Please yourself."

Wigan did Late Turn that day as station officer at Sun. He had a tiring and exacting eight hours, dealing with a complicated larceny charge. Yet when at 10 p.m. he handed over to the night duty station officer there could be no thought of rest. He went to the porters' room at Sun railway station and "flashed" the photo of Dithan Dand. He had done this with photos of Joel and Francis Ferrow and received then the same answer as he received now: "Sorry, guv., I've never seen him before... No, I ain't seen him."

"If he wore a beard, do you think it would make any difference: would you have seen him then?"

"No, guv., certain sure. We would always notice a bloke with a beard."

Wigan returned home about done-up. Mary had his supper ready, and she wouldn't let him say a word until he had eaten it. Then she asked him about the leave. "No leave granted," said Wigan briefly. "The Sub was dead against me."

Mary was silent. She knew the case was getting on her husband's nerves. She knew he tossed and turned at night, thinking of the helpless man behind the bars. But supposing Hampton was in fact guilty? She had followed the case, as indeed had most of the local residents; and Hampton seemed a violent, uncontrolled man likely to commit murder. But to say so to her husband, who thought otherwise, would be disloyal.

"What are you going to do next, Jack?"

"We are getting in touch with a spiritualist chap, Sir Manson Wood."

"How can he help?"

"Mike was playing with the black arts—trying to raise the devil. It is possible that supernatural violence killed him."

"And then stole his book, Jack, and offered it for sale?"

"Yes, yes, I know. It's hard to get over that."

"Well, make your mind easy, Jack. Good will always triumph over evil. God will never allow an innocent man to suffer."

"I wish I could feel that. But innocent men have been hanged before now."

"And guilty ones have gone unpunished—to the outward world. But there's a Divine reason for everything."

Wigan smiled. "There's no getting over you, Mary. I'll go to bed. I only hope Fred Hampton is sleeping easy."

"He is if his conscience is easy. But he doesn't seem to be a very moral man."

"He's got one very good point. He won't let his wife and children suffer. He's in jail and alone, yet he won't let them come near him or even write to him. They are to forget completely about him—that's his order to Harland, his solicitor. It shows courage from a man who is an arrant physical coward and shaking with fear at the thought of being hanged."

"All men have some good points. He may still be a murderer, but if you feel he is innocent, then you are right to help him."

"Well, come along then, Mary: let's have some Devon common sense. You say you followed the case. How would you help the man?"

"I should begin by praying for guidance. Then I should try and check the man's story. He says he lost his knife: he doesn't know where. It may be hard to check that, but when he says that a stolen book was left on his door-step in a parcel, surely that point can be checked?"

"How? Wrapper, string, card—all burnt."

"He must be a very simple gentleman, or a very cunning one. But he cannot have burnt the hands that left the parcel. Cannot that be checked? Did no one see the parcel left?"

"I tried in the street where he lives. It's just the opposite to Chelmer Square. Busy. No one noticed a parcel left, nor saw anyone unusual call at the Hamptons' house."

"I should try again. It's the one point in Hampton's story that can be checked. Now let's go to bed."

# CHAPTER SIXTEEN

## JOHNNY TUPPER SEES A GHOST

The following day Wigan was again Late Turn station duty. He had the morning free, and after an early breakfast he hurried from Sun to Islington, where once more he interviewed likely residents in Hampton's street. He asked the usual question: "About the middle of August, did you see anyone leave a small parcel at the Hamptons' house? Did you see anyone unusual in the street?" And almost at once he struck an extraordinary story from Johnny Tupper, aged twelve, who happened to be playing with the children living near the Hamptons' house.

"I didn't see no parcel, mister, but I see a ghost."

"What kind of ghost?"

"A 'eadless ghost with wings like a bat. I thought it was The Bat. You know, the one in the film that was showing near the Angel."

"I don't go to films," said Wigan patiently. "Just tell me all about it. Don't make anything up. Just tell me what you saw."

"Well, mister, on a Tuesday afternoon during the 'olidays I went to the pictures—the place near the Angel, Islington of course. There was the News, then a serial about cowboys, then the main picture: *The Horror of The Bat*. Very good it was. I was turned out about five, then I went fishing with the Cowley boys along the Lea at Edmonton. I got home late. It was dark. I suppose it would be about half-past ten. I was walking up this street here when I saw a winged 'orror coming along, no 'ead and great black wings like a bat. I thought he was coming after me to suck my blood, like The Bat did in the film. So I ran, and it couldn't run—and that's all, mister."

"Did you tell your parents?"

"Good lord, no. Dad wouldn't half laugh. 'You go to the pictures too much,' he would say, and likely enough he would try and stop me. The same with Mum."

"Are you sure it was like a bat?"

"Dead sure. Great black wings spread out. And no 'ead. Do real bats have 'eads, mister?"

Wigan's natural history was shaky, but he thought they must have heads. They could hardly live without them.

"This one did, mister. It was a Spectral Bat."

"Which way did it go?"

"I didn't look to see, mister."

"Did you see it pause and deposit something—say a small parcel?"

"I didn't see nothing except what I told you. It was 'uge, 'orrible, 'eadless—a Spectral Bat."

Wigan rewarded young Johnny with a shilling and tried hard to find someone else, preferably an adult who hadn't had his imagination stimulated by the pictures, who had seen the bat. But without success. Most seemed to think him cranky, if not gone in the head. Islington, prosaic, busy Islington, wasn't the place for spectral bats. He had to leave the district to go on Late Turn duty. But before returning home he got in touch with Charlie and asked him to take over the search.

"We have got to remember," said Charlie, "that Ruth was once an actress. She could have worn a big cloak and hidden her head."

"Try to confirm the boy's story. I can't ask the C.I.D. to help. I'm pretty sure they wouldn't."

"We're in a very unfortunate position, Mr. Wigan. Only the two of us, and the date of execution fixed, you say. I'll do my best. But Londoners—they don't see nothing. As for spectral bats—pink rats is the limit they go to."

Charlie did his best. He tried door-to-door along the length of the long street. "We're sick of inquiries," said a woman. "We've got something better to do than keep watch on the Hamptons' house. Now the place is shut up and the Hamptons are gone, and a good thing too."

"There was a parcel left, lady. We're trying to trace who left it."

"We're honest people here and don't steal nothing. I expect the postman couldn't get an answer so he left it."

This gave Charlie an idea. He knew how observant postmen are. He went to the local sorting office and asked the men there if they had seen a parcel left on the doorstep of the Hamptons' house, or a stranger wearing a big black cloak.

"I don't remember seeing a parcel," said a man, "the street lamps aren't good enough for that, but as I was going home after making the last collection I do recollect a figure in black. Very queer it looked."

"Man or woman?"

"It looked like Old Nick to me."

"Why do you say that?"

"Well—it's hard to describe—but it was dark or darkish: about 10 p.m. There was a high wind blowing—hell of an August we had—and the figure seemed to fly with wings outstretched. No doubt it was only the wind on a cloak."

"Which way was it going?"

"Towards Upper Street. It—the figure—could get a bus there."

"Did you see feet: big or small?"

"I'm inclined to say small."

"Trousers or a skirt?"

"I can't rightly say. All I really noticed was a big cloak like wings."

"You haven't a clue to the face or head?"

"Now you mention it, it didn't seem to have a head. I might have had a closer look, but I was on my bike and fighting a head wind and I wanted to get home because I had my Pools to do."

"My God," thought Charlie, "it would be queer if Old Nick had something to do with it."

Quite suddenly a lot of people seemed to have seen The Bat—it was obvious that young Johnny had been talking. The story grew and grew. Flying down the street at sixty miles an hour. Uttering weird cries. Great talons extended (it seemed to be changing from a bat to an eagle). Charlie thought he was having his leg pulled and left the rest of the residents alone.

But happening to meet the policeman on the beat (a different division from Wigan), he had a word with him.

"I remember the story about the parcel," said the P.C. "Our C.I.D. were asked to check it, but found nothing. As to the story about a bat, I think it's moonshine. Boys go to the pictures too much, in my opinion."

"There ain't much front garden to the houses. I should have thought a parcel would be seen."

"That's my view. Unless it was left shortly before it was picked up. I can tell you one thing. It wasn't left before half-past nine p.m. because I was round here then and I would have noticed it. I had this beat the whole of August except for leave days, and on the Tuesday—the day the book was supposed to have been left—I was round here as usual just before booking-off time, which is 10 p.m. on the Late Turn. Inspector Saggs, the D.I. at Brabant, asked me about this."

"The night duty comes on at ten o'clock?"

"That's right. It does. The night duty man would do his shops in Upper Street first, and he didn't see the book either. He was asked by the inspector. From 10 p.m. till about 12.30 a.m. he was in Upper Street, kept there by some slight rowdyism. By that time the book had been picked up by Hampton, according to his story. So, as far as the police are concerned, he's unlucky in his alibi. Or he's a liar. Yet I don't think he is guilty of murder, as they say."

Charlie was interested. "Oh. Why don't you?"

"Just a feeling. I don't think he's the type. I think there has been a clever game and Hampton is the victim."

Charlie then told of his connection with Sergeant Wigan and asked the beat P.C. to have a cup of tea and discuss the case, but the P.C., whose name was Thomas Crouch, could not accept. "I can't leave my beat. If my sergeant caught me there would be trouble. But I'll help you in any way I can, short of risking my uniform."

"We can't break the chain of circumstances against Hampton," said Charlie. "We must find someone who has seen the parcel put on the door-step of Hampton's house."

P.C. Crouch was a middle-aged man nearing the end of his service. He had a round red face, a slow manner, and shrewd eyes. "The time for crime," he said, "is about 10 p.m. when the reliefs change. Most criminals know this. Of course the police try to cover it with crime patrols at odd hours; but a crime patrol wouldn't operate in a residential street like this with nothing in the houses worth stealing—they're too poor. Now supposing this bat-fellow you're talking about left the parcel. He would be in the street about 10 p.m. Try the lamp-lighters. These old gas-lamps are always going wrong, particularly on a windy night, and the lighters come round relighting. They are employed by the Council. Try the foreman of the yard. You might get something from him."

Charlie did so. The foreman looked up his time-sheets. "A man called Bond was on duty, street, date, time you mention," he said.

Charlie suppressed excitement. "Can I speak to Mr. Bond?"

"Afraid you can't. He's dead. He died from influenza a fortnight ago."

Truly, the devil himself seemed to be against them in the inquiry.

Charlie went to see Mrs. Bond, a nice old lady of the Darby and Joan type. He asked her if her husband had spoken of seeing anything unusual. "It's curious you should say that," she said, "because one night in August, a wild windy night when Phil, my husband, was busy relighting gas-lamps, he came home and said the devil himself was out—flying down the street, and that these atomic bombs were responsible for the bad weather."

"What made him think it was the devil?"

"He said 'Good night, mate. Ain't it a caution?' and the figure uttered a sort of snarl."

"Man or woman?"

"Phil didn't say. He said a sort of snarl, and then the lamp he had just lit went out again and my husband felt burning and the matches in his pocket, safety-matches, were alight. Wasn't that queer?"

"Very, very queer," said Charlie.

# CHAPTER SEVENTEEN

## FROM THE DEAD

As solicitor in charge of the defence, Mr. Harland was entitled to every help from the police; and without difficulty he received permission to visit Michael Fisk's house when he pleased. He had got in touch with Sir Manson Wood, who wished to hold an inquiry in the house. "I cannot promise psychic assistance," he said, "but we may light on something to help the poor unfortunate man whom you say is innocent."

"I think he is. I feel he is. I can't say more, Sir Manson."

"We will choose midnight next Sunday evening. I am a director of my firm and am very busy. I have also been unwell, but I must make the effort in such a cause. I suffer from my heart. I trust any revelations will not be of too distressing a character."

"Can they be?"

"Oh, dear me, yes. Raising the devil is a dangerous occupation. I shall not of course attempt it. But there may be forces in the Room of Death which will take a long while to disperse. What the public call ghosts. However, we shall see. We shall need lanterns. No doubt the electricity or gas supply has been cut off."

"I will make all arrangements, sir. I should like Sergeant Wigan to be present."

"Anyone you please, so long as he does not disturb the atmosphere by interruptions, or, worse still, jests. I shall bring my dog with me."

"Why your dog, Sir Manson?"

"Because he will defend his master with his life. I really cannot have violent attacks made on me. I don't think I should survive them. But Bruce, my dog, has supreme courage. I would rather have Bruce at my side than a policeman armed with a revolver."

On a mild December night, that seemed to be trying to make up for the shocking summer, the three met at Michael Fisk's house. A handsome black Alsatian dog followed Sir Manson out of his car. Sir Manson introduced Mr. Harland and Sergeant Wigan to the dog as if he were a human being. "He's more intelligent than many humans I know," he remarked. "Is this the house? Hum, Victorian. Well-built. A man could die a violent death here and one might not hear his cries."

Wigan unfastened the front door. In view of the S.D. Inspector's disapproval, he might have been in an awkward position securing the keys himself; but Mr. Harland's order from the D.I. at Brabant had made the way easy. Wigan and Mr. Harland politely stepped aside for Sir Manson to enter. The dog followed at his heels.

"What do you think of the place, Bruce? Full of atmosphere, eh? A man was killed while raising the devil. So don't take any chances."

The dog looked at his master. They entered the study. Mr. Harland switched on a powerful electric lantern. Wigan pulled the curtains across the window. Sir Manson went to the table and looked at the blood-stained volume. "So this is what he was reading? What a lot of blood. This is most unpleasant. Bruce, I don't like it at all."

Wigan and Harland maintained a discreet silence. They wondered what was going to happen next.

"Please sit down. Bruce, stay with me. Don't leave me for an instant."

Mr. Harland found a chair. Wigan sat on an empty packing-case which had probably contained books. He was near the door, and on his right was a high old bookcase filled with books—mostly Mike's occult works.

Sir Manson cleared his throat. "Have his papers been examined?"

"He didn't leave many," replied Mr. Harland. "In the drawer on the right is a cash-book showing receipts—he would have to keep that to satisfy the Inland Revenue. There is another book giving names and addresses of clients and firms with whom he dealt."

"No record of any special enemy?"

"None that we can specifically so state—no." Privately Mr. Harland began to think Sir Manson an old dodderer and rather regretted calling him in. But then he had to take every chance.

"And so you need my help?"

Mr. Harland glanced at Wigan. "That is the position, sir, yes."

"And I must invoke the help of the murdered man."

Suddenly Sir Manson seemed to change his personality. He stood straight and cried in a high clear voice:

"Michael Fisk, I ask your help. I demand it in the name of Justice. Who killed you?"

Silence.

"Michael Fisk, I call you from Heaven or Hell. Who killed you?"

Silence.

"Michael Fisk, I summon you from the damnable book you consulted. I ask you in the Name of God. Speak, man, in the best way you can!"

There was a rumble from a heavy lorry passing up the high-road some hundred yards away. Wigan felt the old house quiver slightly. His eyes were on the dog, tense, alert, its eyes on its master.

Sir Manson took out a white silk handkerchief from the black evening-dress overcoat he was wearing. He wiped his face.

"It may take time," he whispered. "He will have to come from some way…"

The solicitor coughed. He regarded his finger-nails.

The dog yelped. He pulled at his master's trouser-leg, then with the whole force of his body pushed him backwards. He was only just in time. The heavy bookcase with its rows of books, weighing in the aggregate a ton or more, fell forward and crashed on to the table.

"My heart!" gasped Sir Manson. "I cannot do more. The

man let loose the whole forces of evil. It may take years to overcome the influence. We had better leave here. This is a dreadful house. What the man must have been doing with his time! He deserved to be killed."

"He was a good man," said Wigan, "in his own way."

He raised the bookcase back against the wall, tilting it back so that it could not fall.

"You had better let the books remain where they are," said the solicitor.

Wigan's eyes went to a grey volume entitled *The Printed English Bible*, by Richard Lovett, M.A. "Hullo," he said, "look at that!"

"I suppose it is valuable?"

"Not a bit of it. It is worth about three-and-sixpence. I have a copy myself. Somebody has been here. He, or she, has taken one of Mike's books and put this in its place."

"But how would the person get in? The police have sealed the house."

"To get in is easy enough. I'll have a look round."

Wigan went through to the kitchen, taking a torch with him. He found the kitchen window unfastened: it was just pushed shut. He looked for clues, and saw that someone had trodden heavily on the spout of a gas sink-heater, bending it down. There were no other clues—no footprints, fingerprints. Probably the intruder had worn gloves. Almost certainly so.

"We must report the burglary at once," said the solicitor when Wigan returned. "I should like you to remain, Sir Manson, till the Detective-Inspector arrives."

"Very well. But I cannot have any more excitement tonight."

Wigan went to the nearest phone-box. To call out the D.I. at this hour would not be a popular move; but it was of course part of his job to be available at any hour of the day or night. He had a telephone by his bedside. At length Wigan got through to him and stated, briefly, the position. "I'll be over," said the D.I.

When he did arrive, in a short space of time, by police car, he looked about the roughest character Wigan had ever set eyes on. He was wearing an old pair of trousers, rubber boots, and no collar and tie. He was unshaven, and he had forgotten or omitted to put in his false teeth. His hard eyes glared at Wigan.

"What's all this flummery here?"

Wigan discreetly let the solicitor do the talking. "There has been a burglary, Inspector, which should be thoroughly investigated. It may prove my client innocent of murder."

"Don't see why," mumbled J. Saggs. "What's burglary got to do with murder?"

He surveyed the back kitchen, had a look at the fallen books, then said: "What were all you people doing here?"

Sir Manson explained the part he had played. J. Saggs smiled a gap-toothed grin. "So it's come to that, has it? Devil killed Michael Fisk."

"The devil," said the solicitor, "plus someone human. That someone has come back for books."

"Just Wigan's word for it. One book stolen and another left in its place. Sounds doubtful to me."

"This house has been forcibly entered, Inspector. I suppose you don't deny that?"

The D.I. was compelled to treat the solicitor with respect.

"I certainly don't deny it, sir. I will investigate the matter. Sergeant Wigan, what is the title of the book alleged to be stolen?"

"I cannot give you that. I can only say that it is a book probably valuable and that a book worthless in terms of money has been left in exchange."

The D.I. made no comment on this. He spent some time examining the kitchen floor and the floors leading to the study. There was plenty of dust, and footprints should show up well, but Wigan and the solicitor, looking too, could see nothing but smudged marks. "He must have walked backwards," said Harland, "wiping the floor as he went."

"More likely," remarked Saggs, "he wore cloths on his feet. It is a trick which Flannel Foot, the famous burglar, used very successfully. But anyway he's out of it now."

Harland felt that the D.I.'s experience would lead him to be correct, and that, as far as clues were concerned, the chances of capturing the thief were slight. He asked the D.I.'s opinion on this.

"I'll do my best," said J. Saggs, "but I'm not hopeful. I can't make bricks without straw. I'll put a notice in the book trade paper asking booksellers to be on the lookout for any valuable book offered for sale under suspicious circumstances. But I can't name any particular book. I think I'll have a padlock put on the front gate. I'll see the S.D. Inspector about it. Any objections, Wigan?"

"None, sir. But a determined thief can climb over."

"Well, we can't have the house watched day and night. Another lock will help."

The solicitor interposed. "I may wish to visit here again."

"Very good, sir. If you do, just apply to the station officer at Sun. He will have the keys. But I would like to know what's going on, since this house, late property of a murdered man, is still under special police protection and you are making further investigation. Sergeant Wigan, I would like from you a written report as to this evening's proceedings in this house."

The solicitor felt he was being "bounced," yet it was difficult to say anything. Wigan replied:

"I shall be glad to write it, sir. I hope you will send a copy to the legal department."

"That is my intention. Sir Manson Wood, may I ask if you have any views which you wish to put forward?"

"I cannot say that I have, Inspector. I was trying to establish communication with the dead man when that heavy bookcase fell."

The D.I.'s hard grey eyes stared at the psychic expert.

"In your opinion, sir—was there any connection?"

Sir Manson shifted uneasily under the D.I.'s eyes. They were like a couple of boring tools. What a very unpleasant person. No collar and tie. More like a tramp than a respectable policeman. Sir Manson was accustomed to a comfortable office and the deferential attention of all about him. His way of life had not brought him into contact with rough, tough characters like J. Saggs.

"I cannot say, Inspector, that there was any definite connection. But there is evil in this room. Of that I am convinced."

"A man was killed here. Murdered. Some people are inclined to forget that."

The solicitor flushed. "You are unfair, sir, in the way you tackle this case."

"I am not unfair, sir. I'm a paid policeman, and it's my job to protect society. In this case I think I have done it. I ask you again: have you any definite evidence that the man convicted for the murder of Michael Fisk has been wrongfully convicted?"

Harland could only answer: "Not yet. It will help if you trace the thief who entered this house to steal a book."

"I'll do what I can, sir," said Saggs, "but you can see for yourself there are no clues. In most cases of burglary a description can be given of property stolen. Here I only have 'a book.' You can ask yourself what chances I have of recovering it. And there may be no connection between the murder and the alleged theft. With the best intentions, sir, you may be trying to manufacture evidence."

"I resent that."

"Very good, sir. I only want to see justice done. Let me have your report, Sergeant Wigan. Leave it at Sun in the C.I.D. box and I'll have a driver pick it up."

Wigan welcomed the chance to reach higher authority with his views. But when next morning, before going on Late Turn duty, he came to write the report he found it difficult, because he had only surmise and intuition, and when committed to paper these do not sound convincing. He stated Mike's obsession with the supernatural and suggested that this might have something to do with the crime. He hoped thereby to "throw a spanner in the works" and cause further official inquiries to be made. As the D.I. had desired, he explained fully Sir Manson Wood's connection with the case.

At least Sir Manson had a name in the spiritualist world, and had investigated a famous haunted house where all kinds of violent phenomena had been encountered.

Wigan took his report to the station, put it in the C.I.D. box, and saw it collected by the C.I.D. driver to be taken to Brabant.

"I would like you," he said, "to give it into the hands of the D.I. himself."

"Don't worry, Sergeant," replied the driver. "The D.I. sent me here specially for it."

Wigan wondered. Had J. Saggs some feeling that something further ought to be done? Yet somehow it was hard to imagine the rough and tough D.I. letting anyone go.

# CHAPTER EIGHTEEN

## CHARLIE DISCOVERS

While continuing to pay Charlie three pounds a week, Wigan now had to leave him much on his own. "Try to get Fred out," was the only general direction Wigan could give when Charlie turned up to report on the morning following the discovery of the burglary. Wigan was busy getting ready for Late Turn, but while shaving he gave a short description of events.

"Pity you ain't got my memory for books, guv'nor," said Charlie sorrowfully.

"I know. The D.I. doesn't think much of the burglary. If I knew the title of the book taken it might be different. I've got to have my dinner at twelve, Charlie. Have a bite with me, and then you must just do as you think best."

"I think I'll see Ruth again. I'm convinced she knows something. But she will swear black is white for the sake of her precious American. A bit of luck is what we want, guv'nor. For heaven's sake let's have a bit of luck."

Wigan nodded. He was tired. Even the excellent dinner that Mary gave him didn't make him less tired or less unfit for duty. He yawned over a cup of tea. For a moment he thought of throwing his hand in. He was just pursuing a will-o'-the-wisp...

"Wake up, guv.!"

Wigan awakened with a jerk. He got on his uniform jacket, then the heavy police greatcoat. "Don't you worry," said Charlie. "I'll get Fred out of clink. Just leave it to me."

"You're a good sort," said Wigan. He took out his bicycle, mounted, then rode towards the police station. Charlie thanked Mrs. Wigan for his dinner. "I'm worried about Jack," she said. "I'm afraid there's going to be real trouble at the station soon. I know we cannot allow an innocent man to hang if we can prevent it, but all Jack is doing is unofficial—the detective-inspector cannot like it."

"I'll try and do more," said Charlie, "and Mr. Wigan can do less. He mustn't lose his job through this. I've got an idea. Mike's books are valuable. If we can use them as a sort of bait—"

"I'm sure Jack will give them to you if you can make any use of them."

"Use—yes. I'll go and see Ruth, I think. Mr. Wigan needs a good rest. I suppose he can't report to the police and say he's ill?"

"It's called 'going sick.' He can, but he won't be allowed to leave the house. If he reports sick, he must see the divisional surgeon. I'm sure Jack won't agreed to that."

"I'll do my best," repeated Charlie.

"When—when may it be over?" Mary Wigan found that she could talk more freely to little Charlie North than she could to her own husband.

"December 16th, unless a reprieve is granted."

"Do you think it will be?"

"I don't see why it should," said Charlie frankly, "unless we can produce fresh evidence. Surmise is no use—no use at all. Well, I'll go and see Ruth."

He took a succession of buses which brought him to Muswell Hill. In front of the entrance to the block of flats in which Ruth lived was a huge American-built car which shone with chromium-plate and on the bonnet flew a stars-and-stripes flag. "I wonder," thought Charlie, "if the great Di Dand is paying us a visit?"

He was. Ruth opened the door to Charlie, asked him in, and introduced him to a huge man wearing a leather glove on his right hand.

"This is Charlie North—Mr. Dithan Dand."

Charlie humorously appreciated the subtlety of the intro. He was just Charlie North. The great man was "mister."

"Pleased to meet you, sir," he said, and gripped the leather glove, which seemed to grip his hand in return—evidently the artificial hand was the finest possible.

"Charlie North," said Ruth, "knows a great deal about rare books."

Ruth was blazing with beauty. Her glorious hair was like a golden helmet. She had a softness and sweetness about her that Charlie had not seen before. Her thought answered his. "I'm always happy when Di is around," she said.

"I'm always glad to meet an expert," said Dithan Dand. "I should value your opinion on my library. Come to the States some time and see it."

Charlie was charmed by the cordiality of his welcome,

but he didn't let it deter him from the object of his visit. "Mike Fisk's library has been burgled," he said to Ruth, "and one book taken. Have you been offered a rare book, probably occult?"

"I don't think so—have we, Di?"

"Nope. I wouldn't mind, though. Burglary or any other means, it's all the same to me. But why should it worry you, Mr. North?"

"Because I am trying to save a man from the gallows. The book may have been taken by the real murderer."

"I see, I see. That's real interesting. But I'm afraid it doesn't concern us. Ruth, have you committed murder?"

"No," she smiled.

"I wasn't suggesting such a thing," said Charlie, "but if you were offered a rare occult work it might give a clue."

"It surely would. Yep, it surely would do just that. Ruth, be on the watch and if you get a clue, communicate with Mr. North here, who will leave you his address."

"Ruth knows me well, sir. She has bought books from me in the past."

"That's real interesting. Can I see your private stock, Mr. North?"

"Whenever you like, sir. I live in a slummy area and I've only got one room, which is bedroom and sitting-room combined; but I have some choice volumes."

"We'll go right now. I'll drive you there. See you later, Ruth."

Dithan Dand drove his huge American machine in a series of rushes with scant consideration for pedestrians or anyone else. Charlie, seated beside the driver, expected a smash any moment, but the American seemed to be born lucky. He even escaped the attention of traffic policemen. Once a bus-driver swore at him. Dand retorted: "You wouldn't talk to me like that if I could get out of this car." The driver replied with more language. Dand slammed on the brakes and made to get out of the car.

"Easy, sir," said Charlie, "this ain't America."

"I wish it were," growled Dand, "I'd show that guy where he gets off." But he took no further notice of the bus-driver and drove on. Charlie had a knack of getting on with people, high and low. "It's all very well for you, sir, you're a millionaire. But I've got me reputation to think of."

Dand laughed. "O.K., Mr. North. I won't break it up for you."

They arrived at Charlie's lodgings, and Charlie introduced the millionaire to his landlady, then took him up to his bedroom, where, lining three walls of the room, were his collectors' books. Dand appraised the books swiftly. He took out the Bennett first and inspected it carefully. "This perfect?" he said.

"Yes, sir, it is."

"What do you want for it?"

"I don't particularly want to sell it."

The big man's face turned a dark red. "Say, I don't like guys who hold out on me. I take it your stock is for sale, Mr. North, or you wouldn't have let me in this room. I want to buy. O.K. Now what's the price?"

"A hundred pounds," said Charlie, asking more than the book, commercially, was worth. Dithan Dand promptly counted out the money in five-pound notes and took the book. Charlie sighed. He was sorry to see the book go. He could never replace it. He said as much.

"You're a good little guy," remarked the American. "But I guess all first-rate books have to rest in my library. It just happens so."

"Have a cup of tea with me," said Charlie. "It's a long way back to Muswell Hill, even at the pace you drive, sir."

Dithan Dand accepted. Over tea he relaxed entirely. He removed his coat and sat in his shirt-sleeves. "I hate goddam hotels," he said. Charlie exercised his peculiar gift for making people talk to him. "Are you often in this country?" he asked.

"Yep. Pretty frequent. I'm always hunting rare books. It makes me respected in the States more than my money does. I like to see profs nosing round my library. I reckon I've got more rare treasures than the New York Central Library—and that's saying something."

"When were you last over here, sir?"

"About the middle of August. Hell of a climate you Britishers have. It rained the whole time."

Charlie poured out his visitor more tea and pressed him to his landlady's excellent home-made cake. Charlie felt his way with infinite care. "About the middle of August," he repeated. "Well, from about the 9th to the 14th the rain was something special."

"So you Britishers always say when anyone attacks your precious climate. Fine cake this is. Do you think your landlady will sell me one to take back to my hotel?"

"I expect she would rather give you one, sir. Does Ruth buy all your books for you?"

"Nope. She's a good girl, but she don't know much about books. I like to do a bit of snooping on my own. I don't always tell her when I come over here. When she buys for me she buys so expensive because I'm a millionaire. When I buy for myself I pick up a bargain sometimes."

"Mike Fisk had a fine library."

"You mean the murdered guy? Who's got his books now?"

"They have been left to a police officer, a friend of his. But the house is still shut up with the police seals on it. I reckon they'll keep the seals on till the case is over."

"Till the murderer is hanged, you mean?"

"That's right, sir. Have some more tea?"

"No, thanks, though this tea is fine. I don't like tea as a rule. We Americans drink coffee. You seem to know a lot about this Mike Fisk. Do you reckon you can get me some of his books?"

"Don't see how I can, sir, short of breaking into the house."

"Then do just that. I'll pay you well. The occult is one of my special fields."

Charlie passed the huge man more cake. "Why pay me, sir? Why not do it yourself?"

"I'm a bit too heavy for burglary, and this hand of mine is a handicap. I can handle most things, but nothing delicate."

"Burglary is out of my line too," said Charlie. "But Ruth might do it. She has the nerve."

"Yep, she has the nerve, as you say. But I guess I won't discuss the lady, even with you, Mr. North."

The American was suddenly wary. His grey eyes had a gleam in them which made Charlie think that a bomb might go off any minute.

"You're a good little guy," said the American, "but don't you try and pin anything on me. Or on Ruth. I'll tell you why I was over here, middle of August. I came over to visit a guy named Connington, a pal of Ruth's. He does a bit of double-dealing, he's as deep as deep, and I don't like the guy; but he does get hold of rare books, and that's why I have a use for him."

"That's nothing to do with me, sir," said Charlie.

"Nope. When's the murderer due to take the high jump?"

"December 16th."

"Then you had better make up your mind to the fact that he'll take it. Why should I bump a guy off, why should Ruth, when we can buy any book we want?"

"Mike Fisk wasn't always willing to sell."

"Money talks. It always talks. It's talked with you, Mr. North. I can pay a million—pounds not dollars—for any book I fancy worth the price."

"Books aren't like groceries," said Charlie. "The trouble is to find them. There are plenty of collectors ready to buy. When Mike's library is dispersed, the books will go in a flash, or something like it."

"That's a thought, Mr. North. That sure is a thought. I'll have to contact this police officer you speak of. What's his name?"

"Sergeant Wigan. Sun Police Station. But I can tell you in advance—he won't sell to you."

"Then what's he going to do with the books?"

"He has already arranged to sell to another American."

Instantly Dithan Dand revealed his origin, probably Indian on one side or the other. His face twisted with jealousy. "So that's his game, is it? What's the American's name? Or perhaps I can guess. Would it be William K. Makemore of Chicago?"

"I can't tell you the name. I don't know it. I only know that the deal has been fixed. So you will be wasting your time, Mr. Dand, and it's a kindness to tell you so."

"Thanks. I thought you said a book had been stolen from the collection?"

"So it has. But it won't happen again. And, if you're innocent already, don't get mixed up in it, Mr. Dand."

"You sure talk straight, Mr. North. I've hammered a man for less than what you've said to me, or implied. But I guess there's something about you. Ruth likes you, you know. Still, I guess we'll end the conversation right now. Thanks for the tea."

"Look 'ere, guv'nor," said Charlie in his most Cockney, "me pal will swing if I don't do something to help him. Were you in England on the night of August 9th–10th?"

"If I was, what does it signify?"

"Did you visit Mike Fisk's house? I know he had an American connection."

"Nope. I did not. It's still not plain to me what you're driving at. I like folks to speak plain." The American stood by the door, big and formidable, his leather-gloved right hand on the handle. Charlie knew there would be trouble for him if he opened his "trap" too wide.

"There's been a mysterious black figure flitting about, like a bat. I wonder if you saw it. That's all."

"It sounds like Ruth's opera cloak," said the American. "But I guess you can't pin anything on her. She was in Liverpool at the time, on my orders."

"Then you didn't see the figure, sir?"

"Well, I visited a dealer in West Road. It was a wild windy night, real special British weather. I saw plenty of black figures flitting about. I can't call to mind anything particular… Yep, though, I can. I was standing outside Niger's window, looking over the books displayed, when someone ran into me. Queer, the person had no head, or appeared to have none. Then I saw it was a short-necked guy with his cloak well up. 'Pardon me,' I said. 'You're in a mighty hurry.' The figure said 'Sorry.' I saw two eyes deep in the cloak, then the figure hurried on."

Charlie trembled with excitement. "Have you any idea, sir, who it was?"

"Oh yes," said the American carelessly, "I reckon I can tell you that. It was Francis Ferrow. I've had catalogues from Ferrow Brothers, though I've never bought much from them. They print their photos on the front cover, Mr. Francis and Mr. Joel."

"Why didn't he speak to you, sir?"

"Why should he? He was in a hurry."

"And what dealer were you visiting, sir?"

"Bullivant and Jones. They specialise in early manuscripts. Old Mr. Bullivant is a friend of mine. I visit him whenever I am in London, even if it's only for ten minutes. Don't you try and pin a murder on him, Mr. North, or you and I will quarrel."

"I wasn't thinking of Mr. Bullivant, sir. I know he has the highest reputation in the trade. I was thinking of Francis Ferrow. I reckon he's our man."

"That's for you to say. I must go now. I'm taking Ruth out. We are going to the opera, and she'll wear her black cloak. I'll tell her she looks like a bat. That'll wake her up some. Good-day, Mr. North."

"Good-day, sir. Let me show you out."

There were a crowd of children round the huge American

car. Dithan Dand scattered them with a handful of coins thrown on to the pavement. Then he drove away with a surge of power.

Charlie watched him go. "Francis Ferrow," he muttered to himself. "Why didn't I think of that before? He's as tough as Joel, but smoother. He could have knifed Mike, then stolen from the library. And he's quite capable of breaking in and stealing from the library again, even with another man under the shadow of death for his crime. My God, we've got it! We've got it. Now how can we pin him down?"

# CHAPTER NINETEEN
## CHARLIE DISCOVERS TOO MUCH

Policemen's houses are not usually on the telephone unless duty compels them to be. Nor do policemen desire it, for, if they were, the station could call them out too easily! To keep in touch with Charlie, Wigan had given him the station number, Sun 600; but this was only to be used in absolute necessity, for if the wrong person took the call there might be trouble.

At 5 p.m., while he was in the station taking his refreshment, Wigan received a telephone call from Mr. Harland, Simpson's solicitor. At 8 p.m. he entered the station again and was told by the man on communications duty: "There's been a phone call for you, Sarge, from a man called Charlie North. I said you might be in at eight o'clock, and he asked for you to ring a phone-box. I've got the number."

The communications-room was more private than the main office, so Wigan made his call from there. He knew he could trust the man on communications, P.C. Taylor.

"Hullo, guv'nor," said Charlie's voice. "I think I'm on to something at last."

"Thank heaven for that," said Wigan. "I've had a call from Harland, the solicitor. No reprieve will be granted. The law must take its course. That's official."

"That's dreadful news, guv. Still, if we have the evidence we can set him free. I'll try and get a signed confession, and I think you had better keep out of it, guv'nor."

"Nonsense," said Wigan, "I'm not going to let you do the dirty work. There may be personal danger."

"I know, guv., but I'm not afraid. I don't want you to get on the wrong side of the official police or you may lose your job."

"I shall act according to my conscience," said Wigan. "I shall—"

The communications man swiftly wrote something on a piece of paper and pushed it under Wigan's eyes. So intent was Wigan on his telephone call that he had not heard anyone enter the front office. The message said: "D.I."

Wigan concluded the phone call by asking Charlie to advise him of anything that happened, and to call on him if he wanted assistance, then he entered the front office. There was no door, only an opening between the front office and communications-room. The station officer, who was somewhat deaf, was tapping away at a process report. He had probably heard nothing. The D.I. was standing by the counter looking over the crime book.

"Good evening, sir," said Wigan.

"'Evening," replied the D.I. briefly, and Wigan knew that he had heard something, certainly the part about the conscience.

"All quiet outside," said Wigan, the kind of remark that a section sergeant might make to a C.I.D. officer who was his superior in rank yet not his immediate superior in the uniform branch, such as the duty officer or superintendent.

The D.I. made no reply of any kind.


Charlie had told Wigan he was not afraid, and this was true; but he thought he could well do with some help. The Ferrows could be nasty customers, in the auction-room or out of it. Charlie knew about a dozen full-time runners, and about fifty part-time ones. None entirely filled the bill. Finally he decided on Searle Connington, who was a clever man and resourceful. Once he had been bullied at a sale. Charlie saw him raise a long black cane he carried, and reveal a sword-stick. The bully wanted no more. Connington had two sides to him. One day he would dress like a tramp and haunt the markets at Bermondsey or Ladbroke Grove. On the other hand, he could mix on equal terms with the most fashionable people in London. He was said to be a crashing snob, yet Charlie always found him friendly enough.

Charlie contacted Connington at his sister's bookshop and arranged to meet him at 10 p.m. for a cup of tea. Connington was a man for whom late hours would have no meaning. He turned up at the rendezvous wearing a dinner-jacket and a flowing black evening cloak secured at the neck with a silk cord. It was a mild, still December evening, and he looked— yes, thought Charlie, like a bat with folded wings.

Charlie came to the point without delay. He gave his reasons for suspecting Francis Ferrow of murdering Mike Fisk. He told of his plan to try and force a confession, and for this he would need assistance.

Connington listened, silent and motionless. He had a curious high, conical head which would have interested a phrenologist, who might have decided that the conformation indicated an exceptionally brilliant brain, and exceptional cunning. In his time Connington had played many parts: the whining mendicant intent by any means on getting a valuable book for as little as possible; the autocratic bookman dominating others by his knowledge; the astute salesman bent on screwing the last shilling out of a book. But with Charlie he was natural. He did not trouble to act with Charlie. He was a runner and Charlie was a runner.

"Really, Charlie," he said at length, "you haven't got much of a case against Francis Ferrow. I've already had an interview with your copper friend, Sergeant Wigan, and he as good as accused me of murdering Mike Fisk. All this suspicion: it means nothing. If you understood about law you would know that."

"We've got to use desperate means, Searle. No reprieve has been granted, Sergeant Wigan tells me."

"That would depend on the advice given by the Attorney-General. There must be good reasons against a reprieve."

"Will you come with me and have it out with Francis Ferrow? Sergeant Wigan can't do much more or he'll lose his job."

Again Searle Connington was silent. He was silent for about five minutes.

"All right," he said at last, "I suppose I have no right to refuse you. We'll go and see Francis Ferrow tomorrow morning. We'll catch him in the shop about nine. I'll meet you there. All right?"

"Thanks, Searle. We've got to save the poor devil if we can."

Books in the mass weigh about as heavy as lead, and it takes a good man to take out and arrange on stalls several hundred of them. Charlie watched Corky setting out the "shop stuff," and he didn't envy him. Free-lancing as a runner has its hazards; but better that than a regular eight pounds a week and slavery. Charlie didn't approach Corky or speak to him. Presently Searle Connington came up. He was dressed soberly in black and carried a silver-headed black cane—his sword-stick. He nodded to Charlie and they entered the shop together. Corky came in after them. "What do you want?"

"One of these days," said Connington, "you'll get into trouble, Corky, for being so impolite to customers. We wish to see Mr. Francis."

"He's busy opening the mail."

Connington was about to reply that the matter was of importance, when Charlie rushed in. "Say the word 'bat' to him. Got that? Bat."

"You must be off your rocker," said Corky.

"Bat. See? He'll understand."

Corky went to knock on the door of the private room. "You've given the game away now," murmured Connington.

"There's been too much secrecy," replied Charlie. Then Corky returned. "Mr. Francis will see you."

"Thank you," said Connington politely.

The short-necked man, Mr. Francis, was sitting hunched in his chair. On the table before him he had a little pile of American orders, one or two returns, and a bibliographical puzzle—American collectors seemed to delight in splitting hairs over points of issue. Mr. Francis was not in a good temper.

"What do you two want? What do you mean by 'bat'?"

Charlie began: "One night in August, you were seen to flit about the streets in a black cloak with a high collar which made you look like a 'eadless—I mean headless—bat. We want to know the meaning of it."

"Well, I'm damned!" said Mr. Francis.

"Consummate impudence," said Connington, in his part now as Cheery Con, the genial friend of all. His eyes went round the private room, but he saw nothing of any interest. He became silent and let Charlie carry on.

"What were you doing?" demanded Charlie.

Mr. Francis pressed a bell, and the door behind Charlie and Connington instantly opened.

"Corky, show these two out. If they won't go, fetch a policeman."

Charlie suddenly realised that he had nothing to lose. A row wouldn't hurt him.

"Fetch as many policemen as you like, Corky. You're a damned murderer, Francis Ferrow, and you want Fred Hampton to swing for it."

"I'll fetch a policeman, sir," said Corky.

"No—wait a minute. You had better stay, Corky. I know you, Connington. You've got a sword-stick there. If I am in danger of my life, I have a right to defend myself." Swiftly Mr. Francis opened a drawer in the desk and produced a Colt revolver. "This is loaded," he said. "Now let's hear a little more. How did I murder—Mike Fisk, I suppose?"

"You suppose right," said Charlie. "You went out to Mike's house on a pouring wet night. Unfortunately you weren't seen. You hung about somewhere—God knows where. Then you entered his house late at night or early the next morning.

You stabbed him with Fred's knife which Fred lost and Mike picked up—or maybe you picked it up by pure chance."

"Excuse me a moment," said Francis. "You're listening, Corky?"

"I'm listening, sir."

"Because all this is actionable. But go on."

"You killed Mike. Then you rifled his books. You took a Keats first edition, signed and identifiable, which you flogged through Fred Hampton. But you also took another book, using an old runner's trick. You took a book and left a book, a book of no value. It's the second book you took that we want. Recently you paid the house another visit and took another book, again leaving a book of no value. We want this book too."

"The title?"

"We don't know the title."

"Then, my friend, you're on rather a hopeless quest. It's true I wear the kind of cloak you describe, and if I pull up the collar I suppose I appear headless. But I wasn't near Sun on the night Mike Fisk was murdered. I was at home with my brother Joel."

"May I speak, sir?" said Corky.

"By all means, Corky. You've been a good servant to the firm for many years. By all means speak."

"Then, sir, I've seen Searle Connington here wearing the sort of flowing cloak described. Perhaps he knows something about the crime. It's like his impudence to come here and accuse you."

"A good point, Corky. You go about armed, Connington. I believe sword-sticks are illegal, but I can verify the point.

You have discovered too much, Charlie, for me to remain silent; and I shall consider it my duty to inform the police."

"Also the Inland Revenue," said Corky. "I shouldn't wonder, Connington, if you don't cheat the income tax. You and your sister's shop! I wonder who makes the most profits? You or she? Do you book all your deals, and present your books to the Inland Revenue?"

There was silence. Mr. Francis kept his finger on the trigger of his revolver. Connington laid his black cane carefully against the table, then he spoke.

"I don't cheat the Inland Revenue. It's impossible because they can probe and probe, perhaps for years. They know all about my affairs. As to the murder, I can prove where I was on the night in question. So that's disposed of; and your nasty suggestions, Corky, fall to the ground. I suppose it's sweating for a hard task-master that makes you what you are… That and a cork leg and a mind that knows no difference between a first edition and a third edition. You're good enough to rob an auction-room when a rare book has been pointed out to you; and that's about all you do know, Corky."

Corky sneered at him. "What did you mean to stab him with, Connington? The sword-stick? It must have been convenient finding Fred's knife."

"Completely untrue. I spent the night with my sister, and I can prove it."

"So we all have alibis, including Corky, who was working late in the warehouse and would hardly go out to Sun to murder Mike Fisk." Mr. Francis glanced at his watch, then he said suavely: "Gentlemen, I really am rather busy. Oh, Connington, since you are here, I have a four-page letter—American collectors always seem to write reams—about issue points in a Henty first edition—*By Sheer Pluck,* the book is. It's rather out of our line, and the book itself can hardly be worth more than thirty shillings, but I suppose we shall have to try and get it."

Connington took the letter, read it, then instantly gave the information required. "I'll get you a copy of the first issue," he said. "It will cost you two pounds. What you charge the customer is your affair."

"Thanks, Connington, you certainly do understand books."

Charlie was getting redder and redder. He saw the whole affair being smoothed over. He glared round, and his glare included Connington.

"You bloody lot of thieves," he said. "While you fiddle with books poor Fred will lose his life."

"Rather strong language," said Mr. Francis. "I must ask you to leave, Charlie. We have suffered from you already—you and your fictitious millionaires. I have been very patient, but there is a limit to patience."

"I'm not leaving till I'm satisfied. What witnesses have you got? You and your brother."

"May I speak again, Mr. Francis?"

"Yes, Corky. By all means. But please be as brief as possible."

"Yes, Mr. Francis, I will." Corky's sallow face was sweating unpleasantly. He leaned on his cork leg in a twisted attitude as if his body were twisted, and his eyes as they looked at Charlie gleamed with malevolence.

"No one," he said, "has inquired into Charlie North. He knows so much about the murder, I wonder if he doesn't know a good deal more."

"Why, you so-and-so," said Charlie, "Mike Fisk was me friend. He gave me half a dollar when I hadn't the price of a cup of tea, and I've never forgotten it."

"So you say. I may not know much about rare books. I may not be employed as a swell rare book expert, like Connington, and I've got to fetch and carry and my wages ain't been raised for five years and I've got my old mother to keep—" Corky paused for breath, then added: "But I can make two and two into four."

There was silence, then Connington said quietly: "You forget that Fred Hampton is already convicted for the crime. Why should Charlie interfere?"

"Because he has to. He's been roped in by that policeman fellow."

Again there was silence. Charlie left his defence to Connington, but Connington seemed to be changing his personality, like a chameleon. He wasn't cheery Con, or quiet thoughtful Con, or Con bent on justice. He had changed to aristocratic Con. He took his black cane and leaned on it.

"All this is very distressing," he said. "A terrible crime committed for the sake of a few rare books which will probably end up in an American public library. In a few days the rest of the books will pass to Sergeant Wigan. I hope he will take good care of them—or burn them."

Corky leered craftily at Charlie. "You ain't said nothing," he said. "Are you still keen on getting Fred off?"

Charlie turned to Connington. "Why don't you stick up for me more? You know I never killed Mike. Are we going to let these Ferrow twisters get away with it?"

"Proof, Charlie. I told you before, we have no proof.

Good-day, Mr. Francis. Remember me to Mr. Joel. He's at a sale, I suppose?"

"Yes, the Cash Castle sale."

"Ah, there will be some rare incunabula."

"And what Joel can't buy he will steal," said Charlie viciously.

"I'll show you out, Barrow Boy. This way."

"I'd like to black your blooming eye, Corky; and if you weren't a cripple I would too. Accusing me of murdering Mike Fisk."

Corky made no reply. He stomped upstairs to the shop entrance. Furious at being outwitted, Charlie pushed against a pile of books and knocked one down. He picked it up. On the front cover was the title: *The Pious Recollections of Maria Brown*. "Trash!" he snarled, and hurled the book back on to the pile. The leaves fell open. "Hey," he said suddenly, "what's this? *Sabasia. The Black Mass and its Four Acts.* It's a book on witchcraft."

"Give it here," said Corky swiftly. "Those books are not for sale. They haven't been priced yet."

Charlie took no notice. He opened the book at the end—at the back endpapers, looking for Mike's secret mark. It was dark in the shop and he could see nothing. "I'm going to take this in to Mr. Francis," he said.

"You'll do nothing of the kind. Give me the book. I'm boss here now."

"Why, you blasted bloody cripple—"

"Give him the book," said Connington. "You can prove nothing."

Charlie shoved the book into Corky's hands. It was

probably true that the book, rebound, had been provided with new endpapers.

"You may have discovered too much," said Connington to Charlie, as they walked away. "I should watch yourself, if I were you."

"I can look after meself, thank you."

"Small but plucky, eh?"

Charlie was seething. He burst out: "You were a fat lot of help, Connington. You let him talk you over."

"We didn't do so badly. It would be very interesting to see the rest of Mike's books. I expect he had a rare lot of valuable stuff. And now it must fall into the hands of a common policeman. Pity."

"Ain't you got no heart?" said Charlie. "What the hell do the books matter when Fred is going to be hanged?"

"Ah," said Connington airily, "I almost forgot. I bet they raise Corky's money. First he accuses me, then he accuses you. I want to get hold of Sergeant Wigan. Where's he to be found?"

"Sun Police Station."

"Ah, thank you." Connington was now stalking along with great deliberation, swinging his cane regardless of other pedestrians, some of whom gave him black looks. "Ninny," muttered one of them.

At the junction of Tottenham Court Road and Oxford Street Connington paused. "I must be getting to my work. I have my bread and butter to earn." In an old-maidish way he adjusted the fingers of his white gloves. Charlie was profoundly irritated. He had thought better of Connington,

who on occasion had shown himself capable of reso-
lute action.

"Thanks for your help," he said sarcastically. "I had better
do some work too. I'm going back to have another look at
Ferrows' books. I ain't afraid of Corky."

"Maybe you aren't. But you will be wasting your time. Once,
Charlie, I was called to the office of an old lawyer who had just
died. I was asked to bid for his books, and a dreary lot they
looked: all about torts and malfeasances. That is, their titles were;
but when I came to examine them closely I found that the old
gentleman had made an excellent collection of pugilistica. How
the stuffy old lawyer must have laughed as he had *Boxiana* bound
into *Torts of the Nineteenth Century*, or something of the kind."

"Very amusing," said Charlie, "but what's it got to
do with it?"

"The practice is not uncommon. Some books on witchcraft are highly indecent, and a collector might well wish to
hide them from his family. I expect the Ferrows have bought
such a collection. That's all."

"I thought you said I am in danger."

"So you will be if you go on interfering. What do you
think Joel will do if he comes back early from the sale and
finds you rowing with Corky? I've heard that he once threw
a runner out of an auction-room window—and he didn't
wait to open the window."

"Then what can I do to help Fred?"

"Do a bit of running. Visit Niger's and see if you can pick
up some Hentys."

"Just that," said Charlie sarcastically. "And we'll let poor
Fred stew, or rather hang."

Connington smiled, a slight, subtle smile. "Leave things to me," he said earnestly, "at any rate for a time. I think I can handle things better than you can, Charlie."

The junction of Tottenham Court Road and Oxford Street is one of the busiest parts of London. Pedestrians crammed the pavements. Traffic poured into the circus. Yet Connington was detached and intent on his own affairs as if the hubbub never existed; and Charlie, seeing that crafty smile and curious conical head, had his suspicions revived. Suppose Corky, flinging his accusations about, had hit on the truth? Connington now intended to see Sergeant Wigan. Suppose his real object was to secure the rest of Mike's books at a tithe of their real worth?

"You bloody traitor," said Charlie.

Connington turned away. "You're too impulsive, Charlie. Go home and stick a few comics together. Goodbye."

Charlie watched Connington walk to the bus stop, where he boarded a bus which would take him to his place of employment. As a rare book expert, he had a comfortable room to himself. He had two afternoons a week off when he might pursue his own searches; and altogether Searle Connington Esquire did very nicely. So thought Charlie to himself. Some time in the near future he would have to phone Sergeant Wigan. What on earth could he say? What could Wigan say to Fred when he next paid him a visit—perhaps his last?

It all looked pretty hopeless. In his heart Charlie knew that Connington was right. He couldn't go back to Ferrows' and raise a row. It wouldn't have any effect, and he might land in jail. There remained one last card: the bait of the books.

Charlie had a sudden inspiration. After a cup of tea and a

roll and some cheese at his usual Lyons, he started to walk to Sun. Ten miles or so meant nothing to him, who had been a walker all his life. When he arrived at Sun it was afternoon, and he calculated that Wigan would be on duty. He therefore wrote a note in Sun Post Office. The note said: *"No good news to report. Do not sell Mike's books to anyone. Charlie."* He borrowed an envelope and carefully sealed it down. Then he left the note in the front office of the police station to be given to Sergeant Wigan when he came in.

Charlie's next move was to buy some provisions in the town. It was now dark. He walked out to Chelmer Square. Charlie was so tough that he reckoned he could pass most of the night walking about (and dodging the beat police-man), on the watch for any black-clothed "bat" come to have another go at Mike's books before they were dispersed. But he had better luck than that. The house opposite Mike's was up for sale. An agent's board said so. Moreover, the house appeared to be unoccupied—it was easy enough to see that. Charlie, who carried a knife with him, forced the kitchen window at the back. He climbed in. He went through the house and into the front ground-floor room. Then he settled down to watch. There was a gas street-lamp not far away, and he could see the front of Mike's house and the study window.

Charlie rubbed his hands at his own cleverness. "Now then, you blooming Ferrows and Conningtons," he muttered, "'ave another go. Plenty of nice occult items to choose from. What about Caesar von Heisterback's *Illustria Miracula*? I noticed that there. Very choice. Or that work of Lancre's, 1622."

Charlie's pronunciation might have been atrocious; but he knew his stuff, and he knew that he knew it and was pleased.

But he was tired, and he thought it hardly likely that any thief would start operations before midnight. It was now eight o'clock. He settled down to sleep for a few hours.

It was a sleep from which he never awoke. A little before midnight a black-clad figure entered the room, then paused. Charlie was snoring. The light from a gas-lamp opposite entered the room and showed Charlie's face, his mouth wide open. The figure stole up to him. A knife-blade flashed. The figure struck, a single hard blow. Charlie gave a deep groan, then was silent. His body fell forward so that his head rested on the floor. In his back was the knife, driven in up to the hilt. Charlie was wearing an old grey overcoat. The murderer took up the tail and wiped the knife-handle with it. Then, leaving the knife in the wound, the figure left the room.

# CHAPTER TWENTY

## VISIT TO C.O.

Wigan changed from Late Turn to Early Turn. He slept badly, having Fred Hampton's fate continually on his mind now; and he scraped to the station just on time to avoid the stigma of having "done it in"—been late.

About nine o'clock Wigan came in for his refreshment; and soon after there was a message for him from C.O. It came over the wires on the police private line and ran as follows:

*Commissioner's Office to Sun Police Station. Sergeant J. Wigan, No. 583 'U' Division, is warned to attend Commissioner's Office at 3 p.m. today, December 10th. He will attend in plain clothes.*

With this message came a further one:

*Superintendent R. Carisbrook to Sun Police Station. Sergeant J. Wigan, No. 583 'U' Division, after*

*attending C.O. as directed, is warned to report to*
*Superintendent's Office, Brabant.*

The station officer read these messages. They were on the
pad, plain for all to read. "Mhmm," he commented, "you are going
to have a busy day, Wigan. They always choose a man's spare
time for these little visits. What on earth have you been doing?"

"Nothing that I know of," answered Wigan convention-
ally; but he knew well enough, and, as it seemed likely that
he would have to defend his conduct and perhaps fight hard
for the Hampton case to be reopened on a high level with a
Chief Detective-Inspector in charge, he was careful to look as
smart as possible. One sergeant will always help another. With
the station officer's concurrence, Wigan arranged for a P.C.
to come out Acting Jack (acting section sergeant in charge of
the men). Wigan went home early. He had a bath and a better
shave. Then he went out and had a hair-cut. Mary prepared
his dinner early, and, feeling in a better frame of mind and
rested as much as possible, Wigan travelled to headquarters
in good time for the interview at 3 p.m.

Wigan did not see the Commissioner. He did not expect to.
Orders emanating from C.O. merely mean the administrative
side of the police. Wigan was received by an affable gentleman
who occupied a nice room overlooking the river. There was
also present a third man, but throughout the interview he
never spoke at all.

"Sit down, Sergeant Wigan," said the affable gentleman,
"and make yourself at home. Cigarette?"

Wigan accepted one and held a light for the affable gentleman. The third man apparently didn't smoke, for he wasn't offered a cigarette.

"Now, Sergeant Wigan, I have been looking up your record, and it seems to be excellent. What are your ambitions in the police?"

Wigan was a bit puzzled, but he answered politely: "I hope to rise to inspector, sir, before I retire." Wigan hesitated, but too much modesty never gets a man anywhere. "I have even some slight hope of rising to be superintendent."

"Good, good, I like to see a man ambitious."

There was a pause. The third man stared at Wigan like a waxwork. The affable gentleman continued: "Now, Mr. Wigan, have you any strong ideas about justice?"

"Well, sir, like every police officer I like to see justice done; and I always try my best to be just."

"Good, good."

Wigan expected the next question to be about Fred Hampton; and he braced himself to deliver a carefully reasoned appeal for justice to be done in this case. But his appeal was not delivered, for the affable gentleman took a puff at his cigarette, then he said:

"And about religion: have you any views on that?"

"I go to church, sir, whenever duty allows me to do so."

"I see. Of course religion is good too, if not overdone. I once knew a constable who, when directing traffic in London, had impulses to kneel down and pray. That, perhaps, was overdoing religion. Don't you think so?"

"I certainly do."

"And there was another man, quite recently, who felt

impelled to walk his beat backwards. He could then, so he said, deal with thieves who came at him from behind."

In a blinding flash the trend of the interview came to Wigan. They thought him mad!

"Naturally," continued the gentleman, "we had to retire both men at the best financial arrangement for them which could be managed in the circumstances. I expect you agree that we couldn't do anything else?"

"Most certainly I do, sir." Wigan schooled himself to complete calm. The slightest sign of ranting, of even a few words about the Hampton case, and he would be "for it," and his wife and children would suffer. There is nothing harder to disprove than madness. How can a man prove he isn't mad? Most would find it hard if suddenly called upon to do so.

"Well, Mr. Wigan," said the affable gentleman, "I don't think I need say much more. I'm bound to say you seem to me a reasonable man, but you must realise that anything out of the ordinary is out of place in a policeman. We couldn't possibly have our praying friend holding up the traffic, and the public is apt to consider a man who walks backwards as eccentric. I think talking about demons, and writing about them, is also eccentric. What do you think?"

Wigan evaded the eyes of the silent third man. He gave himself a second or two while he deposited cigarette-ash in an ash-tray on the desk, then he said with studied mildness: "It certainly sounds eccentric, sir. My own mind is fixed on my duty, which I like to carry out to the satisfaction of my superior officers; and I am, if I may say so, grateful for your high opinion of me."

"Generally speaking—yes. Well, Sergeant Wigan, I don't

think I need to detain you any longer. I hope you will rise to be superintendent, by sticking to your own business. I'm sure you understand. Good-day."

"Good-day, sir."

Wigan bowed to the silent third man, who inclined his head in reply, and the interview was over.

"Phew!" said Wigan to himself outside the building. "I was within an ace of being sacked. I shall have to be careful—damned careful." Yet how could he abandon the desperate man in the condemned cell? And if he stood by him, if he threw his chances in the police to the winds, what good would it do? They were getting nowhere. He had received Charlie's note. He wouldn't of course sell the books, but Charlie apparently had done no good. He was a good little chap, but hardly clever enough to trap a murderer who was clever enough to get Fred Hampton hanged for it.

Despondently Wigan went to have a cup of tea—he thought he deserved it: and while he was in the nearest Lyons drinking it he wondered what sort of conversation was going on in the comfortable room overlooking the river. It went like this:

"Seems all right," said the third man. "Smart-looking chap."

"Yes, but you read his report about demons."

"I believe in the past demons have been raised from the pit."

"That may be," said the affable gentleman, "but not, however, by policemen."

"I expect he will take a hint," said the third man. "I think he perfectly understood. He's not at all like our praying friend.

Remember how he tried to convert you? He wanted you to sing a hymn with him. A dreadful sinner, you were."

"That may be. Wigan handled his end of the interview very well, but really he promised us nothing. The police force will become unmanageable if the law is administered by men according to individual conscience. I like the chap. So do you. But we shall have to watch him."

There remained Act II—the visit to the Superintendent. Robert Carisbrook had white hair and a flowing white moustache. He was known to his men as "Daddy." He was a good old boy, said all, but Wigan knew that a superintendent is a superintendent, and he would have to be careful from the very fact that Daddy was so decent.

Wigan stood correctly to attention on the Superintendent's carpet; but the Super waved him to a chair. "This is informal, Wigan. How did you get on at C.O.?"

"I just escaped being cast, sir. They seem to think I may be mad."

"Ah, the Fred Hampton business." The Super pulled at his moustache. "I hope you won't go on with it, Wigan. After all, the man was found guilty by a judge and jury."

Wigan hesitated. If he were frank, it might all go back to C.O.

"Trust me, Wigan," said the Super. "Speak freely. That's why I asked you here. I give you my word that nothing of what you say will go further than this room."

"I should like to tell you about it, sir."

"Right, but first, I think, some tea—" The Super pressed a bell. His clerk entered the room, a silent, discreet man. The Super gave orders for a good pot to be brought up from the canteen, then he remarked to Wigan: "I've never forgotten that I was once a P.C. on the beat, cold, tired, and often hungry. I joined the police after the 1914 War. I can tell you, things were strict then. Sergeants used to chase us all over the place. I often longed for a cup of tea, but dared not have one. Now, I suppose, I can do as I please, at least in some respects."

The clerk brought in tea, and the Super poured out a cup for Wigan. "Now fire away," he said.

Wigan gave, as briefly as possible, an account of his thoughts and actions regarding the Hampton case. The Super listened attentively. At last he said: "Well, you know, I think he may be guilty. He's a bad type of man: writes indecent literature, which leads to general moral degeneration."

"Ah, but, sir, it's only for the sake of his family. He's alone now, his last, or almost his last hope gone, but he refuses to have his wife and daughters visit him."

"Really? I didn't know that. It does show courage. I once visited a death-cell, and I confess it made me shudder. I suppose—" The Super stopped and pulled at his moustache.

"I can't abandon the man, sir, I really can't, feeling as I do. I'm convinced that he did not murder Mike Fisk."

"Then if you feel like that, Wigan, I suppose I cannot blame you. You are one of my men, and my loyalty to you is greater than that towards my superior officers. It may be a wrong way of looking at it, but it's how I feel. How can I help you?"

"I may be able to get fresh evidence, sir. It's a long chance, but I may. But how can I make the D.I. listen, if he thinks I'm mad? How can I stop the execution?"

"Listen, Wigan. I dare not grant you annual leave. Anything you do must be done in your spare time and unofficially to me. But if you do discover fresh evidence, if you really feel that you can prove that Hampton did not commit the crime for which he is due to be hanged, then you can communicate with me, day or night—I'll give you my private number: Amherst 14826—and as Superintendent of 'U' Division I shall communicate with the Home Office, who will communicate with the Governor of the prison."

"Thank you, sir. That's a tremendous load off my mind."

"All right. Keep this man you speak of, Charlie North, on the job; and if you can really prove that a definite person did leave the stolen book on Hampton's door-step, then I think the execution should be stopped and further inquiries made. Strictly between ourselves, I can't say I like the D.I.; but he cannot desire a wrong conviction. No policeman would."

"No, sir."

"But just remember this, Wigan." The Super gave a quaint smile. "It took me twenty years to reach the rank of inspector. Don't land me in the cart, will you?"

"I will not, sir. I appreciate the fact that you have trusted me."

"As you have trusted me."


"By God, 'Daddy's' a decent old boy," thought Wigan when he was outside. On the way home he called in at the police station and found that a note had been left for him.

*"I should like to see you. Searle Connington."* A telephone number was added.

Wigan telephoned the number from a public call-box, and Connington, briefly business-like, arranged to meet him at 9 p.m. that evening at Wigan's private house. "Please bring with you," he added, "the keys of Mike Fisk's house."

Wigan took a chance. The station officer on duty was an amiable sergeant named Dooley. Wigan asked him to open the safe, then he took out the necessary keys. "I suppose it's all right, Jack?" said Dooley casually.

"Quite all right, Lawrence. I'll be responsible for them."

And Lawrence Dooley, who was busy on a process report and knew, moreover, that Fisk's house had been left by will to Wigan, thought no more of the matter. He did not ask for a formal written receipt, and Wigan purposely did not offer one. He intended to keep the keys as long as was necessary and damn the consequences, if any. In any case, the bank, as executors, should shortly obtain a grant of probate and police precautions on the house must then be relaxed, if Wigan so desired it.

# CHAPTER TWENTY-ONE

## THE MAN WHO COULDN'T SLEEP

Searle Connington arrived at Wigan's house wearing his book-collecting clothes: sober black, with its suggestion of relentless respectability. No mercy expected here. And none given.

"I have an idea," he said, "that there will be a visitor or visitors to Mike Fisk's house. I think it would be worth while keeping a watch at night, from inside the house."

"You expect someone to steal the books?"

"Yes, they're a great attraction, those books. Book-collecting can be like a fever. All prudence may tell a certain person or persons to keep away. But they won't. It may pay us to watch."

"Very well, sir. Have supper with me, then we'll take with us a flask of tea and a packet of sandwiches."

After supper they had a short smoke, then Connington suggested that they ought to be starting. "I confess," he remarked, "that I shall be interested to see Fisk's books. He must have collected a good many valuable items."

Wigan remembered Charlie's note. "None are for sale," he said firmly.

"That's as you wish. I understand they come to you, and it's for you to say what happens to them. Well, we had better be starting. I'm afraid there won't be much rest for you, Mr. Wigan. Are you on duty tomorrow?"

"Early Turn, 6 a.m. till 2 p.m. I must be at the station by a quarter to six to parade the men."

"Then I shall do the watching. You can just show me round the house and then return home. I will take the flask of tea and the sandwiches which you were kind enough to suggest."

"But what about your rest?"

"I hardly ever sleep. I just doze in bed or in a chair, or I read. Much of my life is spent reading. I claim to be one of the comparatively few bookmen who really do read. Reading is mother, wife, and child to me. If I can't read, well then I think of what I have read. So, you see, to watch will be no privation."

"If you're sure, sir, I shall be grateful enough. I want to do my duty to Fred Hampton, but police-work is no picnic. A sergeant has to be on the go the whole time."

"Right. Then it's settled. I'll watch. And, with a bit of luck, we may free Fred."

The weather seemed determined to make up for the shocking summer. There was a mildness in the air that suggested April or May rather than December. It was dark, but not black. "A good night for burglars," said Wigan.

"It may be," said Connington, "but it's not what I want to see. Even a dealer with a millionaire customer on his books won't be too reckless. Still, of course, he or she may decide to have a go. Therefore we can't turn round and go home."

"It's very good of you, Mr. Connington, to give your time and interest."

"My dear chap—the curiosity of the problem. Detective stories must have hundreds of thousands of readers; and here we have a problem in real life. I met Askew the other day. His hobby is criminology. He's studied this problem, and he thinks he knows the answer."

"Really? Who does he think killed Mike Fisk?"

"You," said Connington.

For a moment Wigan was too taken aback to answer. Then he said: "That's a very pretty compliment. On what does he base his conclusions?"

"You were a friend of Mike's. You knew of his collection. You collect books, or you had begun to under Mike's tutelage. You might well want his books. Now you've got them."

Wigan didn't know whether to laugh or be angry. "Mr. Askew," he said, "ought to join our C.I.D. But we had better be serious. I must say that I wonder that the real murderer should take such an appalling risk as to visit the house again."

"Did you ever read about Don Vincente, a priest of Barcelona and a dyed-in-the-wool fiend for books? He strangled to get a volume he wanted, and then added arson to murder and theft."

Wigan was rather dismayed to see the greed shining in Connington's own eyes when they had entered Mike's house and were in his library. "My word," said Connington, "I knew his library must be good; but I didn't know it was as good as this. All this early stuff in Latin. But of course he could read Latin. A man of knowledge, though a rough diamond."

"He was my friend."

"Of course," said Connington absently. "Dear me, the blasphemous Black Grimoire, which requires murder for the performance of its rites. Some strange things must have happened in this room. I don't wonder that he got himself killed, one way or another. Did he take you into his confidence about black magic?"

"No. I'm a churchman. Mike knew I wouldn't be interested."

"That is so. I must find a suitable place in which to watch and wait. I can hardly remain in the study here, even in darkness. I observed a downstairs cloakroom, unusual in a house of this age; but it will come in useful. I think I will hide there."

"You won't be comfortable, sir."

"Sergeant, did you ever hear of Lavatory Jack?"

"Charlie North told me about him."

"Well, he was a great character. I knew him well. He was one of the greatest living authorities on old colour-plate books, I remember him buying a magnificent copy of Rudolph Ackermann's *The Microcosm of London* with its superb coloured plates. He bought it and he showed it to me, under a gas-lamp. But, alas, he only had tuppence left. 'That's all right,' he said. 'I've got enough for board and lodging. Penny for a roll and a penny for the seat.' I shall be all right, Sergeant. I have my trusty stick and my flask of tea and the excellent sandwiches. So off you go to bed, or you won't be fit for duty in the morning."

"You have a good nerve, sir." Wigan hesitated. "But I don't like leaving you. I really don't. There's danger."

"So I told Charlie North. I hope he hasn't found it out."

"I hope so too. But I think I'll stay, sir."

"With both of us in the w.c.? That would be *most* uncomfortable."

"I can hide in the kitchen."

"I don't think it's necessary. Nothing may happen tonight. A thief is apt to pause and think hard before he strikes again. So be off with you and have a good night's rest, what is left of the night."

Wigan was not unprepared to lose a few books, knowing now something of the ways of book-collectors; but when next morning on his way to the station, or rather a little out of the way, he called in at Mike's house, he found that nothing unusual had happened during the night, and Connington insisted on taking him into Mike's study.

"I wish to show you, Sergeant, that I have taken nothing. Shocking temptation, but there it is."

"I don't need showing, sir. I realise that you are a gentleman."

"My dear Jack Wigan, there's no such thing as a book-collector *and* a gentleman. But I have pocketed nothing."

"You heard nothing suspicious during the night, sir?"

"Not a thing. Well padded on my couch, such as it was, I waited and I watched, but our Ruth was safe in the arms of her Dithan, and the Ferrow brothers were nicely sleeping, and Corky, or Charlie, or anyone else I can think of had something better to do than steal. But I shall come again tonight."

"I'm on leave Wednesday night, sir."

"The night Fred Hampton is due for it, or I suppose eight o'clock the next morning. That's the usual time, isn't it?"

"Yes, sir. On Monday afternoon I'm going to see him."

"I don't envy you, Officer. But keep his heart up."

"Sir, I can't do that. I feel a fraud. All this talk and I have done nothing."

"You have done something. Wigan, I am going to ask you to sell me Mike's books. You needn't really sell them to me unless you wish to, but I want you to say you will; only I am not allowed to take them away till Thursday morning when Fred is gone and the case is closed."

"I'll say so, sir, if you wish. But I cannot make real promises. In fact, I've already told Charlie I won't sell them."

"Have you indeed? Well, I can see you're in a hurry to get to the station. I'm going back to my house. I'll be back this evening about ten. Conscientious Con—that's me."

Wigan saluted and mounted his cycle. Connington visited the public lavatory in the town, tucked away by the old town hall. He had a good wash. Then he had some breakfast in a coffee shop. Then he took the train to town.

# CHAPTER TWENTY-TWO

## MONDAY NIGHT

On Monday evening, before taking up his vigil, Connington called at Wigan's house. Mrs. Wigan opened the door. "I wish you could do something, sir," she said in a low voice. "Jack's in a bad state. He might be going to be hanged himself."

"Pray for rain, Mrs. Wigan. That's what we need: a pouring wet night."

"Then I will pray, sir, and God will see justice done."

Wigan was in the sitting-room. He was utterly downcast. "I went to see him this afternoon," he said. "It was terrible, terrible. Poor chap, he's just skin and bone, and always they watch him, night and day, lest he commit suicide."

"Fred would never do that. He hasn't got the courage."

"He—he cursed me." Wigan nearly broke down.

"Pull yourself together," said Connington. "I may need you badly before the end. What age do you think I am?"

Wigan blew his nose. He looked at Connington in surprise. "I've never thought about it, sir. I suppose between forty and fifty?"

"I'm sixty-two. Before long I shall get the Old Age Pension, which will be a comfort."

"I shouldn't have thought it, sir. You certainly don't look it."

"Maybe not. The reason is I never worry; and I advise you not to. All will come right in the end, with the aid of Mrs. Wigan's prayers. She is going to pray for rain. Friday night was fine. Result, N.B.G., which out of respect for Mrs. Wigan I will not translate, but maybe you have been in the Army too. Saturday night, ditto. Sunday the same. Tonight looks like being the same."

"I don't follow, sir. Why should rain be so important?"

"Well, for one thing, would you take an umbrella out on a fine night? If you wish to hide your identity, an umbrella is a very useful thing. Also, with a sharpened ferrule, it can be a murderous weapon."

"By Jove, sir, that's clever. You mean that an umbrella was to be the weapon to kill Mike Fisk?"

"It might be. Only another and more convenient weapon turned up."

"Francis Ferrow would likely own an umbrella."

"He would. And others. Anyone can own an umbrella. I was nearly spiked the other day in the Tube by a young lady who handled her umbrella carelessly. It had a long thin point, which ought to be prohibited by law."

"Ruth!" said Wigan. In his interest he had forgotten his dejection.

"Maybe yes, maybe no. Catch our fish before we name it. That's good piscology. Will you walk over with me? It will keep you from brooding."

Mrs. Wigan retired to the kitchen. Then she brought in a basket of provisions and a big flask of hot tea for Connington.

"You almost make me wish I was married," said Connington. "What it is to have a good wife."

Mary Wigan was highly gratified. "Why don't you marry, sir? I'm sure you could find some young lady to make you happy."

"Young, Mrs. Wigan? That is a compliment. But I have my sister to look after. Did you ever know the relationship between Charles and Mary Lamb? Mary was insane, you know. My sister is not so bad as that, but she has periodical fits of depression. She is like me; she cannot sleep. Some obscure disease, no doubt. Sometimes I read with her the whole night through."

Wigan had recovered entirely his self-possession. "Well, sir, you certainly look well on it."

"Ah, yes. Mhmm. Good night, Mrs. Wigan. And remember, pray. Pray for rain. A thundering, lashing night of it. I can't speak for the sergeant, but I think your prayers will have more effect than mine will."

"A better man than you never lived, sir!" said Mary Wigan warmly.

Connington was quite embarrassed. "If you go on like that, Mrs. Wigan, we shall give the sergeant cause for jealousy."

They walked towards Chelmer Square. "Look at those stars," said Connington. "Every one shining. No night for fishing. Still, we had better not take any chances."

Wigan, ashamed of his lack of faith, was careful to keep away from the subject of Fred, who in a frenzy of despair had screamed curses at him and accused him of being in league with the f——rs who were hanging an innocent man. But he did say: "The rain had better come quick, sir."

"Yes, we've only till Wednesday night. But I have baited my lines very carefully. I'm to get your books, Wigan, and there will be sensations in the rare book trade when I publish my firm's catalogue, which will be done simultaneously in London and New York. Unique items will be offered. Original manuscripts will be bound in—mark this, Wigan—bound in with ordinary books. I doubt if our murderous friend has examined every book in the library. He, or she, wouldn't take time to do that with the P.C. on the beat liable to come along any minute and try the house for security. But now he or she will probably think again. It will be the chance of a lifetime. I have played Mike's library up and up. My secretary in the office, a very clever woman, has been making indiscreet feelers as to the result if we dispose of items individually; and she has smacked on prices that make even me blink. By the way, Charlie North seems to have completely disappeared. Have you seen him?"

"No, sir, I haven't. I pay him three pounds a week to help me over this business. He didn't turn up to draw this week's pay."

"I hope he's all right. I told him he was running into danger. He's a bit too rash. I believe he told Ferrows fantastic stories to try and see their rare occult works. Of course with no result. They are not fools."

"He was trying to find a book with Mike's secret mark on it."

"A piece of rubber would settle that."

"It might be overlooked, sir."

"I doubt it," said Connington. "Charlie is a free-lance and

he has a good knowledge of books; but he may not realise the careful way in which others work. In my firm, for
instance, when we acquire a fresh book it is collated leaf by
leaf and every mark or imperfection noted. We should certainly note any secret mark. I'm beginning to be very curious
about Charlie."

"I've been too busy to visit his home."

"I'm too busy also. We'll give him till the end of the week,
then, if you don't hear from him, Sergeant, I think some
inquiry should be made."

They reached Mike's house in Chelmer Square. Connington
noticed the "For Sale" board on the house opposite. "That
might suit us for observation," he said.

"I don't think you would be comfortable in there, sir. The
property won't sell. Defective drains, I understand."

"In that case the smell might be very bad. We won't try
it." Connington looked around. "Quiet square this, Wigan.
Not a soul about."

At that moment there came the sound of a car. It slowed
down. Powerful head-lamps swept round as the car entered
Chelmer Square. The car pulled up. The blinding lights lit
the square. There was no chance for Connington and Wigan
to conceal themselves, even if they wished to.

The car had left-hand drive. The driver got out the near
side—a big man. "Good evening, Mr. Dithan Dand," said
Connington.

"Well, Mr. Connington. Just the man we want to see. Ruth
and I thought we would pay a little visit here." A girl alighted
from the other side. "Ruth, here's Mr. Connington. This will
sure save us some trouble."

Ruth was, for her, wearing old clothes. She said good evening to Connington and to Sergeant Wigan. "We thought," she said, "that we should find you guarding your books. We should like to see them. You won't mind that?"

"They are not for sale," said Connington sharply. "They have all been sold to me."

"But I have been a good customer to you," said Dithan Dand. "A good many of my dollars have come your way."

"Well, one look, if Sergeant Wigan doesn't mind?"

Wigan let Connington handle the situation. He said he didn't mind at all.

They entered the house. Connington led the way to the study. He flashed his torch round the books. "Wonderful stuff," he said. "A lot of original manuscripts bound in."

The American looked round. "Five thousand dollars for the lot," he said.

"Sorry, I'm not prepared to sell yet. I have a sheaf of customers for occult works, some of them before you, Mr. Dand."

The American's gloved right hand went to the region of his hip-pocket. It came away again. "I guess I should have come heeled, but packing a gun is not popular in this country. Just remember, Mr. Connington, that I pay and pay well for anything I want."

"I'll certainly remember it, Mr. Dand. I shall send you a copy of the catalogue."

"Are you buying for your firm or buying for yourself?"

"For my firm. I haven't the money to pay for all this."

"You dirty dog," said Ruth. "We've treated you well, Di and I, and this is the way you repay us."

"Yep," said the American. "Would it be William K.

Makemore of Chicago who is first on your list? The rat might pay ten thousand for this little lot, but I guess I'll not be held up. Come on, Ruth, before I sock him."

"He would have socked me, too," said Connington to Wigan, "if you hadn't have been here."

"What has that episode gained for us?"

"Nothing, yet."

"I don't like leaving you here alone."

"Not at all. It will be interesting to see the vultures gather. As I sit and think, or just sit like the countryman who got tired of thinking, I rest very nicely. When Mike's house is finally yours, Wigan, you will have to let me come and occupy my usual post!"

Wigan smiled a bit late, for his sense of humour was in abeyance.

"If you catch someone, sir, a charge of breaking and entering will not clear Fred."

"I know. I hope for something more. Just what, I can't say at the moment. And now I think I had better get in position. It will be too bad to frighten a vulture away."

Wigan, with his keys, opened the padlock which the police had put on the front gate to discourage visitors. When Connington was inside, Wigan locked the gate again and handed him the keys. It was possible to unfasten the padlock from the inside. He saw Connington unlatch the front door and enter. Then he quietly closed the door again.

Wigan walked away. He looked up at the beautiful starlit sky. As a police officer, he was an expert on skies. He had worked "nights" in the blaze of a full moon, in torrential rain, in cold so intense that the motion of the earth seemed to have stopped, frozen still. "It will be fine tomorrow," he thought, "and maybe the next day." And Connington wanted rain. He relied now on Connington. Charlie seemed to have deserted him. His reading of Charlie's character was that he was a roughish diamond, but honest. Wigan thought he had better spare tomorrow afternoon to call at Charlie's lodgings in Lambeth.

Connington sat with closed eyes, resting. He ran over in his mind certain conjurations. He knew how dangerous it is to dabble in the Black Arts. He might, by accident, evoke some uncontrollable force, yet if events took the course he thought they might, it might be the only way.

The night was silent, silent as the tomb. He heard the beat man go by and rattle the chain round the gate and gatepost at the front. Then heard the distant church clock in Sun market-square strike midnight, then one, then two. Connington opened his packet of sandwiches. He drank some of Mrs. Wigan's tea. It was almost as hot as when she poured it into the flask, and she certainly knew how to make tea—a police-man's wife. After drinking the tea, he composed himself for a doze. "Of course," he thought to himself, "they can't get rid of the car."

Three o'clock. Just after three he heard a gentle pull at the front door. It moved a fraction of an inch forward, then back. Then there was silence. Connington reached for his sword-cane. He heard the back door open—it had been left unlocked.

Footsteps passed from the kitchen, past Connington's hiding-place, along the hall passage. They entered the study, on the left. Connington left his hiding-place. He stretched himself, for he was stiff. Then he walked quietly along the passage on stockinged feet. There was a flickering light from the open study door as a torch flashed about.

Connington stood in the doorway. With a swish he unsheathed his sword-cane and exposed the shining Toledo blade.

"Put those books back," he said. "All of them."

"Well, Mr. Connington! I guess we—we were only joking. I should have sent you a cheque for what we've taken."

"Yep, in your own idiom. Put the books back, or I'll run you both through and have the law on my side."

Dithan Dand and Ruth replaced half a dozen volumes in the bookcase from which they had taken them. They both looked very foolish, and Ruth, who was wearing a dark skirt and jumper which emphasised the lithe grace and strength of her body, slammed one volume home.

"I'd like to put you across my knee for that," said Connington. "You ought to know how to treat books. Now get out, both of you. I don't want the trouble of prosecuting, so if you say nothing I shan't."

"That's real kind of you," said the American.

"Yep, and yep again. Over the front gate you go, and I should like to see how you do it, Mr. Dithan Dand."

"On Ruth's back," said the big man. "I'm still open to purchase. Please remember that."

"I'll remember it."

They left. Connington made them leave by the back door.

Ruth helped Dithan Dand over the locked front gate, then she jumped the gate like an acrobat.

"Blast them!" said Connington, as he returned to his hiding-place. He drank the remainder of the hot tea, then recommenced his doze.

At half-past five he met Sergeant Wigan at the corner of Chelmer Square. "Anything doing?" asked Wigan.

"Nothing, except a couple of monkeys playing the fool. But I needn't trouble you with that."

# CHAPTER TWENTY-THREE

## TUESDAY

Charlie's room was over a café kept by an amiable lady called Mara—her real name was Marian. She was said to make the best pot of tea in London, and Wigan, failing to find Charlie at home, sampled a cup while he interviewed Mara about Charlie's disappearance.

"He comes and he goes. That's all I can say about Charlie. I dare say he will turn up in a day or two."

"Have you any idea where he has gone?"

"None. I expect about his business, old books. But he doesn't tell me anything."

Wigan left. He felt he could hardly officially report to the police yet that Charlie was missing. Charlie would be extremely annoyed if he were apprehended by police officers when he was on some secret enterprise of his own—Wigan hoped, to do with Fred. He might hold the key to the whole business. On his way home Wigan looked in at Niger's book-shop and examined some books in a half-hearted way. He now had no interest in books. When Mike's books were really his, he thought he would sell them. It was curious, but he had never considered the money they would bring. He doubted if the books were worth nearly as much as Connington, for his own purposes, had made out; but they would probably fetch a tidy sum, certainly several hundred pounds; and this, if the worst came to the worst, he would share with Fred's widow.

Wigan had reached this sombre reflection. He was examining a book with some coloured plates in it, *Alpine Flowers*, when a voice said: "Good afternoon, Mr. Wigan; or rather, good evening. I suppose it's evening now." The speaker was the runner, tall and thin, Algernon Askew.

"Good evening, sir."

"Any news about our unfortunate friend?"

"None."

"And Thursday morning, I understand… Dear me, it's all very dreadful. I confess that at one time I suspected you. I suspect everyone I know—in the book world—if Fred didn't do it; but I've come round to the belief that poor Fred did, in a violent fit of temper."

Wigan said nothing. There seemed nothing further to say.

"Unless," added Askew, "someone strange and altogether unsuspected has committed the crime. There are extraordinary rumours running round. I've just been to Ferrows' to get an early printed work I want, and their man, Corky, told me that you have sold Mike's books to Searle Connington, but he mustn't remove them till Thursday morning, after, I presume, an unfortunate event. Is that true?"

"Something of the kind, sir."

"Well really, Mr. Wigan, I think you are very rash. I'm friendly with Corky—one of the few people who are. He is not an amiable character, but I manage to get along with him. And do you know what he thinks?"

"Please tell me," said Wigan politely.

Mr. Askew bent his great height till his long horse-face was within a foot of Wigan's face. Then he peered earnestly at him.

"Corky said to me: 'If Fred didn't kill Mike, I know who did. And he's getting Mike's books.'"

"That's outrageous," said Wigan warmly. "Mr. Connington is a gentleman."

"It is evident," said Askew, in his stately English, "that you do not know book-collectors. Many are men of unimpeachable characters. But others are deep, deep, as the sea; and at the bottom one finds a covetous soul. I have only once seen Connington angry. It was at a sale. He was outbid for a volume. After the sale he went up to the successful bidder and said furiously: 'All right. I'll have it yet. I'll have it after you've gone.' And he did. Within six months the man who bought the book was dead, and Connington did secure it at the subsequent sale."

"That is a matter of pure chance."

"I am not suggesting, of course, that Connington murdered the man; but it is a straw to indicate the way of the wind. Connington has a sister, Amelia, who keeps a bookshop in Notting Hill Gate. It's called the Welcome Bookshop—a very nice name. It's in Garden Square, off the High Road, a delightful old-world neighbourhood. You should visit it. It might alter some of your ideas."

"Please be more explicit, sir."

"Well, I mustn't make mischief," said Askew, with somewhat belated thoughtfulness, "but Miss Connington will repay study. I do not say she is insane, but it must take a man of iron nerve to live with her. Searle Connington is such a man."

Wigan didn't know what to think. Surely the vigils Connington was putting in, at great inconvenience to himself, couldn't be so much eyewash? Absently Wigan replaced on the shelf the book with coloured plates he had been considering. Instantly, with the speed of light, like the antenna of an insect shooting out, Askew's long arm seized the volume. "As you have given up ownership," he remarked, "I think I will… Yes, lithographed plates, not aquatints. Still, five shillings is too low a price. It must be worth thirty. I will have it."

Wigan was amused and disconcerted. Book-collectors, even such mild gentlemen as Mr. Askew, were certainly opportunists.

Askew put the volume firmly under his arm. "I must be going," he said. "I specialise in detective fiction. By much reading, I am usually able to spot the murderer, sometimes half-way through a book. I recommend you to visit the Welcome Bookshop."

Wigan looked round. Though the great bookshop hummed with life, no person was very near them.

"Do you mean to imply, sir, that Miss Connington killed Mike?"

But Askew was a man to whom blunt, direct speech, a plain yes or no, seemed impossible. "Once," he remarked, "I was visiting Searle, whom I know fairly well. We were sitting in the back parlour, which is a comfortable room. Over a pot of tea, we were discussing prices and trend and other matters of interest to collectors and dealers. I remember that we were remarking that owing to the attentions of the B.B.C., the first editions of Trollope seemed likely to appreciate in value."

Wigan shifted resignedly. "Well, sir?"

"Well, Mr. Wigan, I chanced to be looking towards the door. Fortunately. I saw it open, and Amelia's head peered in. Then her hand. And in her hand was a carving-knife. Connington looked round, and saw it too. He said quietly: 'Don't be a fool, Amelia. Go to bed.' The door closed. I was trying to find words to express my surprise and apprehension when Searle said to me: 'You're quite safe, Algernon. Her violence is directed towards me, whom she loves. It's the way with the mentally unbalanced.' So there you are, Mr. Wigan. I have told you all I know. Good evening."


Round and round, round and round. Wigan was not much given to headaches, but when he left Niger's he had a splitter. However, his duty was clear: he must visit the Welcome Bookshop. He descended to the Tube at Tottenham Court Road and took the Central London line to Notting Hill Gate. By half-past six he was in the quiet Garden Square. The Welcome Bookshop had an old-fashioned bow front with blown bull's eyes in the glass of the windows. There was a light behind, and in the door hung a sign: "Welcome. We are open. Please walk in." Wigan walked in.

A fire burned cosily at the far end. Round three sides of the room were books, books, almost to the ceiling. At a table sat a middle-aged lady dressed with a Quaker primness of costume. She looked up, smiled pleasantly, and said: "Good evening. Is there any particular book you require? Or would you like just to look round?"

Wigan thought that frankness was best. Indeed, such were his relations with Searle Connington that any other course was impossible.

"Good evening, madam. I am a friend of Mr. Connington's. My name is Sergeant Wigan."

"Oh, I have heard of you. You are a detective interested in freeing Fred Hampton. My interest is chiefly colour-plate books. Just look at this volume on Chinese Punishments. Isn't it realistically done?"

Wigan glanced at a revolting picture of a man hanging upside down.

"Is Mr. Connington in, madam?"

"Not yet. He usually walks home. He will be here about seven. Would you care for a cup of tea?"

Wigan thought of the Borgias and their pleasant little habits with poisons. However, such a thing would hardly happen in a London bookshop. "Thank you," he said politely, "but I hardly like to trouble you."

"It's no trouble. I shall put the kettle on for Searle. He adores tea. He's a real bookman."

"Tea," said Wigan, with a heavy attempt at conversation, "is the standard drink of the police force."

"I think," said Miss Connington dreamily, "that policemen must be rather cruel. Are they?"

"Not usually, ma'am. I've known police officers afterwards help the men they put in prison."

"Really? I should have thought their object would be oth-erwise. Please excuse me while I go into the kitchen."

Wigan glanced over the books, which seemed to be a good general stock. The shop-bell pinged, and a customer came into the shop; Miss Connington returned. The customer wanted a Welsh dictionary. Miss Connington hadn't one in stock, but, with what Wigan thought was extraordinary knowledge, she immediately answered that there was a National Dictionary of the Welsh language with English and Welsh equivalents, compiled by W. Owen Pughe. She could advertise for a copy in *The Clique*. The price would be about two pounds. The customer departed, satisfied.

"Madam," said Wigan, with deep respect, "you certainly understand books."

"It's my business," said Miss Connington lightly. "I have been at it all my life. I learned from my father. He was a very hard man. I wouldn't like to tell you what happened when I once dropped a valuable book and split the endpapers."

Wigan, who was a kind-hearted man, flinched uncomfortably from the strain of cruelty in Miss Connington's nature: she was obviously burning to tell him.

"Such things are best forgotten," he said.

"One can never forget pain, Mr. Wigan."

About seven o'clock Connington came in. He was surprised to see Wigan, and perhaps not entirely pleased. He was wearing his professional clothes, topped off by a round black Homburg hat which sat high on his conical-shaped head. "Since you are here," he said, "you had better share our evening meal. Afterwards I will drive you in my car back to Sun. I expect I can leave my car somewhere convenient, and we can walk to Mike's house."

Wigan felt he had to say it. "If you still think the watch worth-while, sir."

"Why not? It's our only chance. The weather is still fine, I see; but it may rain later."

The shop door was locked, and the card in the window turned from Open to Closed. In the parlour behind the shop Miss Connington served a dainty meal. Her food seemed to melt in the mouth. Wigan respectfully complimented her on her cooking.

"I was trained," she said, "by my father. If I made a mistake, I was whipped for it, wasn't I, Searle?"

"Father was Victorian. His methods were sometimes harsh. Of course we are delighted to see you, Wigan, and glad to repay, in a small degree, the hospitality you have given me. But had you any special reason for coming here?"

"I met Mr. Askew and he sang the praises of the Welcome Bookshop. He suggested that I ought to visit it."

"Ah," said Connington, "did he?"

His car was stabled in a mews converted into garages. After supper he got it out and drove Wigan to Sun. Wigan was troubled and had little to say. Connington seemed to be a thought-reader.

"Askew," he said, "is a born gossip. He gossips for hours with Corky. I suppose he told you all about my sister, and suggested that either Amelia or I killed Mike?"

"Well—he did."

"Askew ought to be shot. One day his tongue will get him into trouble. I was going to let him have some first editions by Sheridan le Fanu, who wrote *The House by the Churchyard*—it's in his line; but I don't think I will now."

"I'm sorry if I have made mischief, sir."

"You haven't. It's Askew, drat him. What is more, you are inclined to believe him, Wigan. I can read you like a book. You know now that Amelia has homicidal tendencies, and you think that she knifed Mike, and I rifled his library. Come on now, give me an honest answer. Yes or no?"

"I don't know what to think, sir. I only know that Fred's life is drawing to a close and nothing can save him. Book-collectors—they are as deep as the sea. Some of them will do anything, anything."

"You have answered me. Very well, think what you like, you can't prove anything. But I still hope to save Fred's life. Curious for a guilty man, eh?"

They came to a traffic block at Camden Town. Connington peered ahead, then he shut off his engine. "We're here for half an hour," he said. "Some fool has taken the road up; now we must wait for some other fool to put it back again." He was in an acid temper.

Wigan hesitated, then he said: "Sir, I must make a suggestion however painful it may be. I feel, sir, that your sister has unfortunate tendencies, no doubt through no fault of her own. She may have had some grudge against Mike. Is it possible that unknown to you, perhaps in your absence, she paid his house a visit? Forgive my saying this."

"Wigan, did you go upstairs?"

"At your kind suggestion, sir, I went up to wash my hands."

"Did you notice the bathroom window?"

"No, sir; the blind was drawn."

"The window is heavily barred. So are all the windows.

The front door has three locks, to all of which I alone have the key. Some of my private stock of books in my bedroom are immensely valuable, and I say that I am afraid of burglars. But I leave you to guess the truth. Amelia must not go out. She cannot leave the house now until I return."

"I hope you're right, sir, but I have a vast experience of burglars; and I've known one slip through a window eighteen inches wide. Where the head can go the rest of the body can follow. So we say."

Connington made no reply. The traffic ahead began to move and he started his engine. At length they reached Sun and he parked his car in the market-square, alongside some lorries, where Wigan assured him it would be safe. Then they walked out to Mike's house.

"Rain," said Connington, "I feel it coming."

"Why, sir, do you so want rain?"

"Because the Bride of Satan will be free to roam."

"You think Mike's killer was a woman?"

"I'm sure of it. A woman, or a man like a woman. Woman, Wigan, is at the base of the Black Mass. She is the sorceress who raises the devil from hell. In the middle ages, many a woman had pins stuck in all over her body to see if she felt pain. The Bride of Satan can feel no pain."

Wigan was hopelessly bewildered. "I wish I had read more about it, sir, but Mike never told me anything."

"Then he did you a service. Good night. I'll see you in the morning, if you're coming this way."

"Wednesday, sir. Fred's last day of life. I shall be here about half-past five."

Connington's sister had made him some sandwiches and

given him a flask of hot tea. He unlocked the gate of the house and passed through. Then he entered the house and quietly closed the door.

About half-past five the next morning, in the December dark lit by gas-lamps, Wigan cycled up to Mike's house. He found Connington waiting outside the gate. He was looking exceedingly cheerful. "Nothing doing," he said, "but I've had the best night's rest I've had for months. My place of abode can hardly be called ideal, and there's a lever at the back which jabs my back; but I managed to get comfortable and went off to sleep as peaceful as a baby."

"That's fine, sir, but I could wish for better news."

"Don't worry. Our friend will come yet. I'll see you here tonight, Wigan."

"I'll watch too, sir. I shall be on leave, and I could never sleep anyway, thinking of Fred."

"Very well, but you'll have to choose another coign of vantage. No room in the lav. for two of us. We can't have you in the kitchen or the study. You'll have to be upstairs. Do you mind the head of the landing?"

"Anywhere will suit me, sir."

"Right. It's just as well that I feel in good shape, because I've a great deal to do. I'm going to call in at Ferrows' and ask to borrow their shooting-brake to take away Mike's books tomorrow morning."

"My offer to sell you Mike's books, sir, was only make-believe, at your suggestion."

"All the same I'm going to ask for Ferrow's brake. Mr.

Francis may not agree to lend it, but he may. Goodbye, Wigan. See you at 10 p.m."

"Come to supper with me, sir, about eight o'clock."

"Well, thank you. That's most generous." Off went Mr. Connington, swinging his black cane in jaunty fashion. Wigan mounted his pedal cycle and rode to the police station, where he paraded his men for Early Turn in the gaslit charge-room. Automatically the men answered to their numbers. Wigan finished posting to beats and took up the station books: the parade book, the crime book, the lists of motor vehicles reported to be stolen.

Wigan read in a flat voice to men who listened with per-functory interest, some of them half-awake. Wigan read without a mistake; but at the back of his mind was the thought: "It's Wednesday. Wednesday morning. Tomorrow morning at eight o'clock Fred will die unless I can save him."

The duty inspector came in, and Sergeant Wigan stood smartly to attention. "All correct, sir," he said.

"That's right," said the inspector amiably. He sent the men out to take up their beats. Afterwards he said to Wigan: "You don't look very well, Sergeant. Don't you sleep well?"

"Not very, sir."

"I suppose it's this Fred Hampton business?"

"It is, sir."

"Well, I suppose nothing I can say will make much difference. By the way, I have noticed that the key to the police padlock on Fisk's house in Chelmer Square has gone from the safe. Have you taken it?"

"I have borrowed it—yes, sir."

The inspector was a man of easy character. "Well, I suppose

it's all right. The house is yours, anyway; and soon you will take formal possession, no doubt. But you'll knock yourself up, Sergeant, if you're not careful. If I were you, when the—when it's all over, I should apply for a bit of annual leave."

Wigan knew the danger of an impassioned reply, that if Fred died, if he, Wigan, failed to save a man he believed innocent, he would never sleep again. Instead, he said with formal respect: "I'll think over your advice, sir."

"That's right. I'm glad to find you so reasonable, Sergeant. I fancy that the higher-ups were a bit bothered about you, Wigan. Dam' awkward, these executions. Years ago, when I was a P.C., I was chief witness in a murder trial. I felt awful when the poor chap took the high jump. But one gets over it, you know."

Wigan forced his lips to a stiff smile. "Thank you, sir."

# CHAPTER TWENTY-FOUR

## HUMBUG

Connington was an actor of ability. He delighted to play what is known in the book-trade as humbug. Wearing perhaps his seediest suit, he would enter a shop—maybe an antique shop, where the knowledge of books is generally shaky—and say: "That's a nice picture-book you have there. I would like to buy it for my little granddaughter. How much is it, please?" Here the shop-keeper, with that strange psychological instinct which seems to stir in the minds of the most ignorant, might hang on to the book. "I don't know that I care to sell it, sir. I think it's valuable. I would like to get an expert opinion before I sell it. It might be worth twenty pounds. It's written by a person who signs himself K.G."

"Dear me, yes. So it is. K.G.—I wonder who that can be? No one important, I'm sure. It can't be valuable—not a book for children."

"Well, sir, there are people who collect them."

"Are there really? I shouldn't have thought it. I feel I must have it, or dear little Dulcie will be so disappointed. Look—I have ten shillings here, ten whole shillings which I have saved up. I will give them all so that my little darling shall have a nice present from her granddaddy on her tenth birthday."

Here the shop-keeper might possibly part with the book. It might require a bit more humbug. But the result would be the same, for Connington had a will of iron and rarely failed: he would walk out with the book, which was in fact a signed presentation copy of a first edition by K.G.—Kate Greenaway.

Connington's star role was probably Cyrus K. Ripshafter from little ol' Noo Yark. He excelled in the part, and any American he had ever disliked was lugged in to be lampooned in the hard, rasping Yankee accent and the silly reverence for age which would buy (for fifty pounds) a worthless piece of pottery, and acquire, as an afterthought, a book he happened to notice while in the house. Visiting a farmhouse, Connington bought in this way a magnificent example of William Blake's work—his *Illustrations of the Book of Job*.

Mother and daughter of the farm laughed till they nearly cried as they watched the "American" depart in his little car.

"Oh, Ma, he gave fifty pounds for a little jug we got at Woolworths!"

"I nearly gave him that old book he fancied. More money than sense. To think that our little jug, which cost us sixpence new, will be carefully packed and transported—that was his word—to 'Noo Yark, where we reverence your beautiful old English craftsmanship, ma'am.' Oh law, Elsie, I shall die!"

Mother and daughter laughed again. They hugged one another and danced. They might not have danced quite so much had they known that the "American" threw away the little jug at the first opportunity, and that the "old book,"

Blake's original work, printed by him and hand-coloured with pigments ground up by himself and his wife, was worth fifty pounds—and the rest.

Connington prepared for more humbug. But first he went home and had a bath and a shave. It occurred to him that out of the mouths of babes and sucklings there sometimes comes wisdom. He liked Sergeant Wigan, who might stand as the best example of a British police officer: honest, kindly, patient, brave as a badger in the face of physical danger. But not, however, overweighted with brains. Still, Wigan might well have special knowledge of housebreakers and burglars and their ways, and what was possible in that direction.

Connington examined the bars of the upstairs windows. All seemed secure except the bars to the window of the spare bedroom, which Connington used as a store-room for his books. The two middle bars seemed to him forced apart a little. He went downstairs to Amelia, who was preparing his breakfast, succulent kidneys on toast, which had been her father's favourite dish.

The danger signs were there. Amelia looked years younger than her real age. Her eyes were shining; her lips were parted as if she were going to meet her lover.

"Amelia," said her brother, "have you been getting out at night?"

"What if I have, Con? I've done no harm."

"Maybe not, but I'd rather you didn't. I'm responsible for you, you know. I promised our Mother that I would always look after you."

"If you didn't, I should be taken to a home, shouldn't I, where I should be tied to a post and beaten?"

"Probably not that. I believe the mentally afflicted are well treated these days, but you ought to do as I say."

"I will, Con. I promise, because I love you. I loved Mother. And Father."

"Yes," said Searle Connington. His friends called him Con; and so sometimes did Amelia.

He began to eat his breakfast, perfectly cooked. His every sense was alert. At a time like this almost anything could be used as a weapon—a tea-pot might be smashed down on his head. He had nearly finished his breakfast when Amelia passed behind his chair. Suddenly, without the slightest warning, she bent down and bit him savagely in the back of the neck. Connington, who was a much stronger man than he looked, gripped hold of her wrists and pulled her off him.

"Oh," she gasped, "I'm so sorry. I'm so sorry, Con. I love you. Now punish me as I deserve."

"I'm not going to punish you. Don't be silly, Amelia."

She was crying and crying, her grey head bowed on the table like that of a little girl.

Connington applied the only cure he knew. "Look," he said, "I'm going to attend Sotheby's sale later today. It's the first part of the Lord Hobson collection. I want you to go through the catalogue and mark values for me."

Amelia calmed herself and did so. She gave an extraordinary exhibition of expertise, which very few booksellers could do with accuracy. Against every item in the catalogue she marked the highest bid which her brother, attending on behalf of his firm, could make and still expect to obtain a reasonable profit on resale.

Connington's neck was bleeding. He went to see his only intimate friend, a chemist who lived near. He did not visit a doctor, because two doctors can get together and sign a lunacy certificate.

"Patch me up, Will," he said to his friend.

"Amelia been at it again?"

"Yes, with her teeth." Connington let down his mask with his friend. "It's a bloody life. I only hope I can stick it out long enough."

"Maybe she will get better with age."

"Maybe. Our father was a sadistic brute. It's not her fault, poor kid; but oh my God, Will, I'm sometimes tempted to have her put away."

"You're the bravest man, I know, Con. There!—now you're ready to face the world again and plunder it of a few more books."

Connington arrived at Ferrow's bookshop soon after 9 a.m. There was a dressing on the back of his neck, but otherwise he was fine and jaunty, and he tried his first bit of humbug on Corky—Corky Edwards, as Connington knew his name to be.

"Good morning, Corky. How's Mrs. Edwards?"

"Well enough, thank you, but I don't see what my mother has to do with you."

"You're a surly devil, Corky, and one day you will get the sack. I'd sack you if you were in my place. Yesterday we had Princess Octavia in and she bought a set of Surtees. I expect even you, Corky, have heard of Surtees. We sold her a set, first edition, five vols., in the sixty-seven original parts, one hundred pounds. How's that for business? And we were courteous, Corky—courteous, my Corkibus."

Corky turned away. He limped awkwardly on his artificial leg and began to set out books. Connington persevered. "Well, Corky, I can see you're busy and want to get rid of me, so just slip in and ask Mr. Francis or Mr. Joel if I can borrow their shooting-brake tomorrow. I'm taking away Mike Fisk's books in the morning, and I haven't sufficient transport."

Corky banged down the books he was carrying. He limped into the inner recesses of the shop. Presently he returned. "Mr. Joel's in. He says you can have the van, but you will have to pay for the petrol."

"Agreed. Will you ask the van-driver to be at Mike's house in Chelmer Square, Sun, at half-past nine? And look, Corky, I once heard you say that you are not overpaid. Here's something for you… Buy Mrs. Edwards a new hat."

Corky's fingers closed over a couple of pound notes. His livid face twisted into a smile.

"Thank you, Mr. Connington, I will. My mother will be very pleased."

"That's right, Corky, always cherish your mother. I always did."

Connington turned away, then suddenly he turned back. "Oh, there's one thing more. Mr. Joel is apt to be forgetful, or he may change his mind about the van; and it's important for me to get the books away early. Sergeant Wigan, the owner of them, may change his mind. I want you to let Mr. Francis know that I am to have the van. You understand?"

"Certainly, Mr. Connington. You needn't worry. Mr. Joel is going to the Hobson sale, but Mr. Francis will be in about twelve. I'll let him know that you are to have the van."

"Thanks, Corky, you aren't a bad chap after all."

Connington walked away, satisfied. In the mood he was in he could have charmed ducks off a lake.

He succeeded in at least one respect, for Corky kept his word. About noon Mr. Francis walked in with an important client, a Mrs. Quihampton Belville from Boston, Massachusetts, who was on a buying trip for an institution library and might spend thousands of pounds. Mr. Francis had met her in his car at Southampton.

"Good morning, Edwards. I'm not to be disturbed. I shall be taking this lady home to lunch, and I shall be busy for the rest of the day."

"Very good, sir." Quite obviously Mr. Francis did not wish to be detained, but Corky did detain him. "Excuse me, Mr. Connington has been in. He is taking away the Fisk library tomorrow morning, and Mr. Joel has lent him the use of our estate car."

Mr. Francis's grey eyes gleamed. Rare books had only one proper destination—Ferrow Brothers. But he would not show annoyance before his client, and he even turned the incident to advantage in his particular line of humbug.

"A promise is of course a promise," he said, "but Mr. Connington's firm can be of little consequence if they cannot provide their own transport. However, I have more important things to think about. Mrs. Quihampton Belville, will you come to my private sanctum? I have some sixteenth-century manuscripts to show you. They are of course—unique."

The word drew the lady as bait does a fish. "That's real interesting, Mr. Ferrow. I think you and I may do business together."

"I hope so, dear lady, I hope so. Edwards, bring in a bottle of the '71 sherry, and two glasses."

When Corky took in the sherry, trying as much as possible to disguise his awkward shuffle, Mr. Francis was showing his client the manuscripts. "Wonderful work," he said, "almost without flaw. I fancy that an error cost the penman extremely dear."

He poured out the sherry with reverent care. "Almost two hundred years old," he said, "brought to England in a Liverpool slave-ship."

"I do not approve of slavery, Mr. Francis."

"But," continued Mr. Francis smoothly, "the last slaver sailed from Liverpool about 1807, and subsequent cargoes were more innocent—this was one of them. Your health, madam. Prosperity to your efforts to secure the *right* books and manuscripts for your library."

It was hard to believe that thirty years ago Mr. Francis, along with Mr. Joel and Corky, had pushed a barrow of books, sometimes to the old Caledonian market, sometimes as far as Epping market; and that they had got their supplies by "knocking"—calling at houses on the chance of getting some-thing good. Corky was Corky. Mr. Joel wasn't much removed from the rough who had once thrown a competitor out of an auction-room window. But Mr. Francis had risen. He was as well-dressed as any bookseller on earth, and his speech and his manners were as smooth as the fine old sherry he was now drinking.

He refilled the glasses. "May I have the pleasure, madam, of toasting the health of the President of the United States?"

"You may. And afterwards we will drink to the Queen of England."

Before they left the private sanctum for Mr. Francis's house, where even more rarities might possibly be revealed, he reverted to business. "These manuscripts are not 'pricey,' as we say in the trade. We are only asking £500 each for them—a mere trifle compared to their real worth. But we happened to buy them cheaply, and we think it wrong not to pass a bargain on to our clients."

Nevertheless, the lady had the shrewdness of her native land. She made Mr. Francis knock off a bit, and then wrote a cheque.

When Mr. Francis showed Mrs. Quihampton Belville out, which he did with easy dignity, Corky was sitting on a stool, his livid face sweating, his eyes glaring at a young man who was in the shop pulling the stock to pieces with no intention of buying a book—Corky was an expert in such matters. He stood up, opened the door for the lady, and bowed. When the lady had passed, a faint, subtle grin passed over Corky's face. To meet a client at Southampton before she had the chance to call on other booksellers, to sell her the accounts of a monastery—Corky couldn't begin to do such a thing; but he appreciated well enough the efforts of one who could. Francis Ferrow was a wonder.

# CHAPTER TWENTY-FIVE

## "HE"

H.M. Prison was built with ingenuity, inasmuch as except for the main gates, which faced a road, it was impossible to get near it. A tall tower rose high above the prison buildings, and at intervals a watchman patrolled the tower, and from the summit he looked around. Once inside the high redbrick walls one was not intended, without proper authorisation, to get out.

On this Wednesday afternoon a van from the Home Office approached the main gates and was allowed, after the usual precautions, to enter. The van carried a plain wooden box which contained a new rope. Shortly afterwards a man entered the prison. He carried a bag which contained his pinion-straps for wrists and ankles. He was taken to the heart of the prison where the hanging apparatus was set up. The great double doors of the trap, each weighing about four hundredweight, had already been tested and now were raised by block and tackle. The bolt had been greased.

The executioner pulled the lever several times. "It seems all right," he said.

"You would like to have a look at him?"

"Yes. What sort of chap is he?"

"He's nearly driven us all mad. It will be a mercy when it's all over."

Fred Hampton lay in a drugged sleep. Prison doctor and prison chaplain had together done what they thought was best for him, and the death-guard were only too thankful for a respite. Fred's hysterical screaming seemed to have sounded in their ears for centuries. The whole prison was upset, and the death-guard were at their wits' end trying to act with humanity and patience. They now, while their charge was unconscious, played a peaceful little game of dominoes.

A port in the cell-door opened and the executioner looked in.

"Just skin and bone," said the chief warder with him. "He can't be more than seven stone."

"No. I shall have to give him a long drop."

The executioner looked at Fred's shrunken face, at the straggling beard, at the eyes half-closed facing towards the cell-door.

"He's not my fancy," he remarked. "I like a brave man or woman. Then we get it over neatly and quickly."

"He swears he's innocent."

"Does he? Well, the last word is with the executioner and I've known some whisper a last confession to me, though of course I don't say nothing."

"We shall have to support him half-drugged. He won't walk."

"Get there he will have to, somehow."

At that moment, by some unfortunate chance, perhaps some obscure telepathic communication which pierced to the unsleeping part of the brain, Fred's eyes opened. The executioner jerked his head back, but not before Fred had seen him.

"He!" he screamed. "He's come for me!" Fred yelled his heart out, as they said afterwards, with all the vitality remaining to him. He rolled off the bed and fought the warders who tried to prevent him getting to the cell-door. He knocked over the table with the domino-board on it and bit a death-guard frantically in the hand.

"Now, old man, for heaven's sake be reasonable. We can't help it, and you can't get out of here. Calm down, there's a good chap... My God, I thought the doc. had drugged him..."

A guard rang the emergency bell and the chief warder brought the doctor in. The doctor gave Fred a "shot" with a hypodermic and he collapsed into unconsciousness. "Still another twelve hours of it," said a death-guard, wiping his sweating face. "Can't you put him out for good, sir?"

"No, I can't. The law's the law. That man was sentenced to be hanged by the neck till he is dead, and he's got to be hanged. I'll look in during the night and give him another shot if necessary, but I've got no right to kill him. I could be tried for murder if I did."

"Then, for his own sake, make him as near dead as you can, sir."

"Yes, but he will probably wake up before the end. He knows in his soul that he is going to be hanged, and there can be no peace for him until he is dead, whatever drugs I may give him. So you had better be prepared. He may wake up and fight like a fury."

The death-guard made no reply. With philosophical endurance they resumed their game of dominoes. With others, they had "drawn" this job from prisons elsewhere; and this time tomorrow they at least would be free. And the poor chap on the bed, poor devil, would be buried in quick-lime; and while hanging was the law, that was the way of it and there was no way out.

The doctor stayed for some time to see that his work was done. Companionably he watched the game in progress.

"I suppose," he remarked suddenly, "that man is guilty?"

"Couldn't say, sir. I never follow it. There's so much in the papers."

The doctor felt his neck. "I wouldn't like to be hanged for a crime I didn't commit."

But the death-guards had too much experience to follow this line of thought. It wasn't their business; and they concerned themselves with what that was. They weren't callous but they were sensible.

The doctor stared at the figure on the bed. His mouth wide open, Fred was breathing heavily. "Don't wake him for any breakfast. Let him stay as he is, if possible."

The elder of the two guards looked at the doctor, who was a young man. He was about to say: "What do you think we are—barmy?" Then he remembered what they owed, and might further owe, to the doctor.

"We shall do all we can for the man," he said respectfully.

"That's right. Don't hesitate to call me if you want me.

I shall be awake all night. I shan't go to bed. I couldn't sleep anyway."

"Your first hanging, sir?"

"Yes, and I hope it will be my last."

# CHAPTER TWENTY-SIX

## WEDNESDAY NIGHT

It rained stair-rods—blinding rain driven down by a fierce westerly gale. Connington, asked to the Wigans' for supper, listened to the sound of it with satisfaction. "Your prayers have been answered, Mrs. Wigan, as I believe the prayers of a good woman always are."

"I hope that's true, sir, about me being good I mean; that's a nasty place you've got on your neck, sir."

"A boil," said Connington briefly. "I think we had better be going, Wigan. I want you to remember that there's a nice thick door-mat just inside the kitchen door. We must wipe our feet well. And there's another thing: I should like to take off the police padlock on the front gate. Do you think the man on the beat will notice if it's gone?"

"He should do, sir. It's part of his job. I can call in at the station if you like and tell the station officer that I want to remove the padlock. As I'm the owner of the house, he may agree. At the same time, he may think that the S.D. Inspector should be consulted. The lock was put on to keep intruders away; and only by the S.D. Inspector's orders should it be taken off. He will be off duty now—his hours are normally nine to six—and I don't think I can call him up after that."

"No. We don't want a shemozzle, with perhaps police cars arriving. The gate isn't very high and it's got a smooth top. We'll let the Devil's Bride climb over or fly over."

"I wish you would tell me what is in your mind, sir."

"My mind has many things in it. Talking won't help. We shall see what we shall see. And now let's fight the gale with mackintoshes and umbrellas and all the comforts Mrs. Wigan can give us."

They arrived at Mike's house. Wigan put their wet mackintoshes in an out-house next to the kitchen. They dried their feet carefully on the mat. Then Connington went to his post and Wigan to his, and they settled down to wait. The house was noisy with wind and rain. The gutters were choked with leaves, and water slopped over on to the ground below. The square outside seemed deserted. There was never the sound of a car, nor a step, nor a human voice. Once there was a loud crash—it might have been the For Sale board on the house opposite blowing over. Connington had a bag of boiled sweets with him, and he sucked steadily: he had a theory that this calmed the nerves. He had had an awkward day, beginning with Amelia and continuing on to the sale. There had been a slight rumpus in the auction-room. A nice copy of Ackermann's *History of the Colleges*, 1st edition, 2 vols., 1816, with forty-eight coloured aquatints, Amelia had marked £80; and following a favourite dodge of his, i.e., bidding when everyone else was exhausted, Connington had at this figure secured the prize from Joel Ferrow. At Sotheby's, among the most famous auction-rooms in the world, one cannot throw competitors out of the window, but afterwards the buccaneer of the Ferrow firm had showed his teeth at Connington and snarled: "You'll be too clever one of these days."

"That's something," replied Connington, "that will never happen to you."

Now he sucked a mint drop and allowed himself to rest.


Midnight came. One o'clock. Shortly after, Connington heard a slight scraping noise. He opened his eyes. He had changed his boots, and on his feet were felt-soled slippers, both comfortable and silent. He pushed very slightly open the cloakroom door. He saw a light pass the door. It went in the direction of the study, on the left as one faced the front of the house. Connington grasped his sword-cane. He pushed the cloakroom door open. Then he silently emerged and stole down the passage to the study door, which was half-open. He looked in. A torch-light was directed on to Mike's books. Behind the light was a figure dressed in a woman's long skirts, with a high old-fashioned black straw bonnet. Against the table stood a wet umbrella.

"Good morning," said Connington.

The figure jumped round, and revealed the face, sweating and gleaming, of Corky Edwards.

"Come down, Wigan," called Connington. "The Bride of Satan has arrived. 'She' killed Mike Fisk. How did you do it, Corky?"

Edwards said nothing. He glared at Connington, and Wigan now behind, blocking the door.

"I want a confession from you," said Connington, "that you killed Mike. We'll take it down in writing, and then you must sign."

Still Corky said nothing. Wigan thought his face, shining with sweat, grotesquely framed in the black bonnet, the most repulsive sight he had ever seen. But under British law the man had his rights, the same as any other. Wigan cleared his throat. "I'm a police officer. I arrest you, Corky Edwards, on a charge of breaking and entering, and it's my duty to warn you that you need not say anything, but anything you say will be taken down in writing and may be given in evidence."

Corky smiled.

"Good God!" said Connington. "An innocent man is due to hang at eight, and you warn this scoundrel to say nothing, Wigan."

"Officially I've got to, sir, whatever my private feelings may be."

"Then thank God I'm not a policeman. I can just see your C.I.D. collecting evidence in the few hours left. Corky Edwards, I think I know a way to make you talk. How's Mrs. Edwards?"

Corky moistened his lips. "Very well, thank you."

"That's right. Always cherish your mother, Corky. I believe you do, too, even if you wear her old clothes on a raid. Don't let her suffer, Corky. She may, you know, if you don't talk; and quickly."

Wigan cleared his throat. "I'm not sure I can allow—"

"Hold your tongue, Sergeant. This is my affair. Well, Corky, it's up to you. Mike Fisk wasn't the only one who dabbled in witchcraft, and if you don't talk I shall certainly pay your mother a visit."

Corky moistened his lips. "I came here to steal books. I'm guilty of that, but I never killed Mike. You'll have to see my employers, Mr. Francis and Mr. Joel."

"Employers be damned!" said Connington. "You own the firm. Francis and Joel are your junior partners, and have been for many years. No doubt you discovered some dirty deed and thus got a hold on them. Now come along, we're wasting time. Are you going to confess or not? If you don't, you will be held in any case on the burglary charge; and while you are in jail I shall be free to do as I like. And I'll do it too, even if Hampton hangs. I shall see your old mother, and I shall take with me a book I have. The title, roughly translated, means 'The Litany of Hell,' and it's about the rarest book in the world on occult practices. Even Mike, apparently, hadn't got a copy. I shall read from it, Corky, and your mother will suffer. She may shrivel small as a pea, or swell up like a balloon. I can't say till I try. But it will be something unpleasant, and I'll do it unless you confess, now, to the truth about Mike Fisk."

"You wouldn't dare!"

"Wouldn't I?"

Corky's face sweated anew. It shone, a perfect mask of perspiration.

"Blast you, you be damned!"

"Damned I may be. But I know you love your mother, and I'm ready to go to any length, however vile it may be, to save Hampton from the gallows—or to avenge him if he does die. I've never been beaten yet, and I won't be beaten now. It's your mother's life or yours, Edwards."

Wigan intervened. "Mr. Connington—we can't. We can't make an innocent woman suffer…"

Connington turned on him in fury. "Be quiet, you! I will start away now, from memory. I hold the book in my right hand, and I confront Mrs. Edwards. I say to her: 'A sacrifice is needed, and you shall be the sacrifice. I summon from hell the Devil and his woman, who will turn you into an acceptable and amusing form. Will it be big? Will it be little? Shall you bellow like a bull? Shall you bleat like a goat? Come, the forces of evil, amuse yourselves. Rise, rise, rise, the women of hell! Seize the sacrifice!' Here, Edwards, your mother will be held by hands she cannot see and mocked by tongues that she cannot, as yet, hear. She will be distended or compressed. She may become very, very small. Pushed, pushed, forced, and crammed. She may scream. From records, a woman has nearly shrieked the house down as a myriad of hands forced her to the size of a tiny little pea. She may cry for mercy, and I will say to her: 'There's your mercy—hanging by a rope.' I will read on from the litany. I call up the Devil himself to approve the amusing shape—the sacrifice. For all this, Edwards, I supply the energy—what they call the ectoplasm; and exhausting it will be. But I can manage the Devil in solid form; and he will laugh at your mother, Edwards: now swelled like a balloon or horned like a bull and bellowing, or rolling about the floor—a pea; or something really nasty, Edwards, something to really make the Devil laugh—"

"Stop it!" Corky rushed forward and smacked Connington across the face. "Stop it! I've had enough of it. My mother is sacred. I'll give you the confession you want."

Connington took out his handkerchief and wiped his nose, for Corky had made it bleed.

"Thank you," he said. "Sergeant Wigan, take down what he says to you."

Silently Wigan produced notebook and pencil. He strongly disapproved of what was taking place, amounting to the "third degree." They had no right to bully the man into a confession.

"I'll take down a statement," said Wigan, "a voluntary statement, if you care to make one."

Connington laughed. He was like a chameleon with his moods; and now he seemed to be a devil.

"'Pon my soul, Wigan, you're a difficult man to help."

"That may be. But I represent the law here; and things will be done in a proper way."

Connington stamped about the room, smacking about with his black cane.

"Magnificent, magnificent! A man, wrongfully accused, is due to hang at eight. We have the murderer here—Corky Edwards. He's ready to confess. But Act A, Section B, Clause C prevents it!"

With Corky glaring and sweating, and Connington raging and knocking on Mike's table with his stick, Wigan kept his temper as a policeman must.

"There's no need to talk like that, sir," he said. "But a criminal must not be coerced."

"Ha!" said Connington. "Coerced. That's good. But Corky and I understand each other. Now get on with your voluntary statement, Corky."

Corky licked his lips. "Because of what happened in the past, I'm the real boss of Ferrow Brothers. Nobody outside knows it. I just work in the shop. But I take one half of the profits, and Joel and Francis one half between them. The profits have been big, but the trouble is to get books. There are more customers than rare books to feed them. For this reason we wanted to get books from Mike Fisk whom we knew had a valuable collection. But he wouldn't sell to Joel or Francis because of disagreements in the auction-room. So I determined to have a try." Corky paused.

Wigan, like most policemen who have done communications-room duty, was a clear and rapid writer. He could take down verbatim if the speaker spoke with reasonable slowness. He nodded to Corky. "Go on," he said.

"Just a minute," Connington interposed. "Did Francis or Joel know of your plans?"

"No, they didn't. We planned together to buy at auctions, but we sometimes got books individually and then charged the firm at cost price. The other day Mr. Francis—I mean Francis—picked up for a penny John Galsworthy's *Villa Rubein* written under the pen-name of John Sinjohn. It was a first issue bound in cherry-coloured cloth, and Francis charged the firm £5 for it. So I would do what I thought. Also I didn't want Joel or Francis to know what I was doing, because I might break the law."

"No trust. Proper bunch of spivs," commented Connington.

"That's as may be. Well. I went out to Sun one afternoon. There I waited. I used an old runner's trick: I waited in a public convenience. There was no attendant to worry me. About 10 p.m. someone came along and closed and locked the iron outer gate, but I have exceptional strength in my arms, and without trouble I climbed over. Then I walked out to Mike's house in Chelmer Square. It was a wild night, the kind I like, wind and rain. I'm at home in the rain like a normal man. Any prints I make are soon washed away. I can move fast if I want to, too. I was wearing a black cloak belonging to Francis, which he kept hanging up in the office, and I went along swift and silent without seeing a soul. Near Mike's house I saw something bright lying in the road. I picked it up. It was a knife. I put it in my pocket because I thought it might be useful. Later, it was."

Corky paused and grinned. He saw Connington's eyes fixed intently on him, and he remarked: "I may not know much about books, Mr. Connington; but certain things I do know. I can plot and plan like a real runner."

"Go on," said Connington.

"Well, I got to Mike's house and went round to the back. I tried the door, found it open, and walked in. A kind of droning noise was coming from the room where Mike was—his book-room. I knew the meaning of it. I knew of his interest in devils and witches. He was reading from the books of the dead. I went in, and there he was, sitting at his table and reading from a volume. He was reading away like mad in what seemed to be a foreign language. I was about to interrupt him; I was going to ask him to sell me some books—persuade him to, if necessary, when he turned round and saw me. His eyes were bleary, like a drunken man's, and he seemed dazed. Then he gave a yell.

"'The Bride of Satan!' he shouted.

"Instantly I thought a bit of humbug might do good. If he

thought me a devil or something, now was the time to get books. My head was sunk in my collar. I advanced towards him. He pulled out a pin and stuck it in my leg, but it happened to be my false leg and of course I could feel nothing.

"'You feel no pain,' he said. 'You are indeed the Bride of Satan. What do you want of me?'

"'Books,' I said in a squeaky voice, 'to read to my sisters in hell.'

"'Take what you want,' he answered.

"Round my waist I had a good sack, which I always carry when I'm book-hunting. I pulled it out from under my cloak and approached the shelves. But I suppose my cloak fell back, for I had only put in one book when he gave another yell. 'You're an impostor. You're Corky Edwards, blast you!'

"He tried to get up from his chair. He was foaming mad, and I knew he would kill me if he could. It was him or me. So I pulled out the knife I had picked up and drove it through his chest. There was a spurt of blood, and I jumped back from it. Now you know all."

"Afterwards?" said Connington.

"I had to make the best of a bad job. There was blood everywhere. And I had left prints on the handle of the knife. But I had come prepared for some unpleasantness. That's why I entered through the back."

"You had meant to steal his books?"

"Maybe, if he wouldn't sell. Now I had to get out of the mess I was in. First I carefully wiped the handle of the knife with a corner of my cloak. Then I hooked on a false beard I had brought with me, as a disguise going home."

"Where's the beard now?"

"I burnt it as soon as I got home. Well, now I had to think about the books. One I had in my sack, but I thought I wouldn't risk taking others. The sooner I was out of the house the better. I had blood on my hands. But fresh blood will come off in cold water if you do it quickly, so I carefully wiped the leather pad on my cork leg and went upstairs to the bathroom. Through the window I saw the glow of a cigarette in a house opposite. Someone was sitting at the window smoking. With my beard on, a witness might be useful, so I turned on the light and let the person (a woman) see me washing my hands. Then I went downstairs and out through the back way. Later I fiddled the sale of the Keats book I had taken. It was too hot to keep. A signed copy—it would always be unsaleable."

"You deliberately threw suspicion on Fred Hampton. Why?"

"Well, he was a bad-tempered chap. He had a row with Mr. Askew I'm friendly with. Also he had a beard. Also again the police might get too near me."

"Why should they get too near you?"

"They might have put someone really clever on the job. I might have left traces. How could I know?"

"So you got another man hanged, or nearly so. You're a black villain, Corky Edwards."

"Maybe I am. But there's Joel and Francis ready to give me away, if they had proof, and they could do it without me telling on them. Anyway, I've confessed. One reason—" He paused. "It's my custom to take up an early cup of tea to Mrs. Edwards. For several mornings she's left it untouched."

"You're a curious mixture, Corky. Got it down, Sergeant Wigan? Get him to sign it, then you had better contact your Superintendent to stop the execution."

Wigan read over what he had written, then he held out his book to Edwards, who signed his name. "There," he said.

"There," repeated Connington. "Now let's get along to the police station. Don't look so glum, Wigan. You've got a voluntary statement. Corky has said so. Think of Fred Hampton. He may be awake, and he'll be in terrible suspense, waiting for eight o'clock. It's ten minutes after four now. Come along, man. There isn't too much time. Any number of hitches may crop up. I don't know how these things are managed, but we've got to get someone at the Home Office out of bed."

"It's the hitches I'm thinking of, sir. For all your cleverness you're not a policeman: and there's not an atom of proof in his statement; and so the Superintendent will think. Corky may have made his story up."

"Tsah!" said Connington. "We can't let Fred hang now. If you hang, Corky, you've asked for it. Where's the cloak you wore?"

"Burnt. Mr. Francis burnt it when you and Charlie came talking about bats. It was obvious what Charlie thought. So Francis got rid of the cloak."

"You made other raids on the books here?"

"Joel did and I did. But Joel trod on a pipe in the kitchen. He ain't no burglar. But we did get some other books, leaving behind worthless ones to fill the gaps."

"Mike's marks in any of them?"

"We erased them of course. I'm not a fool, Mr. Connington."

"You're very far from a fool, Corky Edwards, but give me some proof that you committed the crime and I'll do better than leave Mrs. Edwards alone. I'll look after her after you've gone. I swear it. She can come and live with us as a companion to my sister, who needs someone to look after."

"That's very handsome, Mr. Connington. It's been bothering me all along, what is to happen to my mother. With my money I've made Mrs. Edwards a very respectable lady. Once we lived at Dalston in a back-to-back and with Joel and Francis I pushed a barrow to Epping market and others. Now Mrs. Edwards lives at Crouch End with most respectable neighbours. But I won't deny she's lonely; and with me in this mess I think she had better change her name."

"I shall see to all that. She and my sister will look after each other. I promise you; and Sergeant Wigan here, who's an honest man, will witness my promise."

"I trust you, Sergeant," said Corky. "And I ask you to remember Mrs. Edwards's little fads and fancies. For instance, in her place of worship she's definitely evangelical; she wouldn't feel comfortable in an Anglo-Catholic. She tells me it's very reverent, but she doesn't fully understand it."

"Wigan knows all about that," said Connington. "He's a churchwarden. He shall choose a suitable church for your mother."

"I expect I can," said Wigan. "But I cannot allow bribery here."

Connington glared at him. "Just remember Fred and the high jump he'll take unless we're quick. Now, Corky—proof."

"Well, sir, I killed Mike Fisk, and I cannot add much to that. But for years I have blackmailed Joel and Francis. It arose from a little job they planned—getting a valuable Bible from an old woman. She wouldn't part, so they stole her book.

They didn't let me in on the deal, but I was too clever for them. Theft is theft. I could prosecute them now. But I kept quiet, on conditions. I will admit to blackmail."

"That doesn't affect us." With one of his bewildering changes, Connington became infinitely patient. "Look, Corky, Fred Hampton is due to swing at eight. We want to save him. How can we *prove* you committed any crime?"

"Well, sir, I bumped off Charlie North. He's lying in the house opposite. I don't suppose he's a very pretty sight. I knifed him in the back." Corky's face sweated and gleamed.

"Guard him while I have a look," said Connington to Wigan.

Presently he returned, and even his face was a bit pale. "Charlie's dead. He's very dead. Knifed in the back as Corky said. I reckon we've got hold of the murderer all right; and now we had better hurry to the police station and get the execution stopped. Come on, Corky."

"Certainly, Mr. Connington. As I said. But I ask you to remember your promise to Mrs. Edwards. This may be the last time I'll speak to you. Mrs. Edwards is a very particular lady. She likes to read from her Bible night and morning. She's not choosy in her food, but she likes plain food well cooked. No wine. She's temperance."

"I'll remember it. You've kept your word and I'll keep mine."

"I trust you, sir. And Sergeant Wigan. I don't like coppers. Never did. But he seems to be one of the good kind."

Wigan added a suitable assurance that he would help look after Mrs. Edwards. As a police officer, he had seen many strange sights and met many strange people; but he thought he had never met anyone stranger than Corky Edwards: barrow-boy, blackmailer, hard-working shop assistant, killer.

And a man who undeniably loved his mother, and must have been very, very good to her.

By six o'clock the immense task was done. Fred Hampton was freed from the rope, and Christopher (Corky) Edwards was charged with the murder of Mike Fisk and the murder of Charlie North.

Connington and Wigan walked back together from Sun Police Station to Wigan's house, where after a wash and a shave Connington was invited to breakfast.

As they sat down in the cheerful living-room and Mrs. Wigan brought in supplies, Connington glanced at the clock. The hands pointed to eight.

"Hmmm," he said. "We didn't leave much time, did we? Ah, bacon and eggs. My favourite dish. And a cup of tea. Mrs. Wigan, you make beautiful tea."

"I warm the cup. That's one of the secrets."

"I have a theory," remarked Connington, "that only beautiful natures can make beautiful tea. However, I might find the theory rather hard to prove."

Later, when they were alone, Wigan said to Connington: "That was a terrible threat you made to Mrs. Edwards. Could you really have carried it out?"

Connington had no cigarettes with him, so Wigan offered his pouch and packet of cigarette-papers. Connington attempted to roll one, but gave it up—it was like a pillow in the middle and flat at both ends. So Wigan rolled one for him, politely moistening the paper with his fingers.

"Thanks. Funny your big hands can make one so easily while my slender fingers cannot."

"The secret is to get the thumbs parallel along the paper."

"Common sense, I suppose. And that's really the answer to your question. You must remember that Corky doesn't know much about books. Talk to him of the *Malleus Maleficarum* and he wouldn't know what you mean. Also during the centuries that witchcraft flourished there were thousands of prosecutions, most of them due to malicious gossip. But the judges weren't fools and there were surprisingly few burnings."

"I thought myself that the Sign of the Cross would protect Mrs. Edwards."

"Lucky you didn't say so. As it was, your zeal for British law nearly undid us. Sorry I spoke to you so roughly, Sergeant. It was all part of the act."

"Humbug, sir?"

"Something of the sort—yes. But it is possible to do evil; and to bring forth evil. I leave you to judge what I should really do. And now we have to think of Mrs. Edwards. I can't leave her in the house alone with her son in the cells. I had better tell her that Corky—that is, Christopher—has met with an accident. And she must see no newspapers. Quite likely she doesn't read one anyway. And I shall have to be careful of the radio. Hmmm. More humbug."

"Mary is preparing the spare room, sir. Before you do anything else, you will go up and have a good sleep."

"Sergeant, to you and Mrs. Wigan I show my real self. It's deep down beneath layers and layers of cheating, lying, and sometimes, I regret to say, swindling. I am very grateful."

"One thing more, sir. That dreadful book you mentioned: I should burn it."

"You mean the *Litinas Diaboli*, published at Dresden in 1410?"

"I mean something of the sort, sir, yes. The book you mentioned."

Connington's left eyelid drooped. "Strange Mike hadn't got it. Well, it doesn't exist."

"It was all humbug?"

"Yes. I know evil can be done, and has been done, but it might be somewhat difficult to compress poor Mrs. Edwards into the size of a pea. However, my threats were good enough to impress Corky Edwards."

Wigan looked at Connington as if he had developed horns and a tail.

"You're an absolute wonder," he said. "But I suppose—are you humbugging me now?"

"No, Sergeant. The truth. Just the truth."

# CHAPTER TWENTY-SEVEN

## FOLLOWING DR. JOHNSON

Freed from his frightful ordeal, Fred Hampton left the prison by night, one reason being to prevent any possible demonstration. Wigan could understand that. And he didn't want effusive thanks, but day followed day and he received no word from Hampton at all. Wigan understood from Hampton's solicitor that compensation was being arranged, and that Hampton would use part of the money to open a bookshop in Essex, which as a county has been neglected in this direction. "But," added Harland, "I expect you know all this."

"As a matter of fact," said Wigan, "I don't."

"You mean to say he hasn't thanked you for saving his life?"

"No. But I'm satisfied if he is. I've kept my word to him."

"He's an ungrateful sort of fellow, and of course he's been very ill. The thought of execution must have been a terrible strain. When I was called by the Home Office to go and see him after the good news was known, I barely recognised him. His hair and beard were white, and he seemed nearly dead already. To bring him back to life was another ordeal. But he knows that you were the one who saved him. He's gone into retreat until he recovers his mental balance, but I'm in touch with him and I shall certainly write and say that thanks are due to you."

"I would rather you didn't. Let the matter drop."

"Hold on," said Harland, as Wigan was about to hang up the telephone receiver. "I suppose that, as regards the police, you are not suffering for what you did?"

"Not at all. The Superintendent told me that he could never be grateful enough for what I did, saving an innocent man from the gallows. There have been congratulations all round. J. Saggs, the D.I., is retiring; and the new man is a much more reasonable chap."

"I'm glad to hear that. Well, Sergeant, I'll say nothing to Hampton if you say not. After all, you have the approbation of your own conscience, and, I should think, the respect of all who know you. There are men like Hampton in the world. I shouldn't be at all surprised if he doesn't quarrel with my professional fees!"

Wigan turned with relief to the affairs of Mrs. Edwards. With her son committed for trial for murder, and likely to be hanged, it was difficult to know what to do for the best. He and Searle Connington decided that, if they were careful, she need never know the truth; but she would have to be told that Christopher had met with an accident and she would not see him again. The old lady took this with resignation. "The Lord giveth and the Lord taketh away. Blessed be the name of the Lord."

In his many-sided character, Connington exhibited

tenderness and compassion. It was fortunate that Mrs. Edwards took a liking to him. It amused Wigan to hear their discussions of Holy Writ. Probably, as a collector, Connington knew more about Old Bibles and their values than any man living. He actually owned one leaf of the great Gutenberg Bible, the first book ever to be printed with movable type. But whether his religious beliefs, as expressed to Mrs. Edwards, were humbug, Wigan was unable to say. Connington treated the old lady like his own mother. He moved her to Notting Hill Gate and used Corky's money as the man himself would have wished. She had her own sitting-room, with every comfort; but, as living with people of a different social standing might have been embarrassing to her, Connington found a Miss Docker, in indigent circumstances. This old lady knew Dalston in the old days; and she and Mrs. Edwards were completely happy together. In fact Connington set up a household reminiscent of Dr. Johnson, who in his later years gave shelter to a number of persons, including the difficult Mrs. Williams.

Connington had his reward. His sister Amelia was in the plot to keep Mrs. Edwards happy; and in her interest she forgot her masochistic furies. On the morning that Christopher (Corky) Edwards was hanged for a double murder, Amelia held the old lady's hand while the clock ticked away past the fatal hour; and the old lady knew nothing. She said: "Why are you so good to me, Amelia?"

"I was just thinking that real life and make-believe are different; and that not everyone is cruel."

"I could have told you that. My boy Christopher wasn't cruel. He was very, very good to me. And there is no kinder man than your own brother."

Upstairs, Amelia had a secret hoard of books on sadism and masochism. There was one horrible volume written by an ex-hangman, which related terrible sufferings. Amelia had gloated over them, but now she went up and burnt the lot.

Charlie North had a slap-up funeral, in the opinion of Lambeth and the Old Kent Road. Connington himself attended as a mark of respect to a barrow-boy who had risen to something of a rare book expert. He attended at his most impressive: flowing black cloak secured at the neck with a golden chain, a wideawake hat, and his familiar black cane. Some of the humble mourners thought he was a foreign prince. "Haile Selassie," said a wag. Connington certainly acted like a prince when he was consulted by Mara as to Charlie's books. "Sell them to me," was the first thought of a collector and dealer. Instead Connington said: "I think Charlie would like them to go to a public library. Then he will always be remembered by the book-plate inscription we will put in: 'Presented by Charles North Esq., Bookman.'"

Mike's books Wigan had to dispose of. He had a "blanket offer" from Ruth; but this he refused. He sold the books to Connington at a fair, independent valuation. Not wanting Ruth and others on his door-step, Connington bought on behalf of his firm, and issued catalogues. There were ready buyers for the items; but the buyers did not include Francis and Joel Ferrow, who were prosecuted for a theft committed about twenty-five years ago. Depositions were taken from Corky Edwards, and the principal witness was found still living. Here Wigan approved of the rigour of the law, and the proverbial long arm, for the circumstances of the theft were atrocious, the two men behaving like bandits. They were sent to prison, which broke up their book business. It was taken over by Algernon Askew, with some capital put in by Searle Connington. Connington gave this as his reason: "It is always sad to see a bookshop pack up."

Some months later, in the New Year, a parcel arrived for Wigan. It contained a copy of Henty's three-decker, *All But Lost*, Tinsley, 1869, his rarest book. Probably there were not more than thirty copies in the whole world. With it was a note from Fred Hampton: *"I have tried to get this before, but it wasn't easy. Please accept it with my thanks. You saved my life, and I'm grateful. Fred."*

The letter bore no address; and it was obvious that Fred wished completely to forget the past. The set was fine, each volume complete and nearly perfect. It might have cost fifty or sixty pounds, but it wasn't the value of the gift that appealed to Wigan: it was the thought that Fred had taken a good deal of trouble to secure it, and chosen something that Wigan, as a beginning book-collector, would understand.

Wigan placed *All But Lost* in a position of honour in the bookcase in his front room. It was spotted some weeks later by Ruth Brent when she came to see Wigan on the old business—hunting rare books for Di Dand. She thought he might have kept back some volumes from Mike Fisk's collection. Wigan, who was at home, asked her into the front room, and automatically her eyes went to his books. "Ah," she said.

"*All But Lost.* I must have that. I'll give thirty-five pounds. That's a very good price, Mr. Wigan."

"I'm sorry, Miss Ruth, it's not for sale."

"Fifty," she said, knowing how much Di needed *All But Lost* and a few other rarities to complete his collection of Henty, which was among the best in the United States and the envy of Professor Nickerlo and others.

Wigan shook his head, smiling. "No. Nor a hundred. I'm not going to sell it. I'm afraid Di will have to be disappointed for once. It may even do him good."

Ruth accepted refusal—not defeat—as gracefully as she could. With Fred Hampton, she would have had the book by fair means or foul; but she couldn't treat a man like Wigan in this way. She looked him over. As it happened, Wigan had only just come off duty, and he was in his police uniform, the crown above the three stripes on his sleeve denoting promotion to Station Sergeant. Ruth did not notice this. Nor his kindly eyes. She saw only that he had grey hair. He must be at least fifty!

Wigan smiled again at what was evidently in her mind.

"'Fraid I shan't pop off yet, Miss Ruth, but stay and have some tea with us. You never know—I may choke over a piece of cake!"

Ruth had little sense of humour, but she accepted on the book-collector's principle that one must never lose sight of a desired volume. After all, you never know—do you?

*"If much of the action is set in a bookshop
or a library,
it is a bibliomystery,
just as it is if a major character is a
bookseller or a librarian."* —Otto Penzler

A bookish puzzle threatens an eagerly awaited inheritance; a submission to a publisher recounts a murder that seems increasingly to be a work of nonfiction; an irate novelist puts a grisly end to the source of his writer's block.

There is no better hiding place for clues—or red herrings— than inside the pages of a book. But in this world of resentful ghost writers, indiscreet playwrights, and unscrupulous book collectors, literary prowess is often a prologue to disaster.

With Martin Edwards as librarian and guide, delve into an irresistible stack of tales perfect for every booklover and armchair sleuth, featuring much-loved Golden Age detectives such as Nigel Strangeways, Philip Trent, and Detective Chief Inspector Roderick Alleyn. But readers should be warned that the most riveting tales often conceal the deadliest of secrets...

*"Now tell us about your crime novel.*
*Take my advice and don't try to be intellectual*
*over it.*
*What the public likes is blood."*

The Surrays and their five children form a prolific writing machine, with scores of treatises, reviews and crime thrillers published under their family name. Following a rare convergence of the whole household at their Oxfordshire home, Ruth—middle sister who writes "books which are just books"—decides to spend some weeks there recovering from the pressures of the writing life while the rest of the brood scatter to the winds again. Their next return is heralded by the tragic news that Ruth has taken her life after an evening at the Surrays's hosting a set of publishers and writers, one of whom is named as Ruth's literary executor in the will she left behind.

Despite some suspicions from the family, the verdict at the inquest is suicide—but when Ruth's brother Richard receives a letter from the deceased which was delayed in the post, he enlists the help of Chief-Inspector Robert Macdonald to investigate what could only be an ingeniously planned murder.

# Praise for the
# British Library Crime Classics

"Carr is at the top of his game in this taut whodunit... The British Library Crime Classics series has unearthed another worthy golden age puzzle."

—*Publishers Weekly*, STARRED Review,
for *The Lost Gallows*

"A wonderful rediscovery."

—*Booklist*, STARRED Review, for *The Sussex Downs Murder*

"First-rate mystery and an engrossing view into a vanished world."

—*Booklist*, STARRED Review, for *Death of an Airman*

"A cunningly concocted locked-room mystery, a staple of Golden Age detective fiction."

—*Booklist*, STARRED Review, for *Murder of a Lady*

"The book is both utterly of its time and utterly ahead of it."

—*New York Times Book Review* for *The Notting Hill Mystery*

"As with the best of such compilations, readers of classic mysteries will relish discovering unfamiliar authors, along with old favorites such as Arthur Conan Doyle and G.K. Chesterton."

—*Publishers Weekly*, STARRED Review, for *Continental Crimes*

"In this imaginative anthology, Edwards—president of Britain's Detection Club—has gathered together overlooked criminous gems."

—*Washington Post* for *Crimson Snow*

"The degree of suspense Crofts achieves by showing the growing obsession and planning is worthy of Hitchcock. Another first-rate reissue from the British Library Crime Classics series."

—*Booklist,* STARRED Review, for *The 12.30 from Croydon*

"Not only is this a first-rate puzzler, but Crofts's outrage over the financial firm's betrayal of the public trust should resonate with today's readers."

—*Booklist,* STARRED Review, for *Mystery in the Channel*

"This reissue exemplifies the mission of the British Library Crime Classics series in making an outstanding and original mystery accessible to a modern audience."

—*Publishers Weekly,* STARRED Review, for *Excellent Intentions*

"A book to delight every puzzle-suspense enthusiast."

—*New York Times* for *The Colour of Murder*

"Edwards's outstanding third winter-themed anthology showcases 11 uniformly clever and entertaining stories, mostly from lesser known authors, providing further evidence of the editor's expertise...This entry in the British Library Crime Classics series will be a welcome holiday gift for fans of the golden age of detection."

—*Publishers Weekly,* STARRED Review, for *The Christmas Card Crime and Other Stories*

**poisonedpenpress.com**